CHAOS IMPRINT

ADAM DUNCAN

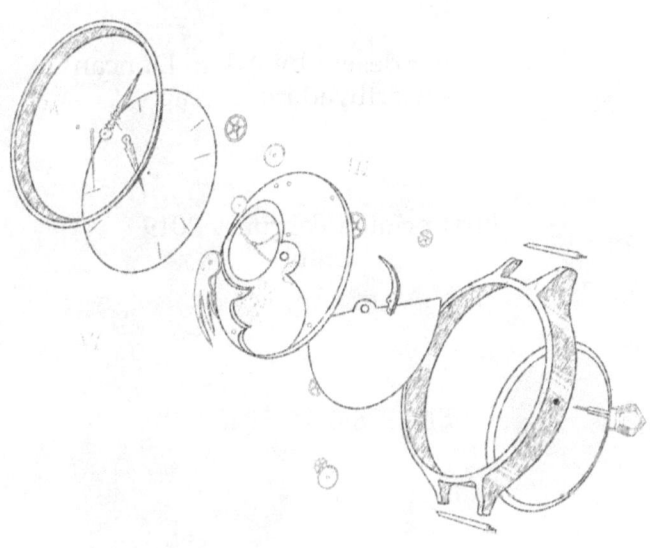

Front Cover design by Adam Duncan
www.artbyadam.com.au

First printed February 2019
Lulu

ISBN: 978-0-6485040-0-9

Dedicated to my Grandad,
who has inspired every bit of writing I've ever done, and whose
wordsmithing has always been the horizon I march toward.

With Special thanks:

First and foremost, to fellow writer David Kachel, for all the writing sessions from the 'Dungeon' at uni together to the countless conversations at the libraries, cafés and houses where so many of the ideas in this book were generated. How fitting it was that the last two chapters were penned in one such session together. This book may be finished, but don't think for a second that you're off the hook – many more ideas are still waiting to be put down to paper. Thanks also to Bek Payne, who encouraged me to share my scribblings with the online world as I went, following her example.

And of course, to my partner Haylea, whose enthusiasm reading the earlier chapters was just one part of the motivation I needed to finally tell the rest of the story. Thanks for your patience all the times I was lost in my own headspace at the end of a good writing day.

Thanks as well to the insights of Michael Riddell, answering my many technical questions as I converted generally accepted police protocols to their more accurate counterparts. Sorry that I fell short of my end of the bargain – the scene with the SRS leader feeding 'Lucky' the goldfish never quite made it into the final pages, but his memory lives on. Should a reader ever find themselves missing some vital detail as they close this book, may they find their solace here.

Thank you to my Mum for, well, so many things, but of note here it was your memory to which I owe most of the details of the iconic buildings near the end of the story. And thanks to Dad, who would particularly have loved the next book I'm working on, set near his childhood home of Mt Mee and the D'Aguilar area.

Thank you to Caylie Jeffery, author of *Under the Lino*, for your insights into the world of self-publication. Words are powerless without a reader, and entertainment purposeless without an audience. Thank you for connecting me to mine.

Chapter 1
On the Farm
April 10, 1985

The young man knelt, cradling the rifle with a practised ease. With one eye peering down the scope, he watched as his father collected branches and twigs through the trees. Slowly, he raised the gun and levelled the crosshairs to his father's forehead. The figure bent in his khaki overalls, stooping for another branch, completely unaware of the silent black cross that had marked him for death just a hundred metres away. As the young man shadowed his father's movements with the crosshair – down, up, a step forward, then down again – he imagined pulling the trigger.

What would happen?

He felt no contempt for his father, and there was no anger in his mind as he contemplated the decision. It was simply an exercise in thought. His finger smoothed over the contour of the trigger, this switch that could determine life or death. Power.

He loved his dad, and they had as standard a relationship as one could have living isolated on their property not far from Broome, Western Australia. He had shown him the ropes in almost every aspect of life; how to live independently, how to work hard and stick to it and when necessary on the farm, how to kill.

His mother had been taken by cancer when he was only four, and his only sibling was his younger sister, Kate. From the age of six he was following his dad around the property, helping to carry water, ammunition, and helping to drag back the night's meal on a successful trip. His father gradually taught him how to handle different firearms, from shotguns to pistols, always teaching him the safety aspects of the weapons first.

"You don't know how much power you're holding when this thing's loaded, son," he recalled him saying the first time they set up a range. "You have to respect the weapon. Too many people get excited and reckless, and that's when people get hurt."

At the age of 16, he had finally been allowed to stay out two nights on the extremes of the 300 acres of land, practising the survival skills his father had taught him on their previous expeditions together. He had set up a make shift tent each evening before the sun went down and shot and skinned a rabbit each night to feed himself. He'd set up a circuit route with his dad before he left, and on the last leg home, he bagged a kangaroo as a trophy for his father and Kate to eat together. His dad had been proud of him, always praising his professionalism, secretly proud of his own influence.

Even as the memories swam through his head, the 17-year-old stared down the scope, hypnotised by the prospect of taking human life. Hypnotised most of all by the comprehension that in his hands, he held the power to change almost everything about his life; who he was, where he'd live and what his future would hold. He played it out in his mind.

He imagined, in slow motion, the .223 bullet leaving the chamber in a burst of flame. He watched in his mind's eye, as it flew between the trunks of the gum and stringy bark forest, whipping passed the leaves in its deadly journey. He watched, in his trance, the bullet hit his father's forehead, imagined the burst behind his head as the round made its gruesome exit.

He heard a noise behind him. A strange, droning wail. As he blurrily woke from his daydream, he recognized his name.

"Aaron… Aaron!"
He turned sharply to face his sister, who held his gaze with concern in her eyes.
"What's going on?" she asked, "Are you alright?"
Aaron stuttered a reply, and without looking back to the rifle, pointed it away from his father and into the distance.
"S-sorry," he stammered, "I guess I was daydreaming again. I didn't hear you come down."

As she smiled, her bouncy chestnut hair fell over her freckled cheeks. She looked lovingly at her brother through her dark hazel eyes, trying to understand how he could behave so unusually at times.

The fallen leaves crunched noisily as their father approached with a stack of firewood in his big arms. Aaron watched Kate's eyes lift first, before slowly turning around himself. As he swivelled, he flicked the safety catch on and reached for the bolt to bring the bullet out of the chamber. With the feel of the cold metal, his mind snapped back to the image of his father falling backwards, a trail of blood hitting his face, and the stack of wood clattering heavily around the body. He blinked his eyes hard and jerked his head to the side as if letting the concept pour out of his mind.

He looked up just as his father flopped his Akubra hat onto Kate's small head and rubbed his knuckles affectionately over the top with his characteristic grin. Kate tucked her chin into her shoulders and giggled with her innocent smile.

Aaron looked back to his dad who always seemed awkward around his daughter now she had started to grow up. It mustn't have been easy raising the two of them on his own, and it was obvious to Aaron that his dad was completely lost on how to raise his sister as a young woman. Still, he knew he loved her dearly and did his best, and she knowingly loved him back. Somehow, she just seemed to fit into their lifestyle. Even though she was the youngest, she seemed to take it on herself to look after her father and brother like her mother would have.

If she had ever wished for a different life, Aaron had never noticed it. She always had such a pleasant disposition and a sincerity about her that Aaron had never seen among the town girls.

Their father had gotten some kindling alight and was stripping out of his overalls to his jeans and red flannelette shirt when he noticed there was no meat to prepare.

"What've you been doing, son?"

Aaron shifted uncomfortably against the log and rubbed a finger into his eye nervously.

"I just… haven't seen anything yet. Don't worry, we won't go hungry," he added with a smirk to cover himself. He promptly turned around and flipped the bolt back into place to make himself focus.

He righted his firing position, and it wasn't long before the ears of a hare poked up, silhouetted out of the long grass against the growing dusk. Aaron stared down the scope and waited for the animal to show its head. As it raised up to sniff the air, the young hunter flicked the safety off silently. As he slowly put pressure on the trigger he watched his mind transform the rabbit into the khaki overalls. He followed the figure as it moved slowly forward, and squeezed the trigger in. The sound split the evening's stillness.

As the hare spun backwards from the round in its eye, the thought echoed again through the boy's distracted mind...

What would happen?

Chapter 2
An Unwelcome Surprise
Canberra
10am, June 28, 2010

Benjamin Terrace pulled the door shut behind him. It was ten in the morning and the streets were silent – the rest of the world locked into their nine-to-five routines and the paths ready and waiting for such a man not long out of bed to take a late morning stroll.

As he sprang down the three red brick steps and onto the footpath, he shut the white picket gate behind him. It still counted as living the dream even if he was still living in his parents' house, right?

It was a typical, fine winter morning in Canberra. The icy chill cut the air, but the sun was high enough to give at least the illusion of comfort. The birds had finished their loud acclamations of the sunrise and had settled into their soothing, slower repertoires. He rounded a corner, following one of his of his typical walking routes. If he were being honest, it wasn't so much for the physical exercise as the reward of the coffee at the other end of the relatively short walk.

House after peaceful house waltzed by the footpath, broken only by the odd cry of a child too young to be shipped off to their own practice of the daily routine. The sun in its warm glory rose steadily with the minutes.

It would have been about 10:30 when Terrace saw the little puppy trot out the gate of a house one door ahead and circle the graceful oak tree by the roadside. It was obvious by the dog's wonderment at the tree's thick trunk and extensive branches that he was not normally allowed to leave the yard. Terrace smiled, and as he approached the tree, he scooped up the little orange Pomeranian and turned to face the house from which it had come out.

The gate was swinging backwards and forwards quietly, and an elderly gardener with thick, brown, curly hair was trimming the hedges behind the fence, oblivious to the puppy's absence.

As Terrace strode forward, a dreadful noise broke the peacefulness of the morning and ricocheted through his bones.

From inside the beautiful, dark-wood, mansion of a house came the muffled but distinct sound of two gunshots!

The gardener perked to her feet with her eyes fixed on the door in docile confusion. Terrace pivoted backwards and pressed his back firmly behind the tree, clinging onto the little dog and desperately trying to gather his wits. He could feel his heart pounding against his chest, and his breath was waving the little dog's flame-red fur.

Reluctantly, he turned his head again to peer just past the trunk and see what was happening. The gardener was now on the little pathway from the gate to the door, slowly stepping forwards, still clutching the hedge trimmers in her nervous hands.

With a bang the front door flew open, and a man with dark, short hair, clothed simply in casual clothes, stepped out in a fast walk. In one motion, it seemed, he strode down the two or three steps, lifted his arm, and while still fast-approaching the gardener between himself and the gate, fired a bullet from his high calibre pistol into the elderly woman's head.

As Terrace shrunk down at the base of the tree, gripping the dog's mouth shut in desperation to be overlooked by whoever this man was, the gardener fell to the ground without a sound.

No change in pace, no second thoughts, the frowning man continued out the open gate, and for the first time Terry noticed the van parked on the side of the road from where he had already come. It was then he also noticed in the perpetrator's left hand, three thick yellow envelopes that he was gripping firmly as he holstered his weapon back into his jacket that was flipping around from the speed his long legs were taking him in his strides.

Terry turned away and clutched the puppy close as the rental van, bright stickers advertising the cheapest rates guaranteed, roared up and screeched passed him in a mad fury. Through swelling tears of fear and breathlessness he tried to catch the numbers on the vehicle's registration, but his blurred eyes were blind to everything but the horror he had just witnessed.

He slumped his head back against the trunk, and let his hands drop to the grass in helplessness. The puppy immediately ran back into the yard, barking excitedly at first, then melting into long-drawn, sorrowful howls as if in painful comprehension of the event that had just changed the neighbourhood forever.

It seemed as if hours had passed before Terrace forced himself to stand up. His heart was still hammering in his ribcage, but his mind was beginning to clear a little. He wasn't a weak person, but he was naturally unaccustomed to such violence, and the suddenness and the brutality of the attack had come as such a shock.

How could he kill the old woman without a second's hesitation?

Terry dragged his feet forward to the gate. She was dead, but he felt compelled somehow to see for himself the woman that he knew would be lying on the path in a pool of her own blood. He had to admit, a morbid curiosity drew him to the corpse. More disturbingly, the curiosity was not satisfied, and at this close a proximity to death, he felt a new question nagging at his insides.

Who was upstairs?

The gate was still swinging as he rested his left hand on the gate post, staring into the blackness left by the open front door. He felt his feet carry him forward, almost in a dream. He walked on the grass beside the gardener, whose blood was already congealing on the cold concrete.

When he reached the doorway, his eyelids felt like lead as he dared to peer into the dark doorway. He inched a step inside and found himself in a small passageway. On the right was an arched doorway onto a polished-floorboard room. He walked cautiously forward.

The room was decorated beautifully, with expensive-looking vases and ornaments. A dark wood grandfather clock ticked from the far corner, beside a grand piano of the same colour. There were a few heavily-decorated lounge chairs and a widescreen television in another corner. The thick curtains over the windows glowed faintly from the sunlight outside, but blocked the light reaching any further. Whether it was the low light or the events of the morning Terry wasn't sure, but the house had a taste of death about it.

He turned to the left and saw a polished staircase going up to the next level. On the right of the stairs was the entrance to what looked like a large kitchen. Still unsure what he was doing there or why he needed to find out so badly, Terry put his left hand on the railing, and put a foot on the first step. The top of the staircase was even darker than the lounge room had been, but he slowly climbed the elaborate steps.

At the top, it dawned on him that he had nothing to defend himself with if there was anyone still up here. The killer had sped off, but if there were other residents hiding somewhere in the rooms, they might mistake Terrace for an abandoned comrade and lash out. The stairs intersected a corridor branching left and right, and just beside another decorative vase on a wooden stand was a golf bag full of clubs. As silently as possible Terry gripped a thick iron club and eased it out of its felt sleeve.

On his right were three doorways, one on either side of the corridor facing each other, closed, and one at the far end that was open. On his left, a single door at the far wall was just slightly ajar. Terry wrapped his hands around the grip of the club and walked slowly toward the door on the left. There was no sound coming from anywhere in the house. It made his passage through this living nightmare even eerier. He held the club to the door and swivelled his head, nervous that someone might jump at him at any moment. The door creaked loudly as he pushed it open, the sound deafening in the deathly quiet surrounding him.

The room was decorated much like the rest of the house. Another grandfather clock watched over the room from the far corner on the right. A large, solid mahogany desk empowered the room from the centre, while looming wooden bookcases towered to the ceiling on either side. In front of the desk lay what Terrace was looking for. The round body of a man lay slumped on his face, in a dark green business jacket, black pants and shiny brown shoes. A thick puddle of dark blood glinted in the low light under the torso and congealed to the old man's greying curly hair.

Still compelled by some mysterious sense of curiosity and courage, Terry placed his hand on the man's bloodied shoulder, and rolled him over to see his face. Immediately, he wished he hadn't. The pale, milky eyes stared past the ceiling of the dark room, a grim expression of surprise and confusion frozen on the man's wrinkled and twisted face. The bullets had opened up two nasty holes in the centre of his chest, revealing fragments of ruptured bone and flesh.

Terry rose to his feet dizzily and looked to the desk behind the corpse. Stepping gingerly over the dead man's legs, he glanced at the papers that were scattered over the desk and floor. He walked to the other side, pushing the leather chair aside noiselessly with the end of the golf club. The desk drawers had been ripped open, and their contents –mostly papers– thrown carelessly around the room.

Why was this man killed? Terrace wondered to himself. His mind raced back to the yellow envelopes he'd seen in the murderer's hands on his way to the van.

This isn't your business, his mind pleaded, *you shouldn't be here.* Ignoring the reprimand, Terrace picked up the closest A4 sheet. It was dusty and old, and had a seal imprinted in the lower righthand corner, but it had long ago been flattened out of shape and was indistinguishable.

At the top was a heading in bold, "Proposed Revision of Firearm Restriction Policy". The slender stained-glass window beside the book case on the left was open slightly, and a ghostly wave of cool air brushed over Terry's arm, doing nothing to ease the eeriness of the dark office. It lifted the corner of another sheet on the desk, catching Terry's eye. It was a newer document, still a bright white colour and the text looked formal. Terrace could read the title from where he stood, "Animal Cruelty in Captivity". He moved his eyes to another sheet and yet another unrelated topic. He began sifting through quicker, scanning the titles, "Their Right to Vote", "Is Abortion Murder?", "Proposed Revision of Legal Drinking Age", "Heavier Fines for Public Nuisance" the papers went on. It wasn't hard to see how the man lying dead on the floor could have gained a few enemies over the years.

Terrace moved to the book case by the window. He glanced over the faded golden titles, the blemish of time on the arguments of potent political issues. At the end of one of the shelves was a dusty photograph in a simple wooden frame. The man in the photo had light brown curly hair and was wearing a familiar green suit jacket and brown shoes. On his knee sat a young girl of about 8 years old, in an old fashioned dress, and her hair in a blue bow. The two were smiling into the camera, and Terry could see the strong passion in the man's dark eyes even in the faded 4×6.

Reverently, he returned the photo to the shelf, and looked to the dark hallway.

Terrace wasn't sure how long he'd been in the study, but he knew it had been too long. It was going to be hard to explain why he hadn't called the police. *Curiosity probably isn't a reasonable excuse.*

Nevertheless, he felt himself fascinated by the morning's events, and felt a strange desire to learn more about the man whose blood was now caking dry on the hard wooden floor.

Events like this never happened in the life of Benjamin Terrace. He lived a plain, and admittedly boring life. Two years ago, he'd graduated from the University of Canberra with a degree in Information Technology. Computers seemed to come to him naturally when he was growing up, and although he was far from passionate about the work, there was nothing else that had stood out to him in the university's prospectus. He was still living at home, though the topic of his moving out had come up many times, always initiated one way or another by his parents. They had a different mental image of what work looked like, and again what constituted success. His younger brother was also living there, and certainly doing much less with his time, but it stood to reason that the eldest had to deal with their protests first before they'd worry about trying to regain some influence on the younger sibling.

Since his course had finished, he'd worked freelance across the world from the comfort of his office chair, and he enjoyed the flexibility of the hours. He'd made enough money to be comfortable, and had enough savings to make sure that whenever his parents did eventually win the argument, he'd still be comfortable somewhere else.

He chose how much he worked and how much he rested, and the jobs were predictable, steady and safe.

Steady, Terrace reflected grimly. That was how he liked his life. Adventure never crept in further than a late night playing online games with opponents he would never meet, or a quickly-resolved drama with some hardware that could be replaced. *This, however, is quickly starting to look like something of an adventure.*

He relaxed his grip on the golf club, and let it swing by his side as he walked out of the study and back into the corridor. Over the railing he could see the little Pomeranian sniffing around through the lounge room aimlessly, wagging its tail in its own little adventure – It's understanding of grief was evidently limited and somewhat fleeting. Terrace looked at the other doors, and considered doing a little more investigating, but his decision to leave was promptly made for him.

From the end of the street came the wailing of sirens. From the unsynchronised drone, he judged there must have been at least two police cars closing fast on the crime scene. Apparently, he was not the only one who'd heard the shooting from the house's top room. And a dead gardener bleeding over the footpath would be a very effective beacon for anyone walking past.

Terrace told himself he'd intended to call the police from inside, but that in the excitement and mystery, logical decisions had long gone out the window.

He ran down the stairs, the noise of his heavy stomping bellowing through the house's deathly, revered silence. He had to tell the police everything he'd seen, everything he'd found in the room. There were a lot of unanswered questions, but as far as he saw it, he was the only witness, and the only one who held the precious pieces to the mysterious puzzle.

Terry reached the bottom of the stairs, panting heavily, and the small ball of fluff barked excitedly at the sight of life in the polished wooden tomb.
The front door was still open, and Terry could see the two police cars had already pulled up in a V formation just against the curb. An officer from each vehicle was already running toward the front door, wearing black flak jackets over their uniforms, pistols already in hand. Two more officers stood behind open doors of the vehicles, one with a handheld radio to his mouth, the other readying his own pistol.

In a second, the lead officers had come through the open gate, and as one slowed his pace around the gardener's corpse, the other moved at a fast walk towards Terry at the front door.

Terry froze midstride, as the officer stood to the side of the pavement with his pistol extended toward him just ten metres away. As if in slow motion, he raised his hands above his head, fingers fanned out, as the authoritative voice booming from the loudspeaker on the side of the patrol car commanded him to stand still and lower his weapon.

Benjamin didn't hear the clang of the club falling onto the porch, or the puppy's bark as it circled his feet. His heart was trying to leap out of his chest, the pulse pounding painfully against his temples.

He tried to bring the words to his mouth, *It's not what it-... I didn't-... I'm the witness! I can help!* -but the silent sentences jammed up in his throat.

He closed his dry mouth, stood stock still, and let the officer approach, resigning to the obvious truth of the situation.

I'm the suspect.

Chapter 3

An Unlikely Suspect
Canberra City Police Station
June 28, 2010

It was an uneventful day in the office. Just the same old paperwork, more bricks to add another level to the tower of forms and folders.

Poking out from corners where the tower's walls didn't quite meet, shone the odd flash of colour from the desk underneath, a solid oak foundation to the tower's growing mass. Coffee mugs on their sides bridged piles to other piles, forming unusual cylindrical corridors, while others resembled round staircases climbing into the tower that had grown over the mouths of the mugs – long-forgotten coffee stains seeping over the edge the only tell-tale signs that human life occasioned the desolate buildings of procrastination and poor organisation.

The detective sighed from his leather office chair. As he sat staring at the miniature metropolis before him, he imagined an open-minded architect taking sketches of the inventive design – years of neglect.

It'd make a hell of a futuristic city, he mused to himself, his mind's eye smoothing the edges of the paper towers into solid rectangular skyscrapers, the mugs into stairwells with circular elevators running through the centre.

Finally his phone broke his daydream with a loud proclamation of reality *bip-a-bip-beep-beep, bip-a-bip.*

The detective slipped the phone from its belt holster and brought it groggily to his ear.

"Oswald," he said.

"Constable Wilkes here, sir. We got the guy from the 303 this morning. Bringin' him in now."

"Suspect, Constable. You have the *suspect,*" Oswald reprimanded, rising to his feet and grumbling inwardly at the growing lack of professional etiquette he found himself surrounded by nowadays. No matter how much he stressed to them that they must be aware of what they say around suspects or their families, they continued to neglect simple forethought.

Regardless whether you think the guy did it or not, Oswald could hear his memory repeating his words, *you can't use words that confirm your own beliefs. Your job is to quell the trouble, bring suspects in, and let the rest of the law system determine if you caught the right guy. You start mouthing off that you think someone is innocent or guilty, you give the guilty ones tips and the innocent ones nightmares.*

"Sorry sir," Wilkes' voice called from the receiver, "my bad, sir."

Oswald started to say that he hadn't heard about any 303 call, when he heard the monotone dial that Wilkes was gone.

He let out a heavy sigh of disdain for his rookie comrades, and slowly replaced the phone to his hip. He sunk again onto the leather chair and wheeled up to the closest tower of paperwork. He carefully moved the stack to the side, and began scrambling through the chaos for the extension number for the radio room.

Yellow post-it notes have a talent for disappearing on a messy desk, though, and Oswald turned to the black office phone on his desk. Squinting intensely at the faded white list beneath the perspex on the side of the number pad, he laid his finger on the greying line with "Comms" scribbled beside a three-digit extension code.

Getting old, too. The paperwork glared at him again as the dial tone continued. A voice on the other line answered. *Behind, and old.*

"Thanks Jim," Oswald said without expression, hanging up after the call to the radio room. There had been a 144 call come in from a panicked resident that morning who had heard gunshots a few doors down from them. Maybe it had been upgraded? The only other details given were that a van had driven passed their own house shortly after, and that the gate at a house not far away was swinging wide open.

More paperwork, Oswald groaned, digging a couple of knuckles into his eye sockets with a frown. It was going to be the usual. He'd seen it all before. *Someone's car misfires and a bystander ducks for cover. A heavy box rolls down a flight of stairs and suddenly there's a report of machine gun fire in a residential area. A shopping centre alarm sounds and panicked customers flee what must be a bomb threat. What's wrong with everyone nowadays? Ever since 9/11 everyone's been anticipating terrorist attacks at every turn.*

Oswald rose with a grimace and grabbed a yellow mug near the edge of his desk. He saw the dried coffee along the walls of the cup and shrugged. *None of the others will be any cleaner.* As he reached his office door, he looked back before flicking off the light. He stood a moment in the doorway, hand still on the switch.

Lights out in the little city. No windows to shine from the towers built on fear, confusion, and neglect.

❖

Oswald entered the clinic-green little interview room to see a smug Wilkes sitting at the desk, arms folded. He seemed to be enjoying asking the questions. He was not supposed to be asking the suspect anything until there was another officer present. Yet further evidence to Oswald's brewing contempt for the undisciplined rookie. Still, Oswald was shocked with Wilkes' school bully approach.

"So you're telling me, you saw some guy shoot the gardener *after* you heard gunshots upstairs, where you *just happened* to be searching the desk beside a corpse when we arrived? C'mon mate…"

Wilkes rocked slightly on his chair and threw a cheery grin at Oswald as if to say *we've got him.* Oswald answered with a fiery frown and strode up to the desk beside Wilkes, looking at the boy opposite. He was only a young kid, about twenty years old. His light brown hair was messy and his bright blue eyes looked wild with fear.

What on earth has he seen? Or done?

"What *Constable* Wilkes here means to say, son," Oswald stressed the rank so as to remind Wilkes he was in fact a Police Officer and not just some thug, "is that you need to make sure you tell us everything that happened today for our report. Any detail may make a big difference to our *investigation.*" Again, that emphasis on professionalism. "Do you understand?"

The boy nodded slowly. Oswald cut him off as he started to speak.

"Now, my colleague and I will give you a few minutes to get yourself settled and we'll return to ask you a few questions."

The boy said simply, "okay," and lowered his head in thought. Wilkes kicked back his chair and the metal scraped the floor to announce his departure. Oswald was close behind, with a quick glance over his shoulder as he shut the door.

On the other side, he flicked the lock and spoke abruptly.

"What the hell was that Eddy?"

Wilkes stammered, but Oswald continued with force. "What are you thinking going all-guns-blazing on the kid? You had no right to start questioning him yet, and especially not like that!"

Eddy Wilkes looked stunned, but parried back easily, "I was the officer who brought him in, I don't have to wait for–"

"Oh you *are* an officer now? Good, because after that display in there I was beginning to think you were just a punk with a pistol in a uniform." Immediately, Oswald knew he'd made a mistake.

"Aaahh," Wilkes was beaming; Oswald had left himself open. "So it's Old Man Oswald and the 'punks' of the new generation again is it?"

There was an unspoken rivalry between the younger officers and Detective Oswald. Oswald disapproved of their rash tactics, and they despised his father-like reproach. The weakness in Oswald's argument was that he'd been getting slack. The metropolis on his desk was a beacon to the whole station that Old Man Oswald was falling behind. The piles of stained coffee mugs needed to keep him awake on shift and the pills to help him sleep when at home worked only further to his detriment. Maybe he really was losing his touch.

The world was so different when he started out on the force. People had more respect for the authorities, and the calls that came in were genuine. Now it seemed that every time someone called the station it was for either petty acts of violence and anger, or a panicked bystander escalating a situation in their mind like he'd suspected of this case earlier.

Oswald had had some great cases in his time. He'd thrived off the thrill of a chase and mystery, and he'd cheered wholeheartedly when he'd solved the case. Even the mundane cases or those that ran cold as the police circled their tails were at least a project to be a part of. Alas, his work seemed so lifeless now.

Maybe the years hadn't eroded the rest of the world. Maybe it was just the sands in the hourglass of his own career that had slipped through his hands. Perhaps he *was* just Old Man Oswald.

"Look," he said solemnly, coursing back to reality. "We have a suspect in there waiting for us to do our jobs so he can go home. Let's just get on with it. Can someone bring me up to speed on what happened?"

❖

The door opened again with a metallic click. Benjamin jumped in his seat, his hands gripping the tops of the thin steel legs. It had all gone wrong. From the way the last officer was speaking, his future was not looking too good. How could they think he'd shot those people? More importantly, how could he convince them he hadn't?

Since the two officers left the interview room, Terrace had tried desperately to recall something of the murderer's face, or something of note about the van. The pistol was long. He could remember that. And loud. Even as he thought about it he could see the gardener spinning around from the shot levelled at her head. Only now did the image of the encrusted blood and gore in the corpse's matted hair start to make his stomach churn.

The officers approached briskly, exchanging only a glance at each other. The older officer nodded and took the chair opposite Terrace. The younger officer who had questioned him before stood near the door, resting his right shoulder against the wall, his arms still folded.

"Hi there, son," the officer in front of him said with a wary smile. He looked like he might be nearing sixty years old. A few strands of grey hair nagged at his short sideburns and above his ears. His mouth was well-pronounced, resting in deep clefts from the sides of his cheeks, though his forehead announced the most evidence of the years of hard work and difficult times. A lifetime of troubled frowns.

But for all of this, there was nothing intimidating about his approach. He addressed Terry as 'son,' and likewise behaved as though he was in fact a concerned father. Beside each of his deep brown eyes, Terry could see the crow's foot lines of laughter, the ink stains of happier times still resonating on the parchment of the old man's face.

The sights Terry had seen today suddenly seemed less of a burden, knowing that for all the man in front of him had seen and done in his life, the good times had still weighed anchor in the biography Terry was reading in his face.

"My name is Detective Peter Oswald. Do you mind if I record our conversation?"

The detective had already pulled out a small black recorder as he was asking the question and pushed a little red button by the time his sentence was finished. It wasn't a question, really, just a polite courtesy to let him feel more comfortable with the little black spy resting on the table. Terry would have to choose his words carefully. After all, his words had equal power to defend him as they did to condemn.

"Not at all," he said as comfortably as he could muster, and added "sir."

"I am going to ask you to recall to me the events of the morning as you saw them. Could you start by telling me your name, please?"

"Yes, sir. My name is Benjamin Terrace. Or Terry, if you prefer."

He managed a weak smile, but he could feel his hands were cold and shaky, and he knit them together under the table to try to ignore his nerves. The detective smiled politely to acknowledge the nickname, and continued.

"Now, Benjamin, at what time did you approach the building that Constable Wilkes collected you from?"

Terry glanced quickly at the young officer still resting against the wall and caught a steely expression in return. The constable seemed impatient and intimidating, and Terry could sense some conflict between the two officers just in the contrast of their approach.

"Uh, I guess it would have been a little after 10am, sir. That's when I left my home just a few blocks down."

The detective frowned slightly, as if this was not what he was hoping to hear. He rested back into the recline of the chair. "That's almost an hour before the Police arrived at the building," he let the sentence hang for the weight of the words to sink in.

"Would you mind telling me what you were doing there?" Slowly, the detective leant forward again, placing his hands together near the edge of the table.

Terry started to shift in his seat. He tried to tell himself to sit still and stay calm, but he could see this escalating against him, and he began to feel scared. The constable adopted the same victorious grin he had shot at the detective the first time he had entered the room, and this made Terry more uncomfortable still. He began to stammer.

"I um... I was walking." The room was absolutely silent between voices, and Terry could hear his own breath coming heavily. He breathed in slowly, his eyes avoiding the intense stare of the detective opposite. "I saw a dog. A little dog outside of the house, and I walked over to it."

"Oh please!" the constable suddenly stood upright from the wall.
He was stopped short by the detective who said only "Constable," without looking away from Terry. "Was there anyone else around?"
"Yes," Terry looked again at Wilkes who had resumed his post beside the wall with his head facing down. He had short, clipped black hair, and a sharp nose set in an angular face. All of his features seemed to mirror his impatient disposition. "There was a gardener, but... she is dead."

As Terry continued to explain everything that had happened, the detective made very few scribbled notes on a pad in front of him, and for the most part continued his inquisitive stare and occasionally nodded slowly.
He grunted when Terry described the dead man on the office floor, a low sound that Terry couldn't decide was threatening or just intrigued. When he was finished, the detective made one more note, and then spoke in the same, comforting tone he had started with.

"I am told that when the Police arrived you were armed. Is that right?"
Terry suddenly remembered the golf club. He *was* holding it when they arrived, but still – armed? That was a bit of an overstatement. The detective was still trying to unnerve him to see if he was telling the truth.

"Well, I wouldn't really say it like that," Terry said, slowly, "I had a golf club in my hand, but-"

"Why?" Constable Wilkes had piped in again.

"Because, *sir*," Terry said, facing him and unwittingly using the same emphasis on his position that he had heard the detective use, "I had just walked into a building that I had just seen an armed man come out of and shoot the first person in his path. I don't think a golf club would have been too much of a threat to anyone – in the circumstances."

An awkward few seconds passed, with Terry regretting speaking so rashly, yet he tried to keep a stern expression. He knew that if he lost his momentum, the officer would pounce on him. Right now, he couldn't afford any enemies. Especially not while the facts were piled against him.

"Very well," said Detective Oswald, finally breaking the silent standoff. When Terry turned back, he thought he could see a glimmer in the old man's eye. Perhaps he was just relieved that he didn't have to be the one to reprimand the unruly officer.

"Now, son, did you ever meet the man you found on the office floor before today?"

"No, sir."

"Although you said you walk past this house regularly?" Again, the silence for the heavy meaning behind the words. "You never saw him before?"

Terry could feel his heart pounding again. He was still on the knife edge of this affair.

"Not that I am aware of, sir. I do tend to keep to myself."

"And I don't suppose you recognised him?" the detective lifted an eyebrow. Terry's puzzled silence was his only reply, so the detective continued. "We believe the man in that office was the well-known political activist Joseph Donald. That at least, is his residence. Of course, the way these things work we do not have a concrete confirmation on his identity." He paused and seemed to look passed the table to the floor for a long moment before looking up again. "Now, son, does that name mean anything to you?"

Terry was careful to look into the detective's eyes as he spoke.

"No, but..." Terry cleared his throat. "but I did guess something like that from the papers on his desk."

Detective Oswald only nodded slowly to himself. Slowly, he pulled back his chair and began to stand.

"These investigations can take any number of days – even weeks. I am going to be honest with you, lad, I don't think you did it."

Terry tried to control his relief, but he hadn't realised how tense he had been until he let his shoulders rest.

"However," the detective added, shooting a quick look at Wilkes by the wall, "I have been wrong before. I don't see the need to contain you here, but that does not mean you are off the hook completely. What I would like is for you to report in to the station daily."

"You mean like bail?"

"Similar, yes. But with less paperwork," the detective grinned at what must have been a private joke. "You simply sign a form each day at the front desk, and you can go home."

"How- how long do you want me to do that for?" Terry asked, unsure if it was okay for him also to stand. Wilkes was still resting against the wall, so he stayed put.

"For now, just over the next fortnight. It may be extended if need be though. C'mon son, you can go home now, I believe we already have all of your contact details?"

"Yes," Terry nearly jumped out of his seat, but as he reached the door that Oswald was now holding open, he slowed. "There was a girl, in a photograph on the bookshelf. Has she been told? She looked like she may have been his daughter."

Oswald smiled, sending his wrinkles to life in his aged face. "She is our next port of call. Son, if you remember any other details later on, you make sure you let me know when you report in. Anything may help."

Terry nodded, then slipped out the front door of the Police Station, sliding his hands into his pockets and bracing against the cold wind outside.

He exhaled a heavy sigh of relief.

Chapter 4
A Walk in the Park
Queanbeyan

Dmitri trudged noisily through the stones beside the footpath, his hands buried in the pockets of his brown leather jacket. The felt collar was high around his neck to shield his skin from the fierce, icy breeze. A wisp of thin fog clouded his face as he breathed through his parted lips. The chill seemed to rip through his dark blue jeans, and his frozen toes felt numb inside his black joggers. He still wasn't used to this weather.

He kept his head down to shield his eyes from the icy blasts and tried to walk faster to keep the blood pumping. He rounded a corner to the right, away from the scattered novelty stores and Chinese takeaway outlets. Dmitri crossed to the opposite side where there was a park with a few evergreen trees dominating the border beside another footpath. His motel was just on the other side of the expansive parkland; it was just a matter of cutting across diagonally.

He'd gone out to try and clear his head, but after the chill, he was looking forward to just getting back behind some fan-forced heat and a cup of instant coffee. He'd be out of the motel in another two days anyway. He'd asked for a basic room and paid a fortnight up front. He travelled light, barely more than a backpack coming with him from holiday accommodation to holiday accommodation. He had learned, perhaps more than anybody, how much possessions can tie you to places. Though he was a collector of sorts, and collections needed a place to stay. So he'd realised the solution to his problem a while ago. His unusual artefacts could stay safely in a storage shed, and he could be free to move around without them when they weren't needed.

There was a lot less paperwork for a storage locker than a house. And a lot less prying eyes.

When he had reached about halfway over the park, he noticed a black and brown dog tied to a tap, whimpering longingly, and staring off, ears pricked, at three figures playing together further in the distance. The dog paid no attention to Dmitri as he approached. It began to bark intermittently as the two children near the playground threw a ball between themselves and their father. The man turned slightly to yell to the dog to sit. The canvas leash was tight between the tap post and the excited pup.

Still walking casually, Dmitri flicked his head around to see if there was anyone behind him, then slipped his right hand deeper into his coat pocket. The knife blade was like dry ice to the touch, but the thick rubber handle didn't seem to absorb the cold the same way. Light flashed off the blade as Dmitri brought it beside his stride and approached the dog that still stood, whimpering, oblivious to Dmitri's presence.

In one swift slice, he split the middle of the leash and continued walking as he slipped the knife back into its hidden sheath.

Like a rocket, the dog had shot off from its rope prison and bounded crazily to the three figures. Dmitri continued with his head slightly to the right, in time to watch the littlest child make a desperate rush away from the dog, gripping the ball tightly. The dog was in hot pursuit, and the father wasn't far behind.

Dmitri couldn't contain his chuckle as the small boy was bowled over, and the prize ball captured and shaken wildly by the possessed hound. The father went to console the little boy who had probably grazed his knee in his foiled retreat.

A popping sound came from the untamed ball of fur in a hurricane of its own euphoria, and the other child squatted in tears as the canine proceeded to tear its thin, rubber prey into strips of spoiled playtime.

Chapter 5
Reporting In

The policeman at the reception desk greeted Terry without looking up from the computer monitor. A heavy-set man was seated in one of the waiting room chairs, and he returned Terry's awkward stare with a menacing intimidation. Terry shifted his gaze to the floor, and back to the officer who was now looking at him expectantly. Terry tried to explain that he needed to sign a form, but feeling the big man's stare still on him, he stuttered mid-speech. When the officer showed he hadn't understood, he tried again, clearing his throat.

"A form. Oswald, uh, Detective Oswald told me I should report in." The man showed no expression that he understood, so he added, "I'm a... witness."

Saying the word aloud, Terry realised that he was in a very dangerous predicament. In the second it took for the officer to respond, he was gripped by a chain of thoughts in a spiral of paranoia. He was the sole witness of a violent murder, and there was no way to know how big the case was. The man he saw may not have been working alone, and he'd have no idea who may want him dead.

"A witness, eh?" started the officer indiscreetly. Terry shot another look to the waiting man, and this time it was he who looked away at last. Terry felt a lump in his throat and leant forward on the desk. Before he could object to the loud proclamation of his vulnerable position, the officer asked him to take a seat.

"Won't be a moment. Oh, what was your name, kid?"

"Uh, Terrace," he said as quietly as he could. "Benjamin Terrace."

"Terrace, huh?" The policeman boomed. Terrace grimaced as the officer's voice seemed to echo a hundred times in the uncomfortable silence of the waiting room and the intimidating figure intent on Terry's business. As he took a seat, he avoided the heavy man opposite, and stared at the magazine rack by the window.

A wall clock above the desk thudded out the long seconds, before the officer's voice ricocheted off the walls again.

"RUDLEY," it echoed, and Terry caught himself wince with the sound. The man opposite clapped his hands to his knees as he rose and brushed past Terry's seat to the desk. Terry could hear the pen scratch out the man's hurried signature, and with a grunt, the man left.

A scruffy, middle-aged woman came through the glass double doors next, and headed comfortably over to the desk. With a flat greeting to the obviously-familiar officer behind the desk, she too scribbled out a signature and went out the way she came with a sarcastic wave. In the space of fifteen drawn out minutes, several other colourful characters came and went – cheery, grumbling or indifferent – and Terry still waited in the otherwise silent waiting room. Finally, his curiosity took hold over him, and he asked from his chair what these people were doing. Without looking up, the officer boomed a sarcastic reply.

"They're all baaaad people," he drawled, "signing their bail." He finished with a cluck of his tongue and continued his paperwork.

Terry frowned at the patronising goody-two-shoes implication and made no reply. It wasn't that stupid a question. *Am I supposed to have signed bail to be a 'big boy'?!*

As he stewed over the officer's attitude, a door to the right of the desk opened. Silhouetted against the fluorescent hall lights behind him, Detective Oswald stood leaning his hand on the handle.

"Heya, son," Oswald said, professionalism and experience etched into his very voice and tone, even in such a casual salutation. Terry felt instantly more comfortable, and he rose to walk over to the opened door.

"Come on in for a minute." The detective jerked his head back toward the corridor behind him. Terry worried for a moment that things weren't to be as straightforward as he'd hoped, but there was nothing threatening about Oswald's manner.

The two walked in silence past a few grey-green doors before Oswald opened one on his right. The room was simple, and very similar to the one he had been in the day before.

Besides a desk and four chairs in the middle of the grey room, a television on a wheeled stand was the only furniture. Terry helped himself to a seat, and Oswald joined him opposite after closing the door. The detective pulled out his black sound recorder, but had not turned it on yet.

"I don't mean to sound rude," Terry spoke first, "but I was under the impression I just had to sign in at the front desk."

"Yes, that is the case," Oswald said, "However I just wanted to touch base and see how you're doing after the ordeal."

Terry could see the man's interest was genuine, but behind that there was still some suspicion – something left unsaid.

"Well, I... I certainly didn't sleep very well," Terry said without expression. The detective said nothing, and Terry wondered what he was meant to tell him about. "I uh, I waited for something to come up about it on the news, but nothing did."

"No," Oswald said simply, "we try to keep these things as quiet as possible. At the very least until we have a better idea what is going on. In this case, however, I daresay it'll leak out quite quickly. Political activists don't tend to go down quietly, and neither, for that matter do gardeners lying in the front yard in a residential area. The neighbours were pretty hysterical, and they couldn't give us any useful information."

Terry couldn't help but feel suspicious of the detective's motives. *Why is he telling me all this? What's he trying to lead me into saying?* Terry decided to play along.

"Who do you think did it?"

The detective smiled warmly. "This guy could've easily had hundreds of enemies. And since you're the only one who was at the scene, you'll have to be careful. You're the best lead anyone's got."

"So it *was* the man from the photos? The activist? Like you thought?" Terry said, changing the direction of the conversation from himself.

"Mmmm," Oswald confirmed, "Yeah, it was Donald. His granddaughter identified him. That brings me to my next point." Oswald reached out to the recorder and spoke the day's date and time, along with the names of Terrace and himself. "You mentioned her as you were leaving yesterday. How did you know about her?"

Terry hoped that the question was only asked so as to put the information on the record, but he swallowed hard before answering, fighting the nerves that suddenly crept up again.

"I saw a photo… in the office. I only mentioned her in concern. If she follows his political pursuits, perhaps she could also be targeted by the same people."

"You say 'people'… yet you only saw one man, is that right?"

Terry sensed the trap, again, and replied appropriately. "That is only an assumption I have made. It didn't make sense to me that one man would feel so strongly as to kill a politician he disagreed with. I figured the man I saw must be part of some sort of organisation."

"You seem to have given this some thought."

"Like I said, sir, I didn't get much sleep." Benjamin added a smile this time.

Oswald appeared to be amused that he should be trying to solve the mystery, and asked, "So then, who do *you* think did it?"

Terry let out a chuckle. "Honestly, I'd have no idea. But I do intend to keep my eyes and ears open, sir."

Oswald turned off and pocketed the recorder. As he stood, he said, "Just be careful, son. This isn't a fun game, trust me. No doubt you've thought about your own dangerous position?"

"Yes, it did occur to me. Should I, uh, do anything?"

"I can't really offer you anything at this stage, but, it'd probably be a good idea to change a few habits, like your 10am walk for instance. If someone *was* to be watching, you wouldn't want to give them a set time you'll be out of the house. In particular, I wouldn't walk down past the same houses." Oswald must have seen the worry in Terry's face, because he softened his approach then. "Don't worry too much. I'm just saying if you want to be on the safe side. At this stage I have no reason to believe you're a target for whoever did this. It seems the only reason the gardener was killed was because she was literally blocking his path."

The two stood and Oswald led them back down the hall to the waiting room. Before he opened the door, he put a hand on Benjamin's shoulder. "It's perfectly normal for you to be thinking about all of this; hell, I'd be more worried if it didn't affect you at all. But don't go snooping. Like I said, the gardener's dead for standing in his way, so you–" he pressed a finger to Terry's chest "–need to make sure you're out of the way."

With another smile, he opened the door and directed Terry to the desk. The loud officer had a form ready for him to sign, and then he headed home on foot.

Chapter 6
New Friends

From the bar, Benjamin Terrace stared at the television screen in the top corner. Sure enough, just as Oswald had said, it didn't take long for the story to leak out to the media.

He placed the rum and cola down on the counter and listened intently to the reporter. Sixty-five year old Joseph Donald had been gunned down at his residence. Witnesses described a rental van driving by at the time of the murder, but the number of assailants was yet to be confirmed. Police believed the murder to be the malicious act of an enraged civilian, and while the motive is thought to be personal, authorities are not ruling out the possibility of a political assassination. The funeral would proceed once the investigation could be finalised.

At least get the facts right if you're going to air sensitive information, Terry thought into the bottom of his glass. *No mention of the innocent gardener, either. I guess the people 'in the way' aren't important enough to reach the headlines.*

A chuckle from a man beside him broke his internal conversation.

"Ridiculous, huh?" the man elbowed Terry. "Political assassinations, pfff." The man shook his head. Terry eyed him curiously; something about the man seemed familiar. Encouraged by the rum, he decided to join in the banter.

"He is a politician, ain't he?" he probed.

"So? Don't mean his death is political." The man swallowed another gulp of beer and drew a breath through his teeth. "Nah, probably his ex-wife or something, pays a thug to whack him. That doesn't sell good news though. It's gotta be *political.*"

"Ah, but who says he's got an ex-wife?" Terry made an attempt at playing devil's advocate.

"Well," the man said, pointing to the screen again, "he didn't make that sweetheart all on his own, did he?"

The news update showed a woman in her mid-twenties, wiping away a tear with a scrunched up tissue. She pushed a lock of brown hair from her face, and made another attempt at a statement, before holding the tissue to her pursed lips and

33

shaking her head. The banner at the bottom of the screen showed her name: Charlotte Harvey, granddaughter. *Idiots. Just publish her identity on the news, why don't you?! Might as well put her address on there too!*

"Besides," the man beside him continued, "his wife died about fourteen years ago." At a raised eyebrow from Terry, the man smirked and continued, "I like to keep up to speed with the fellas in power. Hell, kid, it's not like I'm just in this bar *all* the time." He tossed a peanut from the plate at the bartender and bellowed, "Ain't that right, Rodge mate?" The bartender and the larrikin laughed heartily at the private joke, and Terry made his way to the toilets while the man's attention was elsewhere.

Scenarios raced through his mind, the grip of paranoia fighting for front row seats. It was an internal struggle not to get too carried away.

How could the man know it was fourteen years since the man's wife had died? How did he know that was the granddaughter straight away like that?

Well, he tried to reason with himself, *it had 'granddaughter' written on the banner, that's how you knew who it was, wasn't it?*

Yes, but how did he know before she came up on the screen?

C'mon, he's just a drunk whose constantly at the bar! So, he knows stuff about politicians, that's not uncommon! It certainly doesn't mean he killed him! He doesn't even fit the description you saw!

But he wasn't working alone, I'm sure of it!

His mental debate continued at the toilet sink until the big man himself walked in.

"Hey, hey! How'd you get in here so fast?" he joked. Terry smirked back and dried his hands. As the man passed behind him Terry looked him up and down, trying to get a mental picture of him. Terry heard the steel step of the urinal groan under the man's weight. When his zipper was undone, the fellow turned his head to look behind him. Catching each other's gaze, the man turned his head slowly back. After a pause, and a distinct lack of urination, he re-zipped his fly and turned to one of the cubicles, obviously not appreciating his new audience. Closing the door behind him, he stared at Terry with a menacing look in his eye. Suddenly Terry realised why the man looked familiar. He was the man from the Police waiting room!

Terry broke eye contact, and headed straight for the door, hearing the man lock the cubicle door behind him.

Did he recognise me?!

Once in the foyer, Terrace went straight for the exit. Something about that man made him feel completely uncomfortable, and he couldn't help the feeling that he had something to do with Joseph Donald's death. A Black & White cab was waiting on the street, and Terry suddenly decided walking home was not the best idea tonight. He knocked on the passenger side window, and the driver let him in.

❖

In the morning, Terry walked to the Police station again. He kept an eye out for the heavy-set man from the pub who'd no doubt be coming in to sign his bail. Terry had tried to remember the man's name when the indiscreet officer had boomed it out in the waiting room, but with the hundred thoughts racing through his mind, the name wouldn't come. *D- something... Was it D-? L-maybe...*

As soon as he started on the right track, he'd just remember Oswald's warning; *Stay out of the way.* But maybe he could help. Could he tell Oswald this morning to check out the guy's activity? Maybe why he's so interested in politics... *No, he'd just warn me to back off again.* Unless...

Unless he could find some proper information. *Oswald wouldn't mind my 'snooping' if I actually found something, surely.*

When he went inside, the waiting room was empty. The same officer was at the desk, and this time he didn't have to wait. He signed the form, and the officer placed it absentmindedly beside the keyboard and right next to the last form that had been signed. Terrace didn't have to look long to recognise the name on the top – Rudley. *That was it! Rudley!*

He'd already been there, surely just minutes before! Terry left the building, and with his hands back in his jacket pockets, looked about him before heading on home. He struggled with the disturbing thought that perhaps Rudley had deliberately beaten him to sign the bail. Was he waiting for him to arrive so he could follow him? He'd been there the day before, heard the officer announce his name, and most likely heard Terry tell the officer he was a witness to something.

But then there was his manner at the bar. Before the intimidating exchange in the toilets, he had shown no signs of recognising Terry. He still may not have. It could all have been an innocent misunderstanding.

Hell, Terrace thought, *I was staring at him in the toilets. He could have taken that multiple ways, and he certainly wouldn't have to be after me to find that a bit confronting.*

By the time he had gotten to his own neighbourhood, he had managed to move the paranoid ideas from his mind. His house was in view ahead. But his curiosity pulled him right, to a familiar walking route.

Were it not for the Police tape surrounding the property, the beautiful house could have hidden the pain it knew. From the outside, the house itself showed no damage, and gave no clue to the horrific murder just two days prior. Terry slowed his pace as he neared the building. He stood one house back and stared at the high study window – the one he had looked out of in the presence of the dead. He gazed down to the path, where he'd seen first hand the second callous murder of that day.

And that was the first time he noticed her.

The girl from the picture. The girl from the News – the dead man's granddaughter – Charlotte Harvey. She was sitting by the path, resting her back against the gate.

She was curled over, her legs stretched out to the edge of the concrete. In her arms was a familiar ball of orange fluff – the Pomeranian puppy. As Terry approached, he could see where tears had coursed down her cheeks to her chin, her bottom lip tucked up behind her teeth, biting back emotion. Her wet, brown eyes just stared forward, her mind somewhere else altogether.

Terry thought about comforting her. He knew he should say something. But what? He opened his mouth to speak, but closed it again without a noise.

What *could* he say? *Hi Charlotte, my name's Benjamin, I saw you on the news. No.*

"What are you doing here?" he imagined her reply.

Oh, well, I was here when your grandad got killed. I went upstairs and poked around his office a bit too. Hell, I even turned over his dead corpse just out of compelling curiosity!

No. That wouldn't quite cut it.

The girl's eyes hadn't moved from whatever distant object she was staring at. He could probably wave a hand in front of her eyes and she wouldn't blink. For a moment he let himself wonder what she was thinking. No doubt remembering childhood visits to Grandad's place. Perhaps some phantom conversation was playing out with the ghosts of the building.

Terry realised suddenly that he'd been standing there too long without any explanation. And without having a plausible reason to continue standing in front of the distraught girl, he turned and walked back the way he had come.

❖

It was Terry's overwhelming curiosity again that led him to make the phone call when he got back home.

He thought he'd have to try a few cemeteries or funeral homes, but he was lucky with the first call. Woden Cemetery – 3pm that afternoon. It was not technically open to the public, but these mysterious events have a way of attracting attention. Terry figured he would blend in with the media and the politicians hoping for the recognition of being seen at the ceremony.

It was too far a distance to walk comfortably from his home, and he wasn't about to ask his parents for the car. As a matter of fact, he hadn't told them anything about the last few days. Most families would say it was important to talk about things like that. Maybe he would at some point. For now, though, it was easier left as a secret.

So instead, the taxi had dropped him at the front car park. The plot was in one of the Anglican Lawns. The dress code varied from black suits to blue jeans, and Terry felt a little conspicuous in his three-piece suit. There were less people attending than Terrace had estimated; a few familiar faces from the news, and only one channel covering the footage.

Terry stood a few metres back, suddenly feeling how unwarranted his presence here was. The orator's words were inaudible from where Terry stood, muffled by the figures encircling the grave site, and any words that escaped were sliced to silence by the icy wind.

Terry was about to turn and leave when one of the figures, a tall woman dressed in a black suit jacket and skirt, turned her head as he looked at her.

It was Charlotte Harvey again. Only this time, she locked her gaze at him with a quizzical expression. She kept her hands in her jacket pockets, and though her body was facing forward, she kept her head turned, staring Terrace down.

Even with her hair obscuring her expression in the breeze, Terry felt her eyes piercing through him. He bowed his head and with a shuffle of his feet, turned back toward the car park. When he turned again, her attention was back to the procession. Terry didn't bother calling a cab for the trip home; he could use the walk to help him think.

Chapter 7
Falling Prey
Canberra
June 30, 2010

Yavuz Firat took a seat behind his cluttered desk. He left the office door open to keep an eye on his shop.

Turkish rugs weren't exactly walking out the door with demand in Canberra, but he made just enough money to support himself. There was something to be said, however, for the certain cash operations on the side, but when you can't exactly advertise your product, business moves slowly even in that department.

Usually he could pick the customers. They were always more edgy than those simply browsing the rug store. They'd make pathetic small talk about the weather, or some quip at how many politicians were in town that week. Yavuz realised this was their way of building courage, that they couldn't just straight out state how much cocaine they wished to purchase, hand him the money and go – but still, he grew tired of the hoops they made themselves jump through before they got to the point.

The man sitting opposite him now, however, was another story altogether. In his brown leather jacket and black jeans, he wore a smirk that Yavuz wasn't entirely comfortable with. The way he reclined on the chair offered to him was uncharacteristic of his usual customers. He generally found they paced backwards and forwards through the office, or if they did take a seat, they fidgeted uncontrollably with their fingers or pockets.

The man sitting opposite was calm. Although his hands were hidden in the deep pockets of the jacket, his wind-blushed cheeks and cracked lips told the Turkish dealer he wasn't accustomed to the weather. Not a local, then. A traveller perhaps?

"So, Mr. Firat, was it?" the man asked, gazing over Yavuz' head to the wall behind. He had not told the stranger his surname, but he was aware that his business details were certified on the wall. This man was attentive, a fact that did nothing to ease the uncertainty in Yavuz's stomach. A cop, maybe? Had one of his gutter-bound customers squealed about where he picked up his merchandise?

No, he decided. Surely an undercover cop would try to act like one of his customers, not stand out like this man. But if he wasn't a cop, then why did Yavuz Firat feel such an uneasiness talking to him?

"Just, Yavuz." He stated after a pause, then added, "please."

The man pursed his lips and nodded, saying simply, "Dmitri."

A moment passed without exchange, and finally Yavuz interrupted the man's prying gaze with a question.

"And, how long have you been in town, Mr. Dmitri?" He found himself starting the small talk now, despite his usual distaste for it. Now that he was presented with it, somehow it just didn't feel right to jump straight to business.

The man chuckled to himself and looked at the floor, his legs outstretched with one foot tucked under the other.

"Do I stand out that much?" he asked with a smile.

"Everyone takes to the weather differently," Yavuz replied. *Dammit,* he thought to himself, *now I've even stooped to* asking *about the weather!*

"I've been in and out, on and off," Dmitri replied cryptically. "I've got some time to get used to it."

Another long moment passed, and finally Yavuz found himself fidgeting for the keys to the desk's bottom drawer.

"How much?" he asked, the question equally cryptic in that if this man wasn't after what Yavuz thought he was after, perhaps he'd mistake that he was asking how much *time* he had.

The man now rose slowly to his feet, slapping his knee with his gloved left hand as he rose. The right hand hadn't moved from the warmth of his jacket pocket.

"Just the usual, Yavuz," he muttered as he walked over to the wall on the left of Yavuz, his back turned. With his now free left hand he ran a finger over the spine on one of the books on Yavuz's shelf, then turned his head as he rubbed the dust from his black, woollen glove.

Yavuz proceeded to unlock the drawer and withdrew a small plastic pouch with a plastic tie around the neck. *What's he mean 'the usual'? I've never seen this man before – have I? Is it the usual merchandise? The usual amount people buy? What?*

"Was this what you came to Australia for, Mr. Firat? Is this really the life you envisioned?" Dmitri still had his attention on the book shelf, but Yavuz could sense some sort of trap. He left the question unanswered and began to hope the man would be leaving soon.

"You, uh…" the man goaded, "you ever wanted to be famous, Yavuz?"

Yavuz could make no sense of the man's questioning, and if there was a trap, he couldn't think what on earth it was supposed to be leading to. He decided to play along. He gave a chuckle and leant over his desk, his forearms crossed over the edge.

"Sure," he said, "who wouldn't?"

"Well, here's your chance my good man."

Dmitri pivoted swiftly on his feet. His hand came out of his pocket to reveal a flash of silver which felt cold against the Turkish man's temple. Cold. And deadly.

His heart froze in his chest, but the rest of his body had no time to react. Whether it was the shock of greeting his mortality, or just incredibly good fortune, Yavuz Firat would never know, but he didn't feel the bullet as it bit through his skin, bone and brain. He was well and truly dead before it exploded through the other side of his skull, taking with it the majority of his face.

His body was thrown out of the chair, limbs flailing behind it, onto the floor, his disfigured wounds soaking the ornate wool-on-wool with the gruesome testimony of his murder.

Chapter 8
Finding Answers

When Terrace reached his home, there was a silver Omega parked at the kerb beside his driveway. His feet were burning from the walk.

There's a reason, he thought, *that you don't go walking in formal shoes.*

He kept his head down in weariness as he reached the steps to his front door. He was still fumbling in his suit jacket pocket for his keys, when a voice made him jump to attention.

"You scrub up well, kid." Terry looked up to see Detective Oswald standing beside the door. Terry breathed heavily in relief. He pinched the bridge of his nose and took a moment to recollect himself.

"A bit jumpy, huh, son?" Oswald chuckled.

"Guess I am. A bit. Uh, jumpy." Terry managed. He looked back over to the driveway to check if his father's car was parked there already. Strangely enough, it was not, but that didn't mean he was in the clear. There were no lights on in the house yet, not that he could see at least. He'd have to hope that the rest of the family were out somewhere.

All together? Doesn't seem likely.

"Did you, er, try the door bell, detective?"

Oswald turned behind him to the vacant building and nodded.

"I did. A little while ago. Figured I'd just wait a while."

"So, what did you want to see me for?"

Oswald shuffled his feet and looked back to the door. "It is cool tonight, isn't it? Perhaps we could talk inside?"

Terry looked back down the street, hoping not to see the headlights of his parents' car.

"Of course, uh, sorry." Terry unlocked the door and stepped inside. Oswald followed and shut the door behind him.

The lights were out inside, but a cacophony of muffled metal music roared from an upstairs bedroom.

Jono is home, then.

"Would you, um, like anything to drink?" Terrace asked as he approached the kitchen. He was rapidly trying to work out why the detective was here, while simultaneously trying to think up some way to excuse his presence if his brother came downstairs. Worse yet, if his parents came home.

"No. Thanks, though, "Oswald replied. "I just wanted to touch base with you. See how well you're coping."

"Well, I *was* fine," Terry chuckled. "You uh, you certainly know how to scare the crap out of someone."

The Detective smiled, but looked down at the floor. "You know, in my profession, we're prone to interpreting jumpiness as *suspicious*..." he let the sentence hang for a moment, but at seeing the concern on Terry's face he let up. "...Just saying, kiddo."

The joke had done its job though, and Terry was paying close attention.

"So," Oswald started, resting his hands against one of the table chairs. "Why are you all dressed up?"

Terry cleared his throat before answering. "Funeral." A pause. He found it hard to meet Oswald's gaze. "Donald's... funeral." Oswald looked at him as if there were more to tell, and after another moment Terry spoke again. "I just... wanted to be there. I don't really know why."

A curious '*Mmmm*' was the only response from Oswald. Terry couldn't decide whether it was a good sign or not. He could hear the clock above the small hallway heavily ticking the awkward seconds by, the split seconds between each tick counted out by his brother's soundtrack upstairs. Finally, Oswald removed a chair and sat, indicating that Terry should follow suit.

"Young man," he began, "you have quite a curious nature, don't you?"

Terry smiled politely, "I guess I never really thought about it. But yeah, I suppose I do." He wanted to tell Oswald about Rudley, about the suspicious conversation about politics and the bar he's always at. Maybe Oswald could have him watched, see who he associates with. But Terry held his tongue. This conversation felt more like Oswald was checking up on *him*. After all, the evidence was still only pointing his direction.

"She called me, Benjamin." Oswald said flatly, "Charlotte Harvey, Joseph Donald's granddaughter. She told me that someone approached the house while she was there, and that they backed away as soon as they saw her. She thought it a curious coincidence at first, until she saw the *same* man at the funeral, standing afar off. And again, he left when she made her presence known."

Terry said nothing.

"Now, when I heard this," Oswald continued, "my first thought was that this could be the man we're looking for. It seemed awfully suspicious to me, almost like there was something at the house he still wanted, or perhaps someone he was expecting would attend the funeral. When she gave me a description of the man, however, it led me to you. You, whom I now see, having walked from the other end of the city, after nightfall, in a black suit."

Still Terry said nothing. The house suddenly felt like the police interview room again. The simple wooden table and chairs morphed into the cold, metal furniture from Terry's memory, and the shadow cast by the fridge was now Constable Wilkes, sneering, waiting for him to slip up so he could throw him in prison for something he hadn't done.

Except Wilkes wasn't there. It had been Wilkes that was intent that Terry was guilty, and it was Oswald who seemed to trust him. So then if that was the case, what was Oswald playing at?

"Detective, sir," Terrace began, "I don't understand…"

"What I'm trying to tell you, lad, is that you are not above suspicion. In fact, everything so far places you as an accomplice *at best*." Another pause, and then, "If people start seeing you 'badgering' the family members of a murdered man, things won't go well for you. As it is, we're pushing the limits having you only reporting in daily."

Terry was looking firmly at the table now, avoiding Oswald's gaze altogether. He saw from the corner of his eye that Oswald had stood and was walking over to him. As he placed a heavy hand on his shoulder, Oswald said simply, "I know you think you're helping, but right now you're most helpful to us just by reporting in… and staying out of trouble. You *need* to stay out of the way. Remember that. I don't mean to sound harsh, but my previous warnings don't seem to have done the job. You saw the gardener." Terry winced momentarily. "You saw her get shot just for being there. Think about it."

Oswald took out a pen and a notebook. "I don't think I need to emphasise that I do *not* condone your little private investigation.

But if – IF – you remember something important and want to let me know, you can call me directly at this number. Save it in your phone, maybe."

As Terry reached for it, Oswald pulled it back to add a condition. "Old news only. Jogged memories, alright? Amateur Detective Benjamin Terrace is officially fired, alright? Gun and badge handed in. Back to doing whatever it is you normally do."

Terry nodded. Then he took the piece of paper.

As he headed toward the front door, Terry rose from his seat.

"Anything you wanted to add at all before I leave, son? About Charlotte? Or anything?"

Terry thought again about telling him about Rudley. But Oswald was right. This wasn't his business anymore.

"No. I'll let you know if I get spooked at all."

"Alright. I'll probably see you in the morning when you check in. Remember. Stay out of the way. Don't make me arrest you just to keep you safe."

Oswald threw Terry a wink as he opened the front door and left.

❖

He's right. Oswald is right, Terry thought to himself, still standing by the front door well after he'd heard Oswald's car start up and drive away. He went to the fridge for a drink, flicked on the television and sat down.

He wasn't paying any attention to the pictures on the screen. As he sipped at his glass of soft drink, he did what Oswald said. He saved the number in his phone. And he remembered the gardener. Remembered looking out from behind the tree to see her standing on the path to the front step. He watched her take those few cautious steps toward the door again in his memory. Then the memory flew forward to the man leaving the house.

As he exaggerated his recollection, the monster had grown twice the size, his outstretched gun arm reaching the gardener's head from the door. At least, it had happened so fast, it might as well have been like that.

Thinking of it again now, Terry couldn't really remember the moment of impact, just that the gardener had fallen. But he'd seen the aftermath of the fatal wound. As he held his mental gaze on the mess on the lawn, he thought about the killer.

What must that have been like? How could he just shoot her almost point blank like that? Did the blood spray over him as he walked through the mayhem he'd caused back to his accursed van? Did he hesitate before pulling the trigger? No! He'd just rushed out, seen another target and fired true. *Damn him!*

This wasn't any of Terry's affair. Before this, life had been so… normal. Life had been so… *boring.*

The television now showed snippets from the funeral. The reporter changed the story again now, as she dramatized the scene.
"Police are investigating some items that were stolen during the assassination, and a local witness has been assisting the police with their enquiries…"

The report went on, but Terry's mind was elsewhere already. The stolen items – the yellow envelopes. What was in them? That was the key.

Terry was already running all manner of absurd possibilities in his head by the time he realised that he had taken off his suit jacket and shoes. Almost as if he was watching himself, he changed his formal pants to jeans, his long sleeve shirt to a casual buttoned shirt, took a warm brown jacket, and was heading out the door. His brother's music still droned away upstairs.

❖

The Barrel and Bray Irish bar wasn't that far to walk from his house, but Terry's feet were still aching from the walk home earlier. Once inside, he knew he stood out from the rest of the usual patrons. They all seemed to wear a particular 'look', if that was the way to describe it. A certain expression that said that this particular pub was a second home, that they knew who came and who went, and who was welcome and who wasn't. Terry wasn't.
He sat at the bar where he had the day before and glanced up at the television. The News had long since finished, and the screening had dissolved into the football – something that he had never had the desire to understand.

Terry waved a hand at the bartender, triggering many disapproving glares from the regulars at their tables and bar stools. With all eyes on him, Terry asked for a rum and coke. It would be hard to keep his business subtle tonight, with 'OUTSIDER' practically painted on the back of his shirt, but Terry needed to see if Rudley would show up again.

As he glanced around the dingy room, he noticed for the first time the man sitting to his left. He was dark-haired, with an angular face. He was tall, an attribute displayed in the way he sat up straight on the bar stool. He was staring directly ahead, beyond the bottles behind the bar, seemingly looking through the very wall. He was older, past middle age at least. Youthful, still, exept for a severity that had etched itself somehow in the lines near his eyes.

Terry realised he must have been staring, because suddenly the man snapped his head in his direction. The man had piercing blue eyes, set deep behind his brows, and a sharp nose. Terry couldn't be sure, but it seemed that for a second there, something flashed across the man's eyes. Recognition? No, the look passed too quickly – as fast as it appeared, it was gone. Then, what? The man raised his eyebrows quizzically, prompting Terry that he was *still* staring. He coughed.

"Sorry... mate," he looked down, and found himself looking at the man's shoes. "I, um...," he fumbled for the thoughts. For excuses. At last, he settled for, "Yeah...," turning his head to look back at the bartender, hoping to find some sort of an escape from the awkward moment.

He received instead a single raised eyebrow. A lifetime passed in those moments, but finally Terry decided he had to say something. He'd initiated contact, he couldn't just go introvert, after all. Not if he intended to stay long enough.

He coughed again.

"It's uh, cold out, hey?"

The man beside him suddenly beamed a broad smile, as if he'd been holding it in the whole time, finding amusement in Terry's loss of place.

"Yeah, mate. It's cold alright."

Terry smiled awkwardly, and the man continued, "so you from around here then, kid?"

With a breath, Terry resigned to the realisation that the more he talked, the more relaxed he'd feel. He talked about his work, the weather, his lack of a social life. He mentioned nothing of the last few days. In turn, the stranger talked about his own work. He was in town for a few weeks. Here from time to time, in and out, that sort of thing. Though Terry had already forgotten what he'd said he was selling.

"Well, ain't this cute?" The barman interrupted as he topped up their drnks, "the two new fellas getting along nice and dandy…"

Beneath a thick grey moustache, the man smiled a devious grin. Terry had no idea what to make of that, but thankfully the stranger chimed in cheerily.

"Oh, good of you to join us! How about you, mate? What do you do for a living?"

The barman was thrown off guard by the question. What did he do for a living? Well, wasn't that obvious? But Terry could see that the question had been a deliberate one, and when all trace of the man's grin was gone, he could see that it had worked.

Somehow this stranger had a presence about him. Some sort of power that was beyond his appearance. It hadn't really mattered what he'd said. He had wanted the bartender to keep silent, and it had happened. Words just happened to be the best medium for sending the command.

Wearing a sour expression, the barkeeper took a step back, and moved further along the bar. Terry threw a grin at the stranger, just as he heard a barstool scrape along the floor behind him.

"Evenin' Rodge!" a man behind him boomed. Terry turned to see Rudley, about to take a seat on his right. The man was wearing a wide smile which dropped instantly upon eye contact with Terrace.

Rudley shot a look at the stranger on Terry's left, and then at the bartender he'd just addressed, and stood up straight, tucking his barstool back in. He looked as though he might speak, but then turned back toward the door. As he sauntered in the doorway for a moment, his lips mumbled something like 'my um, um… – be back.'

"Don't think that fella likes you too much, mate," the stranger said. Then he added, "you alright?"

"Uh, yeah, yeah. I'm good. I uh, I have to go too, actually. Nice to meet you, though."

The stranger extended his hand, "Dmitri."

Terry's mind was still on Rudley, and it took him a moment to realise the man was introducing himself. "Oh yeah, uh, Benjamin. But I usually just go by Terry." He shook Dmitri's extended hand. "Nice to meet you, buddy."

And Terry left.

Outside, the cold in the air bit through Benjamin's jacket. On his left, the car park ended at a worn-down wire fence, overgrown with weeds and long grass. A vacant block of land loomed in the darkness beyond, and past that, another fence. A man trudged along in the distance, lit up by a street light, hands in pockets, head down, taking sweeping strides to get as far away from the bar as possible.

Rudley.

Though Terry had no idea what was in the vacant block, he slipped through one of the many gaps in the fence and headed as fast as he could toward the escaping figure, running parallel to Rudley who had the advantage of walking unhindered on the footpath and in the light.

The grass was longer than Terry had hoped, and it was only by sheer determination not to let Rudley out of his sight that he kept a steady pace through the dips and rises of the unkempt field. The fence line was just as worn out as the pub's, but what was left was wooden, warped and missing many planks.

At the edge of the block, Terry slipped back through the fence and onto the path just as Rudley slipped into darkness not far in front. Terrace began to sprint, desperate to follow his only lead in the mystery that had overtaken his life. Terry could feel the footpath beneath his feet, pointing him toward Rudley, but the darkness was hiding the fugitive, and Terry had been consumed by the enshrouding darkness now, too.

Bad move, he thought, just a moment before something slammed into his shins. He lurched forward, and his knees hit the pavement with an agonising crack. Terry's hands stung from catching himself on the concrete, but he sprang back off them to face the attacker. Rudley's menacing bulk blocked out what little light was being given off by the sky, and Terry could see he was holding something long in both hands. His burning shins were telling him it was hard, too.

"Who the *fuck* are you, man?!" Rudley bellowed, as he smacked the object against Terry's cheek, hurtling him to the right. His foot caught on his other leg, and Terry was unable to catch himself this time. The right side of his face hit the concrete, and the left was stinging wildly. Something cold and wet was on his cheek. He raised an arm helplessly to beg the man to stop.

"Wait.... please... wait."

"Answer me, shit bag!!" the monster roared, "Who *are* you?"

Terry rolled onto his front and tried to lever himself up with his arms.

"I said," Rudley muttered through gritted teeth, as he kicked Terry's right arm out from under him, "who... are... *you*?!" Terry hadn't realised his arm was lying straight across the gutter until Rudley's boot slammed down against his elbow.

For a moment, the world went white, pixels filling his vision where the darkness and the madness should have been. A gut-wrenching sound was echoing in the street, and it took Terry a few seconds to realise it was his own scream. He didn't dare to look at his arm – he could guess what state it was in. Despite himself, Terry found he was sobbing against the cold concrete, the salt stinging the splinters in his cheek.

Rudley punctuated each of his next words with a kick into Terry's left side. "You *pathetic- piece* of- *shit!*"

Terry could feel the thuds into his ribs, and he could hear the crack as the boot found the bone. He could feel his arm screaming out in pain, drowning out the relatively minor complaints of his left side. He could hear his breath rattle in his chest as his lungs heaved to take in air. And he could feel his own blood smearing the pavement from his face.

What he didn't hear was the voice yelling out to Rudley from the street. And he didn't feel the fence post crash into the side of his head – Rudley's final, concussive blow before fleeing into the darkness.

Chapter 9
Disjointed
Canberra Hospital
Approximately 11am, 1 July, 2010

A deep drum was beating.

Slowly.

Repeatedly.

In time.

The beat bumped against the inside of Terry's skull, prodding him to stir. After a few seconds, he realised it was his own pulse.

A droning sound layered itself over the drum beat – a garbled, disjointed sound. A discordant melody, perhaps. The world felt bright, but Terry's eyes wouldn't open when he told them to.

The sound droned again, but clearer now, and Terry realised it was a voice, but he couldn't hear the words. Another voice was answering, and slowly, his senses came back. He could hear a tapping across from him.

Metal.

And plastic.

A pen, hitting a clipboard. He could smell copper, as if his nostrils had been filled with it. He tried to move his fingers, and some sensation came back to him. Sensation, and pain! His head was pounding now as if there really was a drum beating inside it, and his throat felt as dry as gravel.

He realised with some alarm, that though he could bend his left hand fingers, the right threw only pain at him as a response. He tried to open his eyelids again, and this time they gave a small flutter.

Focussing all his concentration, he managed to pry them open, and instantly wished he hadn't. White light flooded in and sent the pain in his head roaring.

The voice spoke again, clearer this time.

"...steady Mr. Terrace. Your body's suffered quite a beating." The voice was soft, female, and yellow.

Yellow? What the hell did he hit me with? And suddenly recollection flooded back.

"Rudley!!" Terry called, opening his eyes wide and trying to sit up. He was strapped into a bed, shrouded in white. White floor, white roof, white bedding. A pale green curtain made an attempt at colouring the room, but it served only to highlight the whiteness of everything else. The voice called softly to him again, reassuring him. It belonged to what looked like a nurse. Her shirt was blessedly coloured a dark blue, and her green eyes were framed by locks of light brown hair. Terry's eyes celebrated the darker tone of colour, drinking in her features and slowly piecing together that he must, in fact, be in a hospital.

Another splash of colour stirred behind the nurse, and a familiar deep voice spoke from the other side of the room.

"You're okay, Benjamin. You're safe now." It was Detective Oswald. He was sitting in a chair with one leg crossed over his lap, with a notepad and pen in his hands. He scribbled something quickly and then rose to his feet with a smile. The nurse excused herself.

"How are you feeling, son?"

Terry took a moment to respond. The words caught on the dry shards in his throat, and he coughed weakly.

"Here," Oswald said simply, holding a plastic cup of water to Terry's lips. He couldn't move his arms yet, but Oswald helped him take a small sip. The icy water dribbled streams through the sand that seemed to fill his mouth. It felt as if the fluid soaked into his tongue, evaporating, it seemed, before reaching the back of his mouth. He leant forward for another sip. This time the coolness spread down his throat. The copper taste again.

The water tasted like blood.

Oswald returned to his seat.

"Do you remember what happened?"

Terry frowned, opening a cut near his eyebrow. He winced and tried to refocus.

"Uh... I was..."

"Take your time, take your time. I'll help you if you like. You said, 'Rudley'? Let's start there. Is that someone's name?"

Terry took a moment to respond. He didn't want to tell Oswald he'd been snooping. He shouldn't have been. And he'd failed. And he'd been caught – big time! But he was here now, and there was no point trying to hide anything.

"Rudley's the guy." At Oswald's raised eyebrow, he added, "the guy who killed Donald. At least, I think he is. You know who he is – he's on parole. I saw him for the first time when I went in to sign after the…" A thrash of pain trembled through his body, and he sat in silence for a minute. Terry looked at Oswald, and he knew he was dying to tell him he'd warned him about this. He was grateful Oswald was holding it in.

"Okay, it's alright son. Let's just talk about last night for a minute," Oswald offered. "Do you know the man who called the ambulance for you?"

"Ambulance? Wait- what did you say? Last night? What time is it now?"

Oswald took a breath. "You were pretty badly beaten, lad. You've been mostly unconscious since they brought you in. Or sleeping, at least. A man called for help. He stayed with you until the paramedics arrived. Told them he'd seen you getting attacked… And then by the time you were loaded into the ambulance, he was gone."

Terry instantly thought back to the man in the pub.
What was his name?
It would cause no harm to keep this small detail to himself, surely. Oswald was talking as if the man had done something wrong. He didn't want to implicate someone who'd helped him.
What was his name, anyway?

"I went to the pub to watch him – Rudley. I talked with a guy there, and then I followed Rudley out." He groaned as another wave of pain washed over him. "The sod wailed on me with a fence post, dammit!! He tripped me over and started laying into me with it! Ugh. How badly hurt am I?"

Oswald took a breath and dropped his chin to his chest. "I'll let the doctors fill you in properly, but it seems your main concern is your right arm at this stage."

Terry looked down and saw that what little flesh peeped through the bandages was an uncomfortably dark purple.

"Son, how are you so sure that it was this Rudley guy?"

"I'm positive."

"And this guy at the bar?"

Terry just closed his eyes and shook his head. "I don't know."

"Well..." Oswald struggled for a moment for words. "You're going to be alright. I'll come back in a day or two if you're still in here. Otherwise I'll pop around to your house. Ah, now that reminds me, is there any way Rudley would know your home address?"

Alarm ran through Terry's mind as he backtracked events trying to think. *Why my house? What would he do?* His own mind argued that one back, *Well, you can guess that part, you're only alive because Dmitri called the- DMITRI!! That's his name!*

"Benjamin?"

"Oh, sorry. No. I can't think of any way he'd know."

"Okay. Well, get better soon, kid." Oswald turned and pushed back the curtain. He turned briefly. "And stop meddling. Okay?"

Terry smiled painfully.

"Gotcha."

It must've been hard to keep the reprimand in the whole time.

Chapter 10
Trouble in the Country
Canberra
3:30pm, 1 July, 2010

Detective Peter Oswald was back at his desk. A blank Word document was open on his computer, and the cursor blinked, prompting him to write.

Oswald.

Oswald.

Oswald.

He stirred, then began slowly to type the notes he had made from talking with Benjamin Terrace. He'd just begun when there was a faint knock on the glass of his door. As he swivelled in his chair, the door was opened and in stepped Zoe Sullivan, the young female officer who had joined the precinct less than a month prior.
"Sorry to interrupt again, sir."
"No! Not at all!" In truth, Oswald was happy for the distraction, something to delay the labour of paperwork. Sullivan had only been in the precinct for a few weeks, transferred in from her rural service. To call her a fresh recruit would undersell the skill she had shown even in her small country town placement. In the city now at last, she was eager to help wherever she could, in the hope of making a name for herself.
When it came to mandatory General Duties, well, the sooner the time was over, the better, so the general consensus was to keep busy and let the time fly.

Glancing at a sheet in her hands, she continued, "I looked up that Rudley guy for you. Earl Rudley. He's only been out for four months, nearly five. According to his record, there were some unconfirmed suspicions of mental instability. Says here on his psych report, 'exhibits behaviour congruent with paranoia'. He was initially convicted for assault and attempted murder." She looked up at Oswald, disgust written across her face. "Apparently he crippled a door-to-door salesman, unprovoked. Beat and kicked him against the steps of his front door."

"Hmm... Some privacy issues, maybe. Checked in today?"

"Not as yet."

"Right. Well, keep an eye out. I need to speak with him. He may be the one who's given the Donald Harvey witness a, um-"

"Hard time?" Zoe offered.

"I was going to go with 'thrashing', more like."

Oh Terry... Oswald thought to himself, *what have you gotten yourself into, kid?*

"Sir?" the officer asked, "there's one more thing. A call just came in. A body was found just outside of town. Squad car's already on its way, and I've notified Forensics, but I thought you'd like to know. Could be related?"

Oswald smiled. *Damn enthusiastic recruits. Always hoping something will be a connection to some big case.* "I don't mean to disappoint you, Zoe, but in my experience, related clues don't come this easily. That being said, I'll keep it in mind for my discussion with this Earl Rudley. I'd like to know where he's been since last night." He dismissed the young officer and took the call-out address from the front desk.

It took a good twenty minutes to reach the Greenleigh area, just outside of Queanbeyan. The neatly written address led him off the Kings Highway, down Captains Flat Road and finally onto a white, chalky gravel road. A patrol car was already parked on the edge of the road, and two officers were currently setting up a tape perimeter around an upturned, black Mazda MPV. Oswald was on his way over when his eyes caught another tape perimeter further off the road.

"How's your stomach this morning, Ozzie?" An officer commented as he sidled up beside the detective, breaking his gaze. As they walked over to the furthest cordon, the officer told Oswald what they'd found so far. "Pretty ugly. Looks like the van's been shunted off the road, toppled over, and the driver, we assume, was pulled out, beaten and..." he paused, inhaling deeply through his nose, "–shot. Point blank. And from the mess that's been made of him, it was a shotgun. Found a shell casing from one of those old-fashioned snap-to shotties, still looking for the other one."

"Other one?" Oswald raised an eyebrow.

"Oh, sorry. Two gunshot wounds. One to the head, one to the groin."

"In that order, you reckon?"

The officer responded with a stiff shake of his head. A grimace washed over his face as he jutted his head in the direction of the cordon. Staying well back, he put his hands to his hips, but dropped his gaze back toward the toppled MPV.

Oswald looked at the gruesome facts before him. A wide splatter of blood, cloth and flesh on the white gravel indicated the initial gun shot, and a thick trail of blood leading toward the trees showed where the victim had dragged himself a short way back.

Where the road fell away into the long grass and sparse trees, another splash of gore framed the still, dead and quite decapitated body of a man. The shotgun round presumably aimed at the groin had opened up the majority of the man's lower torso, baring the remnants of his digestive system, and opening up his thighs to expose two white femurs. The head was mostly missing – jagged, torn flesh pointing toward where the scattered puzzle pieces had once formed a face.

"Who the hell still has those outdated things?" the officer called from behind Oswald, the wind's distortion of his voice indicating that he was still facing away from the bloodshed.

"Good question," Oswald replied, finally turning back to the officer. "Might be worth checking the registered guns in the area, *but* I got a feeling this will be one of the hidden ones, from before the ban. Probably been buried, or hidden in a shed roof, maybe. Forensics will get better information than we can, maybe even date the shells, but to be honest, a search for a particular gun in the bush? Needle in a haystack stuff. Who called us out here? Maybe they can help."

"Young girl driving through to Queanbeyan. Happened to take the wrong turnoff. Poor thing. Wilkes has already driven her back to the station. They took her car so we could stay out here till the rest of the guys showed up."

"You left a shaken witness with Wilkes? Crap. The guy's as sensitive as the chalk we're standing on!" Oswald sighed and walked over to the MPV.

The van was dented at the tail where another vehicle had rammed it, and again on the right panel. The letters S.P.B. were spelled out in large gold type against both sides.

"What d'you suppose that means?" Oswald asked, half to the officer, half to himself. He scribbled a quick note in his pad. He moved to the upturned driver side door and was surprised when the door opened with ease. Placing his handkerchief over his fingers, he opened the glove box. Papers spewed out, followed by a dull thump.

"Any chance we may have missed something important, fellas?" Oswald grinned darkly as he held up a snub nose revolver by the tip of the short barrel. "Look after things until Forensics get here, best not to touch anything. I'm going to head back to the station before Wilkes gets a complaint filed against him for being the arse that he is."

❖

Back inside his own silver Omega, Oswald sat staring at the wheel. *What the hell is going on?* he thought. The winter sun was slowly starting an early descent, and the glow was flooding in through the tinted windscreen. Oswald unfolded the shade above the driver's seat to ease the glare, and as his eyes caught the photo stuck to the inside, his heart tugged at his composure.
He slipped the four by six out of the pocket in the sun guard and held it tenderly in his fingers. His eyes took in the soft, round features of his wife, Arlene, longing for the feel of the light brown curls of her hair, and the luring darkness of her eyes. He'd meant to put a picture up of the three of them together, but if it was hard to remind himself of Arlene, it was genuinely heart-wrenching to bring Anna to mind.

It had been almost seven years since the day he'd gotten that fateful phone call. Seven years since he had held his little girl's hand in the hospital bed, hoping with all his might that she'd wake up, dreading against everything how he would have to tell her why mummy wouldn't be coming out of the hospital with her. In the end, she must have figured it out, or maybe Arlene got to tell her, herself. Their graves were close enough, after all.

Since then, it had just seemed like *he* was the one who wasn't with *them*, and not the other way around. The prospect of buying your own gravesite wasn't a thought that Detective Peter Oswald had invested much time into before, but when it came to having to bury his wife and nine-year-old daughter, well, even neighbouring coffins seemed an immeasurable distance apart.

At the time, it had seemed appropriate for Arlene to be on one side, little Anna in the middle, and the empty mound on the right would eventually belong to Peter. Through the tears and the fresh flowers by their headstones, Oswald would picture the site as their own bed, back when life was fair and this heartache was never imagined. He fancied that when it finally came his time to join them, he would again feel the warm curves of his wife's body curled under his arms. He'd feel his little nine year old Anna snuggled close between the two of them, a habit she'd developed around the age of two.

But time went on, and Oswald found that each morning, his bed was just as empty as when he'd gone to sleep. To his disappointment, his lungs were still working fine, and his accursed heart was still beating through the pain, too cowardly to cease and let him slip into whatever lay beyond this life.

In the end, he had to face the facts. He wasn't dying any time soon. And Arlene and Anna wouldn't be coming back either. Of course, no matter how much he told himself that, his heart would still whine, and ask him why. The only solution then, was to bury himself in his work, if not the soil.

He took the late shifts, the morning shifts, the special shifts, anything they'd give him. Letting the coffee and adrenaline keep his mind alive and his heart strings silent, he'd take on whatever challenges his career could throw at him.

But as the years went on, and the tired paperwork piled higher, he could feel himself getting older. Maybe the job was beginning to wear on him.

Oswald returned the photo to its place and decided to close the shade after all. The very sun itself would be easier to take on than those memories.

His reverie was disturbed by the beeping of his phone.

"Oswald speaking."

"Detective Oswald, it's Officer Sullivan. More bad news for the arvo. A Turkish man, Mr. Yavuz Firat, was found dead in his rug shop earlier today. Gunshot to the head, a small bag of cocaine was on display on his desk. Forensics was deferred to check this job out first, probably because of the drugs. They're racing the media crews, too, but it'll probably be on the next news update. Oh, also, there's something you might find interesting."

A pause.

Irritated, Oswald took the cue, "yes, what's that?"

"I just heard that the pistol used is a possible match for the Joseph Donald murder."

As the car came to life, Oswald pulled out back onto the highway and drove toward Canberra. Was it fate that drew him to another side road? Or years of experience telling him when to obey a gut feeling?

Chapter 11
The Road to Recovery
Canberra Hospital
4pm, 1 July, 2010

Terry was bored. He had managed to slip into a troubled sleep a number of times since Oswald had left that morning, but in the intervals, he couldn't help but run his recent adventures over and over in his mind.

Why was he so fascinated by these events?

How much did Rudley have to do with the murder?

And how long would he be held in this hospital bed, unable to do *anything* about what was happening?!

His unspoken question was suddenly answered with the whooshing of the plastic curtain as a doctor marched into his room. Without looking up from his clipboard, the doctor pronounced that he was to be transferred from Emergency and admitted to the Rehabilitation Ward.

"We're satisfied that your concussion is under control," he said, looking up at last with a businesslike expression. "Rehab will make further obs, however, and your doctor there will decide how long you'll need to stay."

"Would you know roughly how long that may be?"

The doctor puffed his lips with a sharp inhale as he made his silent calculations. "This sort of injury can be a bit unpredictable, I'm afraid, it's not your standard fracture," came the breathy reply. "I'll need you to sign a couple of forms for now though, Mr. Terrace, so we can transfer you over."

"Sign? Right. Well my lefthanded skills aren't great, but hey, I'm in good company, aren't I?"

The doctor passed the clipboard with a polite smile that told Terry the man hadn't caught the joke about doctors' writing.

Terry scribbled out something that may have looked at least a little like his name, and the doctor left with the same speed as his entry. However, the curtain remained open and Terry could see out to the hall. A tall figure was bent over the reception desk, one hand shifting aside papers in search of something. Terry tried to shift for a better view but yelped as a fresh wave of pain arced up from his busted arm. The cry had alarmed the guest at the desk, and he spun around with a quick glance each side.

Terry suddenly recognised him as Dmitri, the man from the bar who had called for his help. Dmitri saw him too and threw his head back in a greeting smile. Another glance to his left and right as he advanced toward Terry's bed.

"Hiya! Dmitri, right?" Terry managed, "what are you doing here?"

Dmitri chuckled, "Man, you look like crap!"

"Yeah," casting another glance over his ruined arm and bandaged chest, Terry had to admit it. "Yeah. And hey, I owe you big time, mate! They told me you chased the guy off. Called the ambulance. I think you just might have saved my life!"

The man at the end of the bed smiled awkwardly to one side and broke Terry's gaze. *Probably a bit of a corny line, I guess*, thought Terry. *But it was still true.*

Terry broke the brief silence that had settled on the room.

"Hey, so what were you doing outside anyway? How'd you know I was getting beaten to death?"

"Oh," started Dmitri, able to look at Terry again, "I just happened to go out for some fresh air. I noticed you'd already vanished, and by the time I reached the street I could hear the commotion from the fight. The guy buggered off pretty fast when he saw I was coming. What were you doing out there anyway? Wasn't that guy in the pub earlier on?"

Terry smiled and it was his turn to look down. *Corniness be damned, the guy did just save my life, I think he can be trusted with the truth.*

"Hmph, well," he started, ignoring another jab of pain from his arm, "it was pretty stupid, but... I was actually following the psycho. 'Course I didn't realise he was quite *that* psycho. Life's been a little crazy for me this last week, and uh, I guess I thought this Rudley guy held a few of the answers I was looking for."

"Rightio," replied Dmitri, somewhat distantly. Apparently it didn't make as much sense to him as Terry had thought it would. In fact, if it wasn't for the absence of any other reason for the man to come to the hospital, Terry would have even thought he wasn't really listening.

Maybe he's just not really the curious type.

After a furtive glance back toward the hallway, Dmitri scraped the chair over to beside the bed and stuffed himself into it. "So, uh, Terry, wasn't it? Have they hooked your TV up for you?"

Terry smiled and fumbled for the control under his pillow. Another shot of pain prompted him to give up and ask Dmitri to flick it on for him. Dmitri hammered through the channels until it stopped on a news update.

The screen flickered out an image of a simple, concrete building, somewhere in the business district. The banner at the bottom of the screen read: BUSINESS OWNER MURDERED. The reporter droned out the details of a man being found dead in his office, shot in the head. Terry didn't absorb the information until a familiar face flashed on the screen with a collar microphone. Constable Wilkes.

"We don't want to give any details at this stage, but the investigation will include a sweep of Mr Firat's business dealings for any ties to a drug circle."

The voice on the television continued. Terry cut in, annoyed even at just seeing Wilkes' face again on the screen.

"Pff, this guy!" He started, "such a wanker."

Dmitri smirked but suddenly snapped his attention to Terry. "Yeah? You know him or something?"

Terry frowned, still looking at the television. "Yeah... a little uh, mixup, down on Coorung Street the other day. Had to go down to the station and this idiot Wilkes was ready to lock me away as soon as he saw me – no questions asked." Terry looked away then, lost in another thought. "Reminds me, I'd better let Detective Oswald know I'm being transferred." Then to Dmitri, "Or does the hospital let them know that part? S'pose they would, hey?"

The man in the seat was silent, staring at the floor, a slight frown creasing his forehead.

I've been rambling, thought Terry. "You okay?" he probed.

Dmitri looked up, concentration painted over his face, and another silent second passed before he said, "Yeah. Yeah. Hey, we should keep in touch. I'll come and see you in the new ward."

Terry was taken by surprise. "Oh, yeah, that'd be nice. But, I don't want you to feel any obligation, of course. You've already done heaps."

Dmitri rose from his chair with a smile.

"No trouble, Terry. And hey, everyone can use a friend. Especially when they're going through tough times. I'll see you around."

Another smile, and Dmitri was gone.

Terry rested back against his pillow.

Hmm. That would *be my first friend in a long time.*

The television continued the reporter's spiel, the remote control left dangling by the bedside.

Chapter 12

Tampered Pamper Scam Hampered
Outskirts of Canberra
4:30pm, 1 July, 2010

"What are you looking for, Peter?" Oswald asked himself aloud. He'd slowed down to 40 km/h, scanning through the dense trees for driveways, houses, and above all, waiting for the suspicion that drove him down this little dirt road to lead him somewhere.

A short driveway on the right led to a run-down property. In the few seconds it took to drive passed, Oswald saw the litter of car bodies, wood piles and makeshift tin panel extensions to what must have been some form of balcony. He kept driving.

On the left, a much longer driveway wound up around a small hill. Oswald kept driving. Another kilometre down the road, he slowed down to 30 km/h.

Another property crept up on the left. A white-washed wooden home. Well kept, with a gate in good condition – a rarity in the outskirt properties. A car was parked in the circular driveway, covered thick in chalky white dust. Oswald hands seemed to turn the wheel themselves and lead him off the road and into the driveway. The electronic gate opened automatically. Halfway through the gate, Oswald stopped the car, leaving the gate held wide open by his vehicle. *Just in case.*

Oswald stepped out and walked to the chalky car. It was a recent model Camry, silver under the dust. The bonnet was warm to the touch, and it was then that Oswald saw the sizable dents in the front panels. One of the lights were broken. Oswald hissed in a breath and climbed the few steps to the front door. Inside the lattice-decorated veranda, Oswald knocked on the door.

Within a few moments a woman answered. She squeezed a smile through her cheeks and asked how she could help. Oswald read strain on her face and in her eyes. *Someone has a story to tell.*

"We're just investigating a serious traffic incident in the area, ma'am, and I wonder if I could ask you a few questions."

The woman seemed genuinely surprised. "Certainly. Would you like to come inside? My husband's just out the back."

Oswald stepped in after her as she hurried off around the corner. From the lounge room, Oswald could see out the large double sliding door to the garden out the back. A man was sitting in a deck chair, under a tree, his back to the house.

"Darren," the woman called from what must have been the kitchen or dining room, "there's a police officer here. Can you come inside, love?"

The back of the man's head dipped forward in a slow nod, but he made no move to stand up.

The woman returned a moment later and smiled to Oswald. "Sorry about this, he's been a little out of sorts today. I doubt he even heard me properly. Would you mind if we go out to him?"

Oswald nodded and stepped cautiously over the step leading back outside. He suddenly regretted not calling in the stop to the station. And he suddenly felt that not having his gun with him was not the wisest decision.

Idiot, he cursed himself, *too busy listening to your gut to listen to your brain?!*

The man took no action as Oswald approached, just the balding surface of his head reflecting what sunlight made it through the remaining straggly hairs waving gently in the breeze. Still a few metres from where the man sat, facing the distant hills, Oswald spoke.

"Darren, was it?"

Silence.

Oswald slowed his pace as he rounded to the right of the man. If this was who he was looking for, he could likely be cradling a recently fired shotgun, and odds were the barrel would be pointing left.

He kept a good metre's distance still, and looked back to check what *Mrs* Mysterious Suspect was doing. Another sinking feeling inside as he noted she had disappeared. The man's voice was low. Sad. Lost, somehow. The tone of surrender.

"You guys work fast. I'm impressed."

Oswald snapped his gaze back to the man who was still staring past the jacaranda and over to the distance.

"Sorry, er, what was that?"

"Heard the sirens earlier. Guessed it would only be a matter of time before you came around." The man's voiced lowered then, barely audible, "thought I'd still have a few days at least, though. Bugger."

Oswald squatted so that his head was just under the sitting man's shoulder height, but at this moment the man lifted himself reluctantly from his chair and turned to look at the house. He was not armed, after all.

What the hell is going on now?

Before Oswald could ask anything, the man laid his mystery open. As he spoke, he glanced over the back of his fine house. His eyes lingered on details, shot over to another window, door or post, and lingered again. Oswald had seen this behaviour before, of course. It was the look of a man saying farewell.

Even as he confessed, the man would be seeing new things on the property he'd never noticed before. He'd be wondering how long one of the tiles had been cracked, wondering how it had happened, or how long ago was it he'd planted one of the trees. Everything would look clearer in the man's eyes now. The leaves would be greener, the breeze gentler and the green scent of the nature around him so much sweeter than ever before. The last glances of freedom from a man who knew he was already condemned.

"It was for her, you understand. He'd hurt her, and then... Well, everything happened so fast. I thought I was helping. Now I guess I've just made everything worse for her." Another moment passed, and still Oswald said nothing, waiting for the man to continue.

"It was meant to be one of those pampering packages – a spa retreat, something like that. Found a good deal online, she did. My daughter.

"She said she was going away for a few days, sounded like a real nice place. She could get away for a bit and relax, ya know? Anyhow, they uh... they hurt her, officer."

The man turned his gaze from his house to look Oswald in the eyes.

"I don't know how she got back – I haven't had the chance to ask her yet, I... I just see her come speeding up the driveway in some little black car, not hers. She went straight into the garage. My uh, my wife and I rushed over to her cos of how she slammed the garage door down. We knew she must have been upset. That and she wasn't meant to be back yet. She looked stressed and her hair was all messy, and while we're hugging her she says they were after her."

The man was now staring at the ground, tears not so much falling down his cheeks, but dropping from his eyes as he began to shake. He continued at a higher volume now, reliving a nightmare.

"Everything was ripped and she was bleeding and... DAMMIT!!" he screamed. The man bit down on his own knuckles, his eyes darting around, grief flooding his lungs and causing him to heave out his breaths between strangled sobs. After a few more moments, he continued. "Next thing this big van comes tearing down the road toward the house, but we're all still standing out the front and they screech on their brakes before the open gate. And this guy driving saw me, and me lookin' at him.

"Anyhow, Jess rushed inside with her mum and I was just glued there for a minute. Felt like it, anyway. Then I remembered the shotty in the garage and I started marching up that way, and I hear his wheels spinning in the dirt, and he's trying to get away back down to the highway." Darren was now clutching his temples with both hands, the fingers dripping tears. Despite himself, Oswald felt his heart tighten in his chest, putting the rest the of pieces together in his mind. *Damn.*

The man's wife had reappeared at the doorway, tears streaming down her own face, her arms wrapped tightly around herself, paralysed in the indecision of who to comfort – her husband, her daughter, or herself.

Oswald had seen this sort of thing before, but that didn't make him hate it any less. A private conflict of guilt and responsibility fogged his mind as he pulled the cuffs from behind him and bound the man's wrists in what felt like slow motion. He knew his obligation, but he knew his own mind too. In the black and white world of the law, this man had killed. Premeditated murder. Even if he'd left it at toppling the car he would have been finished.

As soon as he had packed the shotgun in the car he'd sentenced himself on premeditation. It was that simple. The complicated part was that Oswald knew even as he led the man back to the front of the house that even if he could have gone back now, the cuffed man would have done exactly the same thing all over again.

Only a few years ago, Oswald had felt a similar pang of regret for a man that the law considered a psychopath for his crimes at a traffic incident.

A teen in his first year of provisionals had taken a corner too wide and careened out of his lane and into the oncoming headlights of a couple heading home from the cinemas. The impact killed the female driver almost instantly, but when the car had finally stopped spinning, her husband had managed to stagger out of the vehicle in a screaming mess. When the police arrived, they found the husband covered in blood, sobbing helplessly through his wife's window. There was a messy pile of something lying beside the other vehicle, unrecognisable by the time the enraged and grief-stricken man had finished slamming the teen's face against the twisted wreckage of his own vehicle again and again and again and again.

The official story ran that as the teen approached to check if the other motorists were okay, the male passenger had senselessly beaten him to death. That was the black and white. No room for grey understanding. No room for decisions made in grief.

The man was put away as a threat to society, and yes, in one way, that was true. After all, how could a grown man commit such a violent crime against an inexperienced teenager? But Oswald understood the other side of the story, too.

He knew of loss.

And grief.

And anger.

Many times he'd wondered what may have happened if he had been there the day his wife and child left this world in a similar circumstance. Could he have felt the pain and the rage, but still done what was right in the world of black and white? Or would he have spun out of control in what could be called a moment of madness, but could never be called acceptable?

In Oswald's heart, he believed that the man he now held in custody, like that enraged passenger, was not what the world called insane. Furthermore, he wasn't a danger to anyone in the public, he was just avenging a wronged daughter.

However, he was also aware that black or white, grey, whatever, the crime was animalistic. And that is how he found the strength to continue walking the man to his Omega.

Every part of his being wanted to let the man say goodbye to his wife and daughter. Hell, had he even seen her since he had come back from chasing down her attacker? The next time they would be together would be in prison visits, painstaking court cases, bail. And how long down the track would that even be?

No one else is here, Oswald let himself think. *No paper trail to say they hadn't departed immediately to the station.*

But just as gut feelings fought logic in Oswald's world, the voice of each trying to drown out the other, he knew that the heart could get no say. If for no other reason than for his own resolve, Oswald knew it would be harder to pull the man from the embrace of his family than to lead him quietly around the side of the house, into the car and back out to the station.

Once he was in the car, Oswald would put a call through to have someone scour the place for the gun, even though he was sure it wouldn't be hidden. Police would interview the daughter, counsellors would be sent to talk about what happened, and someone would follow up on the story of the assault.

And the only thing that could be undone, was the family itself.

That's how black and white works.

Chapter 13
An Ageless Crime
5pm, 1 July

Dmitri hailed a taxi from outside the Emergency ward. After he rattled off some directions to the driver he sat back, his mind buzzing.

"This should be close enough," he said after a few minutes of driving. He paid with cash and stepped out onto a vacant block of land at the foot of a hill. It was only a short walk to the storage sheds, and he could use the fresh air and the steady rhythm of his feet to help him focus.

Locker 217 was identical to the rows upon rows of private storage sheds in the fenced yard. What was inside, however, was vastly different to other sheds in the lot. It was for this reason that he'd chosen somewhere cheap. Somewhere without video surveillance. It wouldn't do to have someone noticing the odd comings and goings of a man with many secrets.

Once inside, Dmitri turned to lock the roller door. He dug around briefly before taking a seat with what he was looking for – the thick yellow envelope from Joseph Donald's desk.
With his eyes closed and the room quiet, he thought through the Coorung Street murder again.
Sweeping down the steps of the stately building.
Striding out the front door.
Skipping the step on the landing.
Stretching out the pistol to the gardener.
Slipping into the waiting van.

Ah, he realised. *The bugger was behind the tree. That's where the little dog came running out from. He must have stuck around longer than he should've. The cops – he recognised one of them on TV – they must have brought him in.*

He chuckled, amused by the way it had played out.
Still, it was time to let off some steam. He shuffled around in the dark room and his hands closed around a thin plastic card.

❖

It was cold again.
It was always easier in the cold.
The jacket could stay on.
The pockets were easier to get to.
He was walking through the well-tended gardens of the university as the sun was slowly starting to set. The security officer wouldn't miss his card for at least another hour or two when the doors would be locked and the barcode scanner locks would come to life. By then it would be too late to raise the alarm.

Dmitri had already watched the habits of the campus guards on earlier trips. They were sluggard and lapsed, mostly overweight or at least unfit. And why shouldn't they be? What would ever happen here? He had not picked out a target so much as a shift change, a mostly outdoor patrol circuit. He had targeted simply *when* a guard would be there, not which guard it would be.
  So it was Paul Keeghy with his thick mop of curly hair who fate had chosen to place outside the door with his ID card clipped to his belt on an extendable cord. Following Paul was easy. He hadn't even looked behind him once. When he stopped in his tracks to change direction, it had been a simple matter for Dmitri to act as if he hadn't seen him pause on the footpath and crash into him lightly. With an apology, a wave, and an innocent smile, Dmitri had walked on without Keeghy having noticed that one hand had pulled the cord while the other sliced it deftly clear of the belt clip.

Now for some fun.

The next patrol circuit was near the Concourse, the hive of activity which would mute the small building beside it where the guard inside would be checking that the regular office staff were packing up for the day.
  Dmitri didn't need to scan the card to gain access, but he knew it would buzz as Paul Keeghy, and the police would find that very interesting come tomorrow.

Dressed in his jacket and jeans, Dmitri would look like any other student on their way to one of the 24 hour computer labs. He made his way upstairs, and sure enough, a guard was lazily making his rounds through the small corridor.

Trailing him into a small tea and coffee kitchen, Dmitri made short work of knocking him out cold. With a slap to the man's head to get his attention and a jab to the ribs to have him escalate force, he waited for the all too predictable right hook from the confused officer. As the blow went wide of Dmitri's step in, he hooked his left arm over the guard's extended arm, brought his own right hand to cradle behind the man's head and stepped back with a sharp bend to his knees. The kettle and mugs protested with a rattle as the security officer's forehead bounced off the benchtop. The fridge rocked on its uneven feet for a few seconds more as Dmitri pulled the man further into the corner of the little room. Turning the lock behind him, he left the lights on deliberately to attract some attention.

He'd played this game before and learned it was more fun to leave a little trail of little easter eggs for people to follow before they found the main treasure of his visit. Besides, two of the academics down the hall were still talking loudly, their voices carrying enough for Dmitri to hear one mention something she wanted out of the fridge first.

Perfect.

She'd try the door, see it was locked, peer inside and probably catch a glimpse of someone bundled over. Dmitri would have about five minutes until the alarm was raised, and in the meantime, he had business in the next building over, which meant getting downstairs fast.

Trying to keep as casual a pace as possible, he skimmed down the stairs and broke into a purposeful gait as he reached the double doors and walked back out into the air. The last gleams of light were clinging to the leaves, and the Concourse area to his left was already emptier than on his way in. He reached a side door to the main building and again, Paul Keeghy's pass pinged his easy passage into the premises. He glanced around momentarily hoping to spot Paul's shock of curls still in the nearby area.

No matter.

The doorway opened into a stairwell and he legged it straight up to the fourth floor. Once more, Paul Keeghy granted him access past the scanner, and he found himself in an elegant suite with wooden trims wherever they could fit. The air had the sterile smell of professionalism, with only the slightest tell-tale musk that humans spent a lot of time behind these nicely polished walls.

Dmitri took a thick wad of brochures for a makeshift doorstop, then continued down the hall. The door would beep if it was left open, but he knew he'd have enough time before even that alerted his prey to his presence.

Office suites aren't designed to be safe houses, nor the wooden doors to hold secrets, so the names on the polished brass signs told Dmitri exactly where his quarry would be. He had made even better time than he estimated, because the Dean was still shuffling around flicking off the lights to his room. The bespectacled figure half emerged from his office, cradling a thick assortment of forms. As he leaned to pull the door behind him, some loose sheets on top fell from their cradle. With a resigned sigh, he bent to collect them.

It was with utter confusion that he looked up from his crouched position and saw the face of Dmitri staring down at him, loaded glock pistol in hand, pointed at the academic's face. Dmitri could almost see the cogs ticking and whirring behind the man's eyes – decades of academia training his brain to comprehend and analyse, seemingly even over the immediate human reaction of fear.

The aged eyes squinted as if trying to focus behind his glasses, but before any logical explanation could be pulled from his bank of knowledge, the bullet had sprayed his well-learned brain over the doorpost behind him.

In the silence of the offices, the shot rang out with an omnipresence. Dmitri didn't stray a moment longer. As he brushed through the jarred door, and away down the steps, he kicked the pile of brochures blocking it so that a snow-like shower of advertising marked his speedy retreat down the concrete stairwell. One final scan to ice the cake that would implicate the unsuspecting Keeghy, and he was on his way down the hill.

Lying low in the trees, he waited until his breath had settled before emerging to stroll out of the university grounds like any other student on a normal day. With a strain of self-control, he resisted turning his head when he heard the woman's voice calling out from the first small building.

"Get security! There's a man upstairs who's hurt. The door's locked!"

In the confusion of the gunshot and the cacophony of panic from the tea and coffee room, it would take a while to stitch together the story of what had happened at the university campus.

One thing was certain, though – campus Security Officer Paul Keeghy would soon be asked some very tricky questions.

Chapter 14
Family Matters
Canberra Hospital
2 July, 2010

"Benjamin."

The voice drifted softly to him - nearby, yet the figure was standing so far away.

"Benjamin!" Urgent now.

The figure fell, a shadow on the dark footpath, and a monster emerged from the vacant lot beside it. A blur of movement landing blow after blow on the man who had been walking. Terry could feel the blows on himself as his mind replayed the events from the disembodied viewpoint. The voice calling him was drowned out by the curses the demon was bellowing at him.

Watching the last blow was enough to startle him from his troubled sleep, accompanied by the searing pain that shot through his bandaged arm.
He'd rolled onto it in his morphine-fuelled rest and the sedation had not been strong enough to blot out the pressure on the busted elbow.

"Benjamin." The voice was real.
Calm, though.
Familiar.

He rolled onto his back, and looking around the room in a panic, found the face of his mother leaning over the bed. She smiled a mother's reassurance and the nightmare fled.
"How are you feeling?" she asked.

Terrace had been transferred to the recovery ward late the night before and was yet to see his rehabilitation physician. He didn't see how he'd be ready to do any sort of exercises with the arm that was hurting through the painkillers, but he figured it was more a case at this stage of finding out what would be involved in his recovery.

"Yeah, I'm okay," Terry replied with a smile. "Sorry to worry you all."

His father was at the end of the bed with his arms folded, and his younger brother slouched over his mobile phone, hair covering any expression he may have had on his face.

"Are you ready to tell us what on earth's going on yet?" His father's voice was calm, but stern. Nothing unusual then.

"Lee, for God's sake, leave him be! You haven't even asked if he's okay yet!" his mother's reprimand came quickly, but she couldn't conceal her own curiosity.

Lee scratched a finger through his thick grey stubble before replying.

"We're in the hospital aren't we? I just want to know what the hell he's gotten himself into. A detective signed him in, Miranda. We don't even know where he's been the last few days, then next we hear the boy's in rehab."

"*Physical* rehabilitation, Lee. It's not like he's on drugs... Are you?" The look she shot Terry was a cocktail of concerns.

Terry nodded at the drip poking out of the top of his wrist.

"Morphine count?"

His father's arm dropped to his side with a slap.

"Jokes again. Great."

"Hey Jono, how about that? Looks like I got on drugs before you. Didn't see that coming, did we?" Terry aimed the joke at the face illuminated by the phone screen. His brother only grunted in reply. Again, nothing unusual.

"Jonathan, for God's sake, put the phone down. Your brother's in a serious condition," mother again. "I think we all need to give Benjamin some space and let him tell us all about it."

Terry considered pointing out that she hadn't given him much option for staying quiet, but his father started up again before he had the chance.

"What are you going to do about work? Have they said how long this will take to heal?"

Crap. Terry hadn't thought about that yet. Trust his dad to be the one to bring it up. His family made no secret of their dislike for his home business, especially when it was in *their* home, as they often said. Since his parents put more emphasis on being outdoors and "working for a respectable firm" or "holding a respectable position", they maintained that Terry had led Jonathan away from his talents on the soccer field and further into his phone and game consoles.

He could hear the accusations again clearly. How his website building and game designs were encouraging Jono to stay inside during his growing years, setting a poor example for someone to get out there and find some 'real work'. They knew he was making some decent money from it, but Terry suspected their real issue was that the money wasn't taking him up a ladder. Or better still, to another dwelling.

His father's question hadn't really been out of concern then, beyond whether he could pay his board, but rather it was a way of saying "you chose a job where only your hands are moving on a keyboard, and now whatever you've gotten yourself mixed up in has made that impossible."

So he took the bait and responded in kind.

"Well, that's the beauty of technology. I can do most of it one handed or use voice to text software, I guess. Hey, good thing I didn't choose a career in sports, eh? I'd have been screwed! Carpentry? Phew, I'd be out of work for who knows how long. Actually, I'm not sure I could have even chosen anything in the corporate line of work - I wouldn't have cut a good public figure with my arm in a cast." He pushed the advantage, "Man, I can't think of *anything else* I could be doing where an injury to my arm wouldn't stop me from working. Hear that, Jono?"

A grunt from Jono. The roll of his father's eyes was followed by a bemused smile to concede defeat this time. His mother chimed in again now to bring the conversation back.

"Alright, you lot. I think we've asked enough questions. I'm sure Benjamin will tell us if there's anything we should be concerned about."

The exchange was interrupted by the efficient swishing footsteps of a doctor approaching. No one would have been able to explain how they knew it was the physician before seeing them, but even Jonathan looked up from his phone a moment before the doctor rounded the corner and stepped into the room.

She would have been in her late thirties, by Terry's estimate, and had bouncy chestnut hair, almost red even, rolling back in waves over her shoulders. She had an air of professionalism but not the sterile clipboard-bound manner of the emergency doctor Terry had seen earlier. This was someone who cared about what she did for a living and knew she was good at it. The assessment had been made within a few seconds of her introducing herself, but as quick as she had conveyed her professional nature, the façade dropped, and her smile failed her.

The chart she had whisked from the end of the bed was now hugged close to her chest, and whatever she had been saying was cut short, replaced by a stammer, and left hanging in the air as she swivelled back into the hallway out of view.

Terry looked at his mother.
His mother looked at his father.
His father looked at Terry.
Jono looked at his phone.

Another awkward moment passed before the doctor spun back into view, her composure delicately forced into some version of calm.
"Hello," the doctor began. She paused again for a brief moment, but continued before the awkwardness could set back in. "I'm Doctor Kate Tetherman, I'll be looking after you, Benjamin... er..." she glanced back down at the clipboard she had still been squeezing to her chest, "...Terrace. Benjamin Terrace."

As she continued to explain the process, any awkwardness was soon forgotten, faded into a wash of medical jargon and steps to recovery. Most of it washed absently over Terry, whose ears only picked up on the timeframe before he'd be back home with a working right arm.
"We'll leave the arm bound for only a day or two, then we'll begin with some very mild exercises. It's important to keep the muscles moving early on. For the most part, we should be able to treat you as an outpatient, but I'd like to admit you for a few days to begin with - just to make sure there are no surprises."

She stood for another moment in silence after returning Terry's chart. She flashed an odd smile and disappeared again.

Chapter 15
Blast from the Past

Theodore considered himself a social man. He enjoyed the company of the others in the village, and of the crowd that frequented his market stall. He liked to think that it would be difficult to discern who was there for the produce and who was attracted to the chance to have a good chat. He was a *conversational gentleman*, as he would put it, and *a man what believes there is always something to be said for everything*, as he often regaled his daughter on their long trips to and from civilisation.

Which is why it was unusual that he should feel so uncomfortable about his daughter talking to the stranger leaning against the wooden stand-to just a few yards from where Theo was tying down the unsold stock for the journey home.

"Petulia, dear," he called, his worn voice almost faltering over the faint breeze.

When she turned to him, her face was awash with mirth. The kind bred in country folk who dream of adventure far away but in truth could never be happier but in their rustic little ruts - married to the land.

Theodore had caught the stranger's gaze, too, and found himself uncharacteristically lost for words. He mustered a cough and jerked his head back to beckon her over. The wind carried away whatever it was Petulia said to excuse herself from the stranger and with a polite straightening of her pleats she had skipped the short distance to her beloved wiry father.

"Just, uh, help me with this crate will you?"

Together they placed the load of vegetables onto the cart and the old man snuck a suspicious glance over his shoulder to see what had become of the stranger. He was no longer leaning against the pole but walking further down the dirt road with an irregular gait. His clothes weren't anything like the sort Theodore had seen in the area.

Nothing of the sort any local tailors would have put together, and whatever it was he was wearing on his feet came from no cobbler Theodore had ever heard of - a mess of bright colours and strange symbols. Theo was not a learned man, but he knew a word that could fit this fellow rightly.

Different.

The very way he walked seemed to ooze this difference, and not just because of the strange, slightly-blue material he wore over his legs. Indeed, the only thing about him that seemed to belong to this world was the brass door handle he cradled in his left hand, and even that itself was odd enough. Who carries a handle without a door?

Secretly, perhaps, Theodore was a little hurt this man had come for neither his stall nor his conversation, but something equally convinced him that he and his daughter had somehow dodged something very dangerous.

It went unnoticed by both Petulia and Theodore as they closed up the back hatch of the wagon that the handle was missing, the lighter load allowing the wooden back to sit against the planks of the sides unfastened.

❖

Dmitri sauntered into the small town, his face unreadable though his eyes flickered around, absorbing the details of the dusty street and the quaintly ramshackle houses that lined it.

The first time he had been by this way, the old farmer had gotten his full attention, but though the man was clearly wary of him, he seemed to have no memory of ever seeing Dmitri before.

It was a new experience, walking away. But then the same question that had started his journey in the first place simply begged for new horizons. Even as Dmitri stepped off the road and into the guard's station (which were it not for the hand painted sign he would have dubbed more appropriately, 'a shed') he found himself wondering...

What would happen?

By the time the loud reports sounded out like cracks of thunder in a jar, shattering the silence, Theodore was already shaking his head like a madman and turning his startled horse back towards the village.

"I knew there was something odd about that man! I tell you I'd bet my life that whatever that evil sound was, that stranger is behind it and I don't like it! I can feel it, right down in my gut, something terrible has happened! I just know it. And to *think* you were talking to him, Petulia!"

It didn't take long to reach the outpost and some of the townsfolk were warily approaching the spartan hut. In a blur of communal confusion, Theo dragged out the bodies of two townguards, blood still pouring from mysterious holes punched into their leather hide vests. One guard had died still clutching the hilt of his sheathed sword.

As Theo rode back toward the farm many hours later, Petulia heard him muttering to himself.

"To think it could've been *us*."

Dmitri opened his eyes and looked around his storage shed.

The collection of items was starting to grow. That much was clear. Still, each had its own place. Carefully he placed the handle from the back of the wagon in its place on the shelf. Aside from the roller chair, and a laminated white desk, the shelf was the only furniture in Locker 217. It stretched across the whole lefthand wall, a honeycomb of odd bits and pieces, each in its own cell in the array. Dmitri adjusted the handle again so that it sat perfectly in its usual outline in the dust.

Slumping into the office chair so that it rolled back to the other wall, he pressed a finger to his temple in contemplation of the chaos represented before him. The neat panorama – a contradictory calm to showcase the worlds turned upside down behind each mundane object.

His gaze fell to the empty shelves toward the right of the honeycomb.

Perhaps some travelling was in order.

Chapter 16
Questions to the Answers

"Paul Keeghy."

The name hung in the tiny room, suspended by the silence.

Detective Peter Oswald was sitting upright, a manila folder open on the table in front of him. He scratched the corner absent-mindedly as his eyes scanned over the documents in front of him for the umpteenth time. He had read it over and over, and though he still couldn't believe the report, he was familiar with the details by now. *It was important to put on a show though*, he thought to himself.
He turned a page.

The figure opposite had his head in his hands, propped up by his elbows. He flinched at the sound of the folding paper and lolled his head to one side.

"Says here," Oswald drawled, "you've worked at the university for over seven years. Is that right?"
A groan from the embodiment of despair in the chair opposite.
"And your firearm licence is up to date."

Another page.

"Even though you don't need to carry one in your role as security officer."
"All of this information is in the record, detective. My client Mr Keeghy has provided much of that information of his own free will. He is aware of the details in the file you're perusing." The solicitor's voice was blunt, hostile, even.
Oswald dismissed the tension. *Another part of the show.*
"As am I," Oswald said, closing the folder and sliding it to one side. "I am aware that Security Officer Paul Keeghy has been implicated in the murder of an esteemed academic in his place of employment. I am aware that it was *his* security pass that was used to access the building and I am aware that said security pass is still missing. I am aware that Mr Keeghy is unable to provide any information as to how someone got hold of his pass,

as he claims, not to mention the knowledge of the layout of the academic building to execute the assassination so efficiently.

"Yes, I used the term assassination. Just as the media have been. I am also aware that Mr Keeghy did not report his security pass as missing in a timely fashion. Only when the investigating officers were able to match him to the card used to gain entry to the building, did the claims of a stolen security pass surface."

Paul Keeghy slammed his hand to the table and looked up. Oswald continued calmly. "It is my hope, Mr Keeghy, that you will be able to help me fill in the blanks – for your own sake."

"I already told them, I don't know, okay?!" Keeghy was breathing heavily, his eyes darting, wet, the pupils wild with anxiety. Not unduly. "Someone must've stolen it from me, you know. I didn't see anyone. I can't remember anything about it. One minute I was walking, you know! I was at work, I was walking, and the next thing there's chaos around me and people screaming, and you know next thing... next thing you guys are already asking me questions, and I don't know the answers! Alright? I don't fucking know!"

The disgraced security officer sniffed loudly and put his head back in his hands. The solicitor started to speak, but Oswald cut him off.

"Are you aware we have been able to identify the weapon that was used?"

The man looked back up.

"The firearm used was a 9mm glock pistol. Typically used by security and police alike. A weapon you are proficient with and have used each month at the firing range to keep your firearm licence."

"That doesn't mean shit! I mean, that's a good thing for me, right? I don't *own* a glock. I check one out each time at the range - you check your records and see if that's right. That's what you're saying, right? I hire a glock at the range, that means I don't have one. How does this possibly point to me?"

"You're right, Mr Keeghy. The model of the gun does not point specifically to you. But it doesn't rule you out, either. Does the name Mark Corday mean anything to you?"

"Who? No. Should it?"

"Forensics checked the striations on the bullet, and by an unfortunate coincidence for you it matches a pistol registered to a Police Officer."

"Do I look like a-?"

"A Police Officer whose pistol was forced from him and shot dead with his own gun, just over three years ago. The weapon was never recovered."

Paul Keeghy's mouth was moving, but the words were choked in his throat.

"As I said, Mr Keeghy, this evidence does not point directly to you. But it also does not point away from you. And given the precision of the seemingly senseless and unprovoked violence toward such an esteemed academic, the Police Service and indeed the justice system itself is very interested in finding puzzle pieces that match.

"As I understand it, you are currently viewed as an accomplice at best. Your card had not been scanned at any checkpoints for at least an hour before the attack, and no video surveillance can attest to your whereabouts until after the fact."

"I was on the outer circuit! I didn't scan into any buildings because I wasn't *near* any buildings! Get it? None I needed to go into, anyway. I don't know why there's no footage of me anywhere, I mean, that's the Uni's fault isn't it – if their cameras don't cover all the grounds? Right? I mean, and how is this cop's gun tied to me in any way? How would I end up with it? I mean, you're not suggesting I killed a cop too, are you?!"

Oswald's face showed no expression. It was the solicitor who spoke next. The words were professional, but the delivery was dripping in defeat.

"I would remind you at this point, Mr Keeghy, that you are not required to answer these questions until such a time as the police are able to provide some evidence of their suspicions. I would advise at this time, Mr Keeghy, that you say no more in this interview."

❖

Canberra City Police Station
6pm, 7 July, 2010

Oswald lifted his head from his hands and looked wearily once more at the paperwork sprawled out in front of him.

Yavuz Firat. Dead in his own shop.

Joseph Donald. Killed in his own study.
Not to mention the gardener.

He had already sifted out Darren Booth's file from this particular inquest. The murder on the country road was not in the same ball game. It was no less violent, but it made sense. Worse, the killer in question was, dare he think it, justified in his actions, some would argue, if not within the confines of the law.

But Firat and Donald. These were even less cut and dry, and something was nagging for Oswald's attention on the pages before him. Yes, the bullets were a 98% match, but that wasn't it. The bullets meant little without the shooter, especially without the gun.
Which is exactly why Oswald was puzzled even further to find his mind wandering back to Paul Keeghy and the University Dean two years earlier.

Firat and Donald had each been taken out with a single round from a high-powered pistol, heavy calibre.
Big guns. Not the sort you encounter all that often in civilised suburbia. The Dean had been hit with only a 9mm round, a stolen police issue pistol.
There was no comparison. Not in the weapons, anyway.
But something.

What was it that Oswald had found so disturbing about the case those few years ago? The efficiency, perhaps?
Earl Rudley. The man who'd put Terry in the emergency ward a week ago. That was the sort of character who filled the prisons. Hot-headed, a little less than sane, dealing out heat of the moment violence.
And of course, the characters like Rudley weren't all that hard to track down again after they misbehaved. He'd been just clever enough to work out that once they ambulance came for Terry, he'd be able to point the police to his assailant. So of course, he'd breached his bail and taken off.
And he'd managed to score about two days of freedom before he was back in the clink, awaiting a new sentence for assault once the defendant was well enough to testify.

No, the Rudleys of the world were not capable of this level of callousness. The cold and the calculated were harder to pin down. You had to exhaust all the avenues, and the baddies good enough to give you the slip were the ones most aware of just how many avenues there were to slip down.

There was nothing to be done but close them down one at a time.

Oswald decided it may be worth checking up on Security Officer Paul Keeghy's custody arrangements. Last Oswald knew, he'd been transferred to the Alexander Maconochie Correctional Centre when it had been built the year before. He brushed aside a few papers and dug out the office telephone.

Who knows? Anything could have changed in that time, and a conversation could go a long way.

More Than One Way...

It had been a long week.

Sometimes deciding on targets was simple. Easy. Like Dmitri was responding to some sort of direction. Other times it took more deliberation. This was one of those times. Purpose had always been a loose term to apply to what he did. He wasn't here for any greater good or for a higher calling. In fact, he'd maintained that that was a dangerous way to look at the world - deciding what was fair and unfair, who should live and who should die, or whether the end justified the means.

Nevertheless, here he was making the final decisions.

But only for himself. So if purpose was the wrong word to use, then what was the right one?

Sport, Dmitri mused to himself as he stood from the park bench and folded the newspaper back to the seat. He reached a hand behind his back to check the gun was still sitting properly. He'd chosen the desert eagle again. The .44 round was undoubtedly powerful, a hand cannon for all intents and purposes, but in fact the choice of weapon had more to do with his sense of anarchistic entertainment than practicality.

Better to leave a controlled trail of bread crumbs. Gotta keep the fans on the edge of their seats.

The rest of his inventory he checked subtly as he approached the Holden Hotel. Tapping his right trouser pocket, he felt for the fibre cord. In his left pocket was a spare loaded magazine for the pistol. Another in the left jacket pocket. Another clipped into the gun itself. He wasn't counting on needing the 24 rounds in total, but it always helped to be prepared on the first visit when surprises worked against him.

The right jacket pocket was empty, waiting for the most important part – an artefact to start the game.

The hotel itself had spared no expense in its presentation, as one would expect from a five-star establishment. The circuit driveway was decorated with topiary hedges and the centre island looked like a miniature tropical jungle. The stairs leading up to the glass doors were a tan marble, and an abstract awning reached out to greet and shelter the high paying guests.

Dmitri turned his attention instead to the ornate fountain by the staircase. A cascade of clear water tumbled over jutted slate beneath the stock standard stone cherub. It stood on a stone disc ringed by ornate steel doves that in turn spewed more water from their beaks into the pool below.

Dmitri slowly rested his weight against one of the birds. The fixture was weak enough. With a quick glance behind him to check he wasn't being observed too closely, he slumped his full weight into his grip, coughing loudly to mask the crack of the concrete as the little bird snapped free.

As the water rolled out of the thin, exposed pipe, Dmitri shot a guilty look at the sculpted cherub before leaving him to toil away with his futile bucket that would eternally drain as fast as it filled. Dmitri strode quickly up the polished stair case and the glass doors welcomed him inside.

❖

The lobby was typical of most high-end hotels - a spacious room with comfortable pastel-coloured furniture splayed at unusual angles. Patrons roamed aimlessly, lost in a holiday preamble of destinations without deadlines. Slim, sleekly dressed women stood behind the dark marble counters, their hair clinging tightly to their heads in efficient buns or ponytails, each with matching makeup to reflect that their professionalism was as polished as the room itself.

Dmitri looked past the families checking in or out, past the lone businessman reclining at the bar off to the left, and toward the decorated staircase that weaved intricately up to the in-house restaurant. An elevator bell pinged and out strode another businessman walking purposefully in contrast to the mother and child who stepped out behind him on their own separate quest.

The restaurant would be the best place to observe his quarry. He knew the sort of person he was looking for, and he knew they'd most likely be staying on the top floor. In his jeans and brown jacket, though, he would hardly look the part of a guest who had lost his key. Asking at the counter would not be an option.

Up the stairs, he ordered a drink and took a menu, sitting closest to the window where he could look out at anyone coming or going.

The slow process again.

It was almost forty minutes later that Dmitri found himself tailing a guest to the elevator. If he'd had to guess, he'd have said it was a politician. A tall, lop-sided man with thinning hair but a well-practised smile that split his face into a tapestry of wrinkles and perfect teeth. Dmitri had watched him grin through his entrée, spilling sentences from his lips as easily as he took breath.

The man's lunch partner had gone downstairs after the exchange, but the politician looked to be heading back to his room. At the elevator well, Dmitri waited until the man pressed the 'up' button. When they made eye contact, he gave a friendly nod, swivelled so that his back faced the man, and pressed the 'down' button of the opposite elevator. The politician's elevator opened first. Dmitri waited until the man withdrew his keycard from his jacket pocket and touched it to the dial inside the lift before he made his move. As the doors just had began to close, he seamlessly slipped through, whipping out the fibre cord from his pocket. By the time the doors shut, Dmitri had twirled the cord around the man's neck, kicked out his knee from behind him and let the man's body weight choke out the oxygen from his lungs as Dmitri held his head up, balanced between his own spread knees.

Going up.

Dmitri looked to the dial as the man flailed helplessly. The top floor had been selected just as he'd hoped. The digital display counted out the floors, tapping out the politician's last seconds in reverse. 9... 10... 11...

He'd need to move fast once it got noisy, and he'd need to find a good way back down afterwards.

12...

The man had already gone limp, panic accelerating the rate his body was spending the available air.

The elevator slowed. 13.

Hadn't that traditionally been an unlucky floor?

Dmitri returned the cord to his pocket and crashed the butt of his pistol to the man's head just to be sure. The door opened as he straightened, stepping over the lifeless limbs splayed before him.

He was on the far left side of a well-lit corridor. He moved to the right and saw there was another elevator shaft at the opposing end.
Perfect.

The doors to each room were a heavy wood, inlaid edges but otherwise nothing fancy beyond the keycard lock. Already the plan for next time was forming, but for now there was some more research to be done.
He had collected the dead man's keycard, but it was only labelled with the Holden Hotel logo and nothing to suggest which room it was for. Dmitri moved to the first door on the lefthand side. 1301. The scanner flashed but beeped with a red light.
1302. Right hand side. *Beep beep.*
1303. *Beep beep.*

Behind him the elevator door pinged closed, and the arrow flashed to show someone had called it downstairs. Taking the politician with it.
Ah, fuck.

Dmitri slammed into the door of 1304. *Beep beep.* But this time a muffled voice came from inside.
"Hello?" feminine.
"Room service," Dmitri called back.
The door clicked open and Dmitri was met with a confused expression.
"Good evening!" He chorused as he swung his arm from behind his back.
"We didn't order any-"
The sentence was left hanging as the shot echoed mercilessly in the tiny entrance way. Dmitri strode further into the room and found a man still hurriedly pulling up his pants at the edge of the bed.
Definitely another politician, Dmitri thought as he took in the blotchy red face, the paunchy belly and the stuttering expletives spitting out of the panicked face. Another loud shot saw the ruffled linen sprayed with gore as the man's head snapped back

with the bite of the bullet. Dmitri slipped back into the hallway. No one had stirred yet, but then it had only been less than twenty seconds or so.

Room 1305. *Beep beep.*
Room 1306. *Beep beep.*
1307 - Dmitri froze.

Back the way he'd come, the door to 1302 clicked open. A head cautiously peered out.

Panic does strange things to the human mind. Fight or flight is so often an unreliable response. Which is why instead of retreating into the relative safety of his room, the man a few doors down bolted for the lift. Dmitri stepped away from the door and fired into the man's path. One, two, three shots before one connected, and then it served only to drop the man noisily. Dmitri strode quickly toward the stricken guest and fired again at close range. The high calibre bullet thudded through the man's torso and bit into the floor below with a loud crack.

Two bullets left in the clip. Sloppy.

Another door opened further down the hall, but this time slammed immediately shut again. Dmitri's own heart rate was building by now, and he ran to the door just past 1307. He fired the last two shots in quick progression into the door, aiming chest height and a little to the left of where the door would have opened onto.

Clicking out the clip, he reloaded, listening for any movement beyond the door. The far elevator door pinged and Dmitri slid the gun behind his back again as he made out the blue canvas of the cleaner's trolley. Apparently news hadn't travelled too far yet, as the middle aged cleaner seemed to show no unusual surprise to Dmitri's sudden appearance before her cart, blocking her exit from the lift.

"Hi there," Dmitri started. "I think I got off on the wrong floor. Tell me, have you cleaned my room already?"

The woman stammered, and Dmitri continued. "Uh, second floor. Third floor, sorry."

"Third floor? Yes, all done this morning. Not me. Other cleaner take Three, Four, Five this morning. I clean top down."

Dmitri stepped to the side so the woman could leave the lift. "Excellent! Thank you. That's *very* helpful."

As she drew level with him pushing the trolley, he could see the keycard dangling from her belt. She suddenly stopped midstride as she noticed the blood lightly spattered down his right arm for the first time.

Calmly she looked forward into the corridor and took in the carnage soaking into the carpet near the opposite lift. Then, as her own bullet rocked her forward from the back of the head, she tumbled half way into the linen cart, and Dmitri tore off the master keycard from its zipline on her waist.

Now at the opposite side to where he'd come in, he started to work his way through the doors.

Room 1315. A beep and a green light. A figure stood on the other side, knees wobbling and a dark patch forming rapidly on his pants. Again, the shot echoed out and this time cracked the window beyond.

Room 1314. *Beep.* Three people in the room, huddled in the bathroom. A teen and her parents.

Five shots. Sloppy, man! Sloppy!

Room 1313. *Beep.* Was that a siren in the distance? The room appeared empty. But there was a wallet still on the counter, beside a set of keys. The bathroom was empty, but there was a scuffle of feet on concrete from beyond the billowing balcony curtain.

Dmitri stepped out to see a man leaning over the top bar, looking desperately for another way out, phone pressed firmly his ear. To the man's credit, he met Dmitri's gaze and lowered his phone. He knew what was coming.

And so did Dmitri.

The pistol arm was raised and the force of the high calibre bullet through his skull lifted him into an almost slow-motion tumble, dangling bodily over the high glass boundary of the top floor balcony. Teetering, but not falling. Dmitri stepped forward and looked over the edge. A seemingly tremendous height to the courtyard circuit below. And the fountain.

Sadism, per se, was not usually part of Dmitri's game.

Entertainment, sure, but not quite sadism. He'd learned the difference the hard way a long time ago, and he knew where the boundaries lay. This moment was more about curiosity. About seeing something he hadn't seen before.

With the gentlest force, Dmitri lifted one of the man's feet from its tentative position. And slowly, the balance shifted. He watched spellbound as the body rolled over the edge and plummeted to the ground thirteen storeys below.

Heads up, cherub.

Definitely sirens. And they were coming fast. The lights of the patrol cars were visible now, speeding toward the hotel as Dmitri stepped back into the room and loaded the last clip into his pistol. He'd seen what he needed to see for now. Now it was time to finish it properly.

He stepped back into the corridor and moved toward the next room. As the door beeped green for his entry, the first elevator pinged to announce company. Room 1312 was empty - actually empty. Apparently, it seemed even with only fifteen rooms on the top level the hotel didn't overbook.

Dmitri locked the door behind him and wedged the door stop against it. He walked into the bathroom, closed the door and sat on the tiles as the room went completely dark. He stowed the pistol and took out the ornate metal dove he'd collected from the fountain.

And as the first of the footsteps came thudding through the corridor, he concentrated.

He squeezed the contours of the metal dove and filled his mind with the smells, sights and scenery he'd taken in at the foot of the fountain before he'd stepped inside.

And found himself there again.

...To Skin A Cat

As the water rolled out of the thin, exposed pipe, Dmitri shot a guilty look at the sculpted cherub before leaving him to toil away with his futile bucket that would eternally drain as fast as it filled. Dmitri strode quickly up the polished stair case and the glass doors welcomed him inside.

This time around, Dmitri skipped the restaurant. It would still be about ten minutes before the politician would be meeting his friend for an entrée and small talk.

The elevator door opened and again the businessman walked purposefully out while the mother and child branched off to the opposite direction. This was the same elevator that he'd taken up the first time.

The same elevator that the politician would be riding to the thirteenth floor in about forty minutes' time. Except this time, he'd decided this elevator would serve better as an exit.

The corridor branched to the right and Dmitri followed the mother and child around the bend and out into the open. The footpath wound around to the left and out to the leafy guest car park.

On the righthand side was a utility area, with skip bins tucked out of view behind a thin wooden fence. A closed door marked the entrance to the laundry room, but the upturned milk crates, discarded Coke bottles and greasy footsteps staining the concrete were the tell-tale signs of a smoko area for the cleaners.

It would mean more waiting, but overall it was a more efficient way to do things. Dmitri leaned against the opposite wall, far enough away to avoid attention but close enough so he could jump into action when an opportunity presented itself.

After only a few minutes the laundry door swung open and a blue linen trolley led the way. Dmitri stiffened, but stayed where he was, dismayed when a young cleaner appeared behind the trolley, his head still spun behind him to finish a joke with someone inside. Dmitri was pretty certain he'd heard the voice of the cleaner who would later be upstairs, but there were definitely other voices chorusing in the mirth behind that door, and there was still plenty of time on the clock.

The young cleaner passed without even looking in Dmitri's direction. Down through the corridor and toward the lobby.

Possibly the cleaner she'd said would be sorting out the lower floors.

The rooms would be less spacious on those floors, he was sure, so presumably there would be more rooms. More rooms would mean more cleaners, and it was impossible to know how many more would be coming out before his first target. He wondered briefly why the cleaner he'd be looking for would use the far elevator well instead of the one just inside from the laundry room.

The thought began to nag at him and he decided that since she wouldn't be going up for a while, he might as well tail the younger cleaner in the meantime and solve the small mystery.

With a few long strides he was back in the corridor and near the elevator. Ahead, the young cleaner had stopped in the lobby. At the far end she was neatly piling clean linen into the laundry trolley from a stack on the counter by the farthest lift.

Not very efficient, Dmitri almost muttered out loud. *Perhaps the hotel wants this part of the process on display? Showing the guests the linen was cleaned daily by having the newly crisp whites waiting for them as they came in.*

Whatever the reason was, time had passed watching the cleaner stack the trolley, and if it was part of the show, maybe his target would be out of the room sooner than he'd expected. But where to deal with her if she'd be heading from the busy laundry room into public view…

As he returned to his post by the door, inspiration struck, and he headed instead to where the skip bins had been fenced off, keeping an eye out all the time for when the cleaner would emerge. Another twenty or so minutes ticked slowly by before the door opened at last and the familiar cleaner hobbled out with her trolley.

As she pushed off toward the side entrance, Dmitri called out.

"Miss! Excuse me, miss? Do you work here?" He'd taken only a few steps, but feigned exhaustion, panting with his hands on his knees in exasperation. He'd gotten her attention, and she stepped away from the trolley toward him. "Could you help me, please? I've dropped something in the bin, and I need it."

The cleaner's reply came in broken English. "Oh, please no use staff bin. No need - we take care of for you in room."

"I know, I'm sorry, it's just – I've managed to drop my car keys in there and I can't reach them. Here, I'll show you – maybe you'd have something long enough to reach it?"

Reluctantly, the cleaner followed. There were three skips in a row, arranged so the fenced gate could open at collection time, but otherwise they'd be out of sight. After all, no one really wants to see what happens to their refuse at the best of times, but especially so on holidays.

Dmitri flicked open the lid of the second skip. In another circumstance, it would have been amusing – tall Dmitri asking for help from the tiny lady who could barely see into the skip on the tips of her toes.

But it did expose her neck, and Dmitri pounced on the opportunity. Ripping the fibre cord from his pocket, he wound it around her throat and pulled back, the height difference making it barely necessary to push into the backs of her legs at all.

Ever reflective on whether this was the best way of doing things each time, Dmitri found himself thinking of alternative ways he could have executed the task while she was still kicking out the last confused breaths.

Sure, this wasn't as quick as the bullet she'd taken on the first visit, but maybe a few seconds of panic was preferable to being left in a mess. At any rate it had to be better than crashing something over her head. Besides, however the scenario played out, she'd have to die. To simply pickpocket the keycard would just raise the alarm the moment she reached the lift and found it was gone. The method of the murder was the only concession afforded her.

Finally, the cleaner stopped moving – to her credit she put up a longer fight than the lop-sided lobbyist had. Dmitri cut the keycard from her belt and left her between the skips, sufficiently hidden from view. Stepping out onto the footpath again he saw for the first time the sign on the right labelling the staff car park, and he kicked himself for not thinking of this solution sooner. He casually strode back to cleaner and checked her pockets.

You've really been most helpful, he acknowledged in his head, as he pocketed her car keys.

Moving quickly now, Dmitri moved past the trolley left standing alone on the path, through the side entrance, past the first elevator well, through the lobby and past the stack of neat linen his first victim should have been collecting.

A moment after hitting the 'up' key, the elevator door pinged open.

At the top floor again, Dmitri tried to remember who he'd seen in the earlier visit just now, because coming from this side, they'd be playing out in the opposite order. This time the first door was on the right, 1315, and it was where last time the man had wet himself before being shot. This time he'd die with a little more dignity, having not known what was coming.

Dmitri swiped the cleaner's keycard against the reader and it beeped once, then glowed green. In the second it took for the door to swing open and to see the man propped on the end of the bed watching television, Dmitri reflected.

Going back in time to perfect a crime scene was not always as simple and straightforward as the time traveller might hope. People did not always act the same way that they had the first time around. Of course, the slightest change in timing could mean that someone was in a completely different place altogether, or for whatever reason sometimes they simply decided on a different reaction. It was as if the choice between fight or flight were a coin toss, and going back somehow reset the odds.

This was important to note, because on his first trip, the man down in 1302 had bolted for the far elevator before Dmitri had opened 1307. There were still a few unexplored rooms and Dmitri didn't want to waste bullets at a moving target again.

Better to keep it quiet for a bit longer this time.

The man before him looked up with a look of sheer confusion as Dmitri took the pistol out and raised the handle like a club. The weight of the hand cannon crashed under the man's jaw and the momentum saw him roll off the bed with a thud. Dmitri was on top of him in a second and brought the butt of the gun down twice more on his bleeding head.

As he stood, he saw the dark stain form again on the man's trousers.

Well I guess a full bladder doesn't change the second time around.

Dmitri stepped back out into the corridor, and this time moved along the same side to 1313, ignoring for the moment the family in 1314 and focusing instead on the man who'd called the police last time.

The keycard again granted him access.

Inside the room, the wallet was in the same place on the counter, but the balcony sliding door was closed this time. As was the bathroom door.

The man must have had his phone with him though - it wasn't anywhere in sight. So, Dmitri perched himself at the front of the bathroom door in time to hear the flush of the toilet. Footsteps. The door opened and again that look of confusion was painted on the man's face as Dmitri fired a shot into his heart, hurtling the man backwards so that his head cracked the glass of the shower.

The report of the high calibre pistol roared in the acoustics of the tiled room.

Noisy now.

Dmitri considered briefly whether he could leave the family in room 1314 alone. The teen girl reminded him slightly of someone from long ago. But then, most girls did in some way or another. In fact, it was usually for that reason that he tended to spare them during decisions like this. The trouble was, though, if there was anyone likely to have their phone in their hand at the time the shots were fired, it would be a teenager.

The door beeped, and Dmitri swung it open. This time he was there in time to see them madly scrambling to figure out whether what they'd heard was as bad as it sounded. The teen was even peering bodily out from the bathroom and around into the small walk space by the door when Dmitri raised the pistol.

Only one shot each this time.

Neater.

Back in the hallway, Dmitri looked down toward 1302. Sure enough, the door was just starting to open cautiously. If it *was* a coin toss, this guy had been just as unlucky each time.

Certain he'd bolt for the elevator again, Dmitri sprinted to close the gap. He caught up in time to hear the man curse as he scuffed his feet in the mad dash to the lift. More out of frustration that the runner would continue to spoil his streak, Dmitri dived for him in a crash tackle that brought them both skidding roughly to the carpet. The man flailed and slapped to get away and was too panicked to focus properly on keeping Dmitri's arm from coming up and taking aim. He'd rolled himself onto his stomach and was clawing at the carpet to pull himself from under the time traveller's weight when Dmitri rested the hot barrel of the gun on the back of his head.

And fired.

Again, the gore splashed over the carpet as the bullet bit into the floor beneath, but this time the runner only needed one shot.

In case Dmitri needed any more encouragement that he'd taken care of things more efficiently this time around, a rare opportunity presented itself as he stood and levelled the pistol down the hall at the entrance of 1309.

Seemingly in slow motion, as the door creaked open, Dmitri squeezed the trigger. By the time the guest's head came into view it snapped back in a smear of blood against the door post. The distance had been a gamble, but all the more rewarding that it had worked.

He hadn't actually been sure he'd hit anyone the first time, firing through the door at the person who'd poked their head out and ducked out of sight. This time it was just a matter of not knowing *who* he'd hit.

Dmitri wanted to get back down the hallway and go through each room in sequence, leaving the elevator for the final exit. Still, the remaining rooms were unknown quantities, and he knew 1304 matched the number of bullets left in the clip.

The escort who had let him in unknowingly last time was not standing in the doorway this time around, but instead Dmitri found the two of them huddled behind the bed. The woman was clearly afraid, but the portly and presumably political man looked absolutely terrified. He clawed at the sheets as though they were a shield and buried his sweaty face as low as he could get into the back of the woman who he'd left in front of himself.

As much as sadism didn't fit Dmitri's perspective of killing, actual dislike of a person also rarely played a part in the decision. It was more of a general indifference. But as he watched this toad of a man worm around behind his hired escort, Dmitri found himself utterly disgusted in the creature. Dmitri pulled the woman out of the way by her arm.

"Bathroom. Go. Lock yourself in." He'd surprised even himself by saying the words.

Efficiency momentarily thrown aside, Dmitri smacked the half-dressed man hard across the face with the pistol before firing two shots. One into the man's belly and one into his pained and bloated face. Dmitri stormed out of the room, loading a second clip into the gun. He strode back the way he'd come to room 1311, glancing only briefly at the mess outside 1309.

Beep. Green light.

Two guests inside. Two bullets.

Room 1310. *Beep.* Two guests. Two bullets. One cracked window.

Room 1308. *Beep.* One guest only, an old man who seemed to have no idea of what was happening outside his room *–bang!–* and never would.

Room 1307. *Beep.* Empty, except for a briefcase and a laptop, each with gaudy bright decals lathered over them. It was possible this was the room of the politician still finishing his entrée downstairs. Dmitri yanked the laptop from its charger and tucked it under his left arm.

Every good murder needs a motive.

Or at least it needs to look that way.

Room 1306. *Beep.*

Nothing inside but the guests' luggage sprawled out everywhere in the dark.

Room 1305. *Beep.* Again darkness, but this time something nagged at Dmitri's gut, and he followed the feeling out to the balcony. Outside, a woman screamed to his left. She had climbed over the edge of the glass balcony and was attempting to shimmy across the thin ledge.

"Fuck you!" She wailed at Dmitri, her voice breaking into sobs.

And with that, she jumped.

Dmitri was stuck frozen to the spot for a moment or two. He must've moved in that time, because he looked over the edge as she fell, but he seemed to float to the edge like it was a dream, and he noted for the second time just how tremendously high the top floor was.

However, the unexpected event had temporarily thrown him. He could feel his focus slipping. This death hadn't been part of his design – yet it was still very much his fault. Where the edges blurred, some old and very much forgotten feelings stirred inside himself.

Dangerous feelings.

Feelings of helplessness.

A wail from the hotel alarm system stirred him out of his stupor in time to recognise the distant flashes of sirens on their way again. He hurried back into the hallway. There were so few doors left, but so much less time as well.

He still needed to get down to the main lobby and out. And now, with his scene tainted by this most tragic act of free will, something told him deep down, he wouldn't be revisiting this place again. If he was cornered, and he had to reset and stand again out by the fountain, somehow he knew he'd be more likely to just walk away and not go through with it a third time.

It had all been much more intense than he'd anticipated.

But it wasn't over yet.

As he eyed off the lift to his right, the door to 1304 opened again. The spared escort had foolishly taken a second chance at the odds and decided to make a break for the lift. In a noble but hopeless effort, she threw a small vase at Dmitri in passing, but the look on her face showed she knew the game was already over. Maybe she'd seen the body of the man in front of her who'd had the same idea to run earlier.

Dmitri took a reflexive step back as the ceramic piece burst well in front of his feet. Expressionless, he levelled his gun and fired. Twice. She crashed in a heap, spilling the contents of her large purse.

Dmitri sucked in a breath through his teeth.

Disappointing.

The light was glowing on the lift and Dmitri decided he'd spent too long there already. He ignored the last two doors, stepped past the carnage on the floor and called the elevator.

It opened almost immediately, and it was only once he stepped in that he noticed the form of the original politician huddled in the corner. How long had he been there? The alarms had only just started, and surely he wouldn't have gotten into the lift once they were blaring. Dmitri calmly pressed the button for the ground floor and made a quick mental recount of the bullets he should have left in the clip.

The man must have entered the lift below, then huddled in the corner when the gunshots sounded outside, frozen before pressing any of the buttons. He wasn't so much sitting as forcing his weight into the wall, as if by wanting it enough he could slip through to the other side and away from the nightmare.

So it was strange that in such a state of panic, a familiar sight caused him to stammer out a ridiculous statement.

"That… That's mine."

Dmitri looked at the man as the elevator shuddered into life and descended. He looked down at himself to where the man was feebly pointing, to the sticker-covered laptop cradled in his left hand.

Dmitri smirked at the eccentricity of the moment and, satisfied with the number he'd reached in his clouded mind, replied.

"Is it? That's unfortunate."

He stepped forward and fired the last bullet of the clip into the man's head.

Chapter 19
Chasing a Shadow

The phone call should've been enough.

In fact, Oswald knew it was enough. But he hadn't called the Alexander Macanochie Correctional Centre to save himself a trip – he'd called to make sure the trip would be worthwhile. Though if he was being honest, the trip was likely not going to be all that fruitful anyway. How could an already imprisoned man have anything further to do with an ongoing case?

Pulling the Omega into the visitor space carpark, Oswald corrected himself internally again.

An ongoing series of murders. Calling it a case suggests there are suspects, witnesses, leads… something.

Here goes nothing.

By the time he'd reached the front door, Oswald was already making a mental note of everything he was carrying and what he'd have to check in before he was admitted into the prison's interview rooms.

After the incident in the country the week before, Oswald had made a conscious decision to keep his pistol on him, even if it would've been easier to skip the extra security step at one of the most recently built maximum security prisons in the country.

He'd managed to arrange the interview with Paul Keeghy the night before. Though Keeghy had been sentenced for accessory to murder, his conduct on the inside had reportedly been above standard. He was therefore in one of the self-contained cottages, and for all intents and purposes he was not seen as being any continued threat to anyone within the prison walls. Visiting hours for his section were not usually until the evening, but having the investigating detective ask for a follow-up interview was apparently grounds enough to book an interview room during another wing's visiting hours.

Judging by the inanimate face of the ginger haired clerk standing behind the desk, however, Oswald resigned himself to the fact that that would be the only concession he'd receive in the arduous process.

The clerk was shuffling some papers absentmindedly when Oswald approached. Without moving his head, he had snapped his eyes up to see Detective Peter Oswald's name badge and then address his questions to the paper in his hands.

"Visiting the North Wing, officer?"

"Just the interview room, thank you," Oswald replied, his keys jingling as he placed them onto the concave of the bench beneath the glass screen. "I called through yesterday-"

"There's a locker for those after the next desk," the clerk interrupted. "You'll need to register your finger prints if you haven't been here before."

Contorting his brow into the semblance of a facial expression, the clerk concentrated on his own papers still as he pointed to his left and mumbled, "finger printing and weapon storage to your right. Smile for the camera."

At the next desk, Oswald realised the bored attendant had evidently attempted a joke, as he was met with a digital finger print scanner and a sign showing a passport-style example of how to look at the camera fixed behind another glass screen.

Next, a security officer motioned him over to a wall where an array of solid steel safes was set like absurdly secure PO Boxes. Here he unclipped his pistol and ammunition. The detective also turned off his phone and deposited it, knowing he'd left instructions with Constable Zoe Sullivan to contact him at the AMC if need be.

Reminiscent still of airport security was the next checkpoint, where a uniformed officer passed him a tray to empty his pockets into before going through the 360 scan metal detector. Once through, he re-pocketed his plastic biro and spiral notepad, and refitted his magnetic name badge under the watchful eye of the humourless security team.

Like donning a medal after completing these rites of passage, he was awarded with a lanyard with ESCORTED VISITOR written in bold letters.

❖

Further inside the compound, Paul Keeghy's feet were getting sore. He'd already lost count of the laps he'd walked of the yard, but that wasn't uncommon. What else was there to do in the long hours of the afternoon?

Paul Keeghy had always considered himself an alert man, his former years as a security officer convinced him of it. After two years in the AMC, however, he'd learned what it really meant to have eyes in the back of your head. Before he'd even fully rounded the fence line he'd already recognized the daggy gait of Ian 'Bolt' approaching him, complete with his regulation grey trousers dangling generously off his diminutive frame.

Paul slowed his own steps to allow Ian to close the gap. As he drew up close, a big grin split across his face – so he was carrying news. He was confident for his size, a proper weasel who knew the rules of survival in this sort of place. He wore his nickname of 'Bolt' with pride, supposing it referred to his speed. Another reason for the inmates to chuckle at the irony that it clearly labelled where his loyalties lay.

"The screws are lookin' for ya!"

"For me? What for?" Keeghy slowed to a stand still, crossing his arms to mimic the stance Bolt had just assumed, but without the mostly toothless grin.

"Someone to see ya, they reckon," Ian drawled. He raised his eyebrows, and Keeghy couldn't help rolling his eyes at the pulling gesture Ian made at his own crutch. "Lucky Paul!"

He stepped aside so Ian could pass and let Bolt's laughter at his own joke fade behind him as his mind began to race.

Who's here? Why outside normal hours? Why couldn't one of the bloody guards have passed the message on themselves?

With no sense wasting more time, and being so close to the officer station already, Keeghy approached the window and addressed the officer.

"Keeghy, 8-17. Got a visitor."

The officer swivelled on his chair and ran his finger across the plastic ID cards dangling on the wall behind him. Handing it over through the cut out beneath the window, he was at least friendly.

"8-17. Cheerio."

The gate buzzed and Keeghy went through. As he continued along the fence line the possible explanations in his mind were growing rapidly. Was it an official visit? Was something wrong?

It's gotta be bad news, right? Why else would someone be here unscheduled?

The passageway opened onto another open yard. He didn't bother looking around himself now, his vision tunnelling on the next gate and what mysteries lay in the building beyond. So much so he'd almost crashed into the gate before remembering he'd need the officers to open it for him. One guard was shuffling through the name boards on the wall, but the officer in front was frowning as he held out his ID card.

"Where are you going, again?"

"Visits," Keeghy replied.

"And who's visiting you?"

"I... don't know."

"And you know it's not your unit's hours, right?"

This was getting ridiculous.

"I know," Keeghy said, fighting the feeling of prickles in his cheeks. "They gave Bolt a message for me. Someone's here to see me. I don't know anything more than that."

"Well, well, well!" the officer at the name board turned now with a grin. "Pardon me, sir – can't argue a reliable source like Bolt! Ah, what the hell, let him through. They can always send him back."

Again the gate buzzed, this time opening up into a well-lit but distinctly grey interior. He'd only taken a few steps when a voice boomed beside him.

"Oi! Where do you think you are?" Though the officers all wore uniforms, there were those who somehow fit it better, as if their demeanour were somehow strapping in the sides and keeping the creases out of the cotton. Keeghy had worked with plenty of these types in his own profession before incarceration.

"Visits. Got a-"

"Not dressed like that you're not. Go back and get a shirt."

Paul looked down.

Fuck...

In the excitement and confusion, he hadn't even thought about his singlet top. Apparently no one had thought to point it out along the way, either.

Without arguing, he turned around and went back through the two gates, handing back his ID as he headed to his room. At least he'd had the right footwear, so he only needed to run inside and get a shirt and he could go back through.

The AMC was one of the few prisons to offer self-sustained cottages for many of the inmates - one of the strategies to focus on rehabilitation. Still, it wasn't *quite* as luxurious as it sounded - the sentenced guys weren't trusted with their own cooking, and he did have to share it with four other inmates. One such housemate of course was Bolt, lounging now in the common area between the bedrooms. "Christ, that was quick, mate!" Ian Bolt, ever the one for the drama, had even slapped his hand to his forehead as he cackled. "She must've been a looker!"

Keeghy ignored him and went straight over to unlock his room. He was still pulling the shirt over his head as he walked back out the main door, with Bolt still writhing on the chair in peels of laughter.

"Yeah, yeah, fuck you."

He shook his head, partly to loose the sound of Bolt's incessant high-pitched cackle from his head, but mostly in frustration that he'd now have to go back through each process again.

Collecting his ID card a second time and buzzing through to the next yard, he approached the officers tidying up the name boards again.

"Yeah, I remember," replied the officer. "But tough luck, mate, it's *no movement*."

"You're kidding."

"Kitchen staff are coming back in. Might as well take a seat. This could take a while."

Again the prickles in the cheek started to rise. A buzzer went off at another gate to the side. Keeghy was sure he heard a stifled laugh behind him as he slumped onto a wooden bench and watched the queue of kitchen staff approach the officer's station one at a time to get patted down and buzzed through.

It must have been at least ten minutes before the guard waved to him to come forward.

"Alrighty, you're clear to go through. Wanna hurry though, your visitor's probably been waiting a while."

Keeghy swallowed hard. His knuckles were white as they gripped the door, but with a buzz, he was back in the visits area.

He looked around for the fashion police – he wasn't hard to spot. The officer now resembled a proud father, maybe a benevolent king, giving an almost imperceptible nod as he pursed his lips into a subtle smile. Apparently approving of Keeghy's new attire, he had bestowed his blessing.

Unbelievable.

At the desk, he hoped the drama was over with.

"Keeghy, 8-17. I have a visitor?"

"Do you?" the woman behind the counter looked like she'd spent too many years in retail before this gig to continue dealing with people on a daily basis. It was the face of someone who was sick of you before you'd started speaking. "Sentenced unit? Not your hours, hun."

"I know. Please, I had a message that there was a visitor for me though."

"A message? Who-"

"I have no idea who it is. I'm sorry. Could you please just check?"

She dropped her eyelids further and worked her lip unpleasantly against her teeth. The look said, *now you've done it. Now I've gotta move all the way behind me and look at this clipboard.*

Luckily for Keeghy, the monologue only happened in his head, and as she said her next line he was free to go back to worrying about who had come to see him, what it meant, and exactly what he needed to brace for.

"Paul Keeghy, you said? Yep. Looks like you're in booth three. Go on in."

He sucked in a quick breath as the officer led him to the door to booth three. It opened into a small and brightly lit cubicle. There was a bench in the centre, walled off from the other side by another perspex screen. Cautiously, he took a seat as the officer closed the door behind him and left Paul facing the empty chair on the other end.

He rested his arms against the pale wooden bench. It couldn't be his wife coming to see him. *She would've come in the normal visiting hours.* They would've let him know she had scheduled a visit.

His brother hadn't seen him in over four months. *It could be him.* But again, why outside normal visiting hours? *Something could be wrong.* It could definitely be bad news. *What sort of bad news would they need to come in to tell me? Oh god, please tell me no one's died while I've been stuck in his hell hole.*

What if it was to do with his sentence?

Wait, what if it wasn't bad news at all?
What if they'd found the real killer?

He shifted in his seat and put his hands back into his lap.
He shifted again and placed his hands at his hips.

Folded his arms.

A shadow appeared on the head-height blurry glass of the door opposite, and the handle started to turn. Keeghy shifted forward so that his hands rested on his knees. The man who began to enter looked official. *And familiar...*

The man turned to face behind him, calling out a 'thank you' presumably to the officer who had let him in. The notepad in his outstretched hand was leading his entrance.

*So it is police...*What was that detective's name again?
The man came in and sat delicately. He looked at Paul fleetingly before reaching into his jacket pocket for a pen.
Definitely familiar. Must be the same guy I saw back then.

He cleared his throat and addressed Paul at last.
"Hello, I'm-..."
The door behind the detective opened suddenly again and an officer leaned down to the man's ear briefly. There was a moment where the visiting detective seemed torn between standing or sitting, but finally he stood and followed the officer past the door.
As it shut, Paul stared intently at the shadows on the glass.

He wiped his palms on his knees and cleared his own throat. Blinking through the possible meanings of this interruption and desperately clinging to that thin shred of hope that the news may just be good after all, he had no choice but to wait.

And the shadows left the window.

And he was alone again.

After a minute, he began to work through the scenarios. He decided it must not have been the worst of news - surely they wouldn't interrupt that. So assuming everyone one the outside was still alive and well, the news had to be about his sentence.

Maybe it was only an update. Maybe there was just a *suspicion* that someone else could've done the awful crime he was serving time for. Maybe they just had a few questions.

Or maybe they were just screwing with him.

Surely that was the same detective from the interview years ago.

Another full ten minutes passed before he was startled by the door behind him opening.
"Paul Keeghy?" It was an officer.
"Yeah?"
"Visit's been cancelled. You'll have to head back."

"For fuck's sake!"

❖

Oswald retraced his steps through the prison security and retrieved his pistol and phone from the safe. He was in a rush, but not so much that he couldn't observe his own behaviour in a highly secure compound. The image of a detective madly strapping a pistol to his chest wouldn't help anyone, so he tried to breathe normally and go over the facts as he prepared himself to leave.
He'd missed the emergency call of course, but Sullivan had followed his earlier instructions and called the AMC as soon as the update came through. There'd been a mass shooting at a hotel.
A high-powered pistol had been used and it was suspected to be a lone shooter.

Unapprehended.

Chapter 20

Day Pass
Canberra Hospital
2pm, 11 July, 2010

"Hospital food sucks."

A clink of metal as Terry pushed away the tray table carelessly. He swung his legs out of the bed, his arm still cradled in the blue cloth sling he'd been wearing on and off for nearly nine full days. His strangely skittish doctor had been very specific that he was only to rest the arm when he was in the worst of the pain.

For the most part, he was meant to keep the elbow moving so the joint wouldn't completely freeze up on him. He stood straight and pumped his legs in the air a few times to get the blood moving.

Wincing as he eased his right arm out, he threw a comment to his so-far-silent visitor.

"God, I feel like I've been in here forever."

As he waited for a response he looked around at the rest of his silent room. He'd been in the private room now for a week, a blessed reprieve from the beeping and bustling of the emergency ward.

Dr Tetherman would no doubt be in shortly to check up on him. She'd seen him a few times every day and worked through some exercises with him to keep the muscles mobile. Terry had only been into hospital a few times in his life, even taking into account visiting other people, but he'd never seen such dedicated attention from a doctor before.

Not only was she focused on his recovery, but she seemed genuinely interested in his overall wellbeing. With friendly professionalism she'd asked about his work, which interests and hobbies he had to balance out the work with leisure, and on one occasion had even enquired about his future goals.

"So is counselling part of your expertise in physical rehab, doctor?" he'd asked at the time.

She'd flashed that odd smile of hers again and had taken a moment to respond. She even sat at the edge of the bed.

"I believe health is multi-dimensional, yes. There's only so much I can do for your arm physically; part of your healing will come with time, and there's something to be said for having a healthy mindset."

"Wow, I didn't know you guys were allowed to believe in all that positivity stuff."

"Oh trust me, I've seen a lot in this place that medical science alone can't account for. Seen people who strictly speaking, shouldn't have recovered the way they did but for their outlook. And I've seen too many who failed to bounce back from seemingly minor conditions. Only thing I could put it down to was their mindset along the road to recovery. We're a strong species, Benjamin. The cruel irony is we seem to need to believe it for it to be true. We have to believe things will get better, that they'll all work out in the end."

Terry hadn't expected such an answer and he'd been taken aback. When she'd stared off into the corner, he found himself pressing further.

"Sounds like you've survived some things yourself."

Her red-brown hair bounced over her shoulders as she turned away for a second, hissing in a breath. She swivelled back as she stood up. "Let's take a quick look at how the other cuts are healing."

That had been a few days earlier. Terry brought his good hand to his face now and rubbed at one of the nearly invisible bruises.

"I've asked her for a day pass," Terry blurted, bursting the crushing quiet of the room, and his visitor stirred in his seat at last.

"Hey? Oh yeah. Good idea. Stretch the legs," Dmitri had also been off in his own thoughts. The events at the Holden Hotel had played over and over in his mind and it was taking some concentration not to cross that line and go back. He'd decided to distract himself the way most people did – by talking to someone.

His particular pastimes didn't lend him well to social situations. Friends weren't something he'd come across too often in the last twenty or so years, but something had drawn him back again to the broken boy he'd seen pummelled to pieces in the street the week before.

Except the kid wasn't doing too good a job of distracting him. They'd both just been mostly sitting in silence – Dmitri unable to give a good explanation for his presence, and Terry too bored and restless to start a decent conversation. What was it he was hoping to discuss anyway? He certainly couldn't divulge anything that was actually on his mind… could he?

He imagined the conversation in his head. Somehow it didn't seem realistic.

What've you been up to recently?

Me? Oh you know, completed the single bloodiest rampage in the country's history.

Really?

Yup, didn't even end up dead.

That's great! How'd you get away with it?

Well, I had the advantage of knowing where everyone would be, so I could get out of the building by the end of it without being seen. Oh and I had the car keys from one of the workers so I could just drive on out of there in the opposite direction before the police arrived.

No kidding.

Unlikely.

So instead, in the silence, he was free to chase his own questions around in his head.

Where was there to go from here?

What could be a higher hit of adrenaline than getting away with something like that?

He knew he could go back, but he also knew he didn't want to. And worse, *that feeling* was starting to creep up again. That one that replayed the scenery over and over, and he knew where that could lead, and it was bringing up worse memories.

Don't go back there.

The one place he didn't ever want to go back to.

Fight it.

The only thing he truly regretted.

Fight. It.

The feeling passed as the voices started to echo in the little room, grounding Dmitri to the present.

"Are you okay?"

Dmitri looked down at his wringing hands and the object he'd been unwittingly throttling. Somewhere in his reverie, he must have taken hold of Terry's nurse-call remote. Mashing the buttons, he'd turned on Terry's television set, and a news update was bellowing out behind the kid with the broken arm.

"Hey, maybe turn it down a bit? It's so quiet in the rest of the place." Terry eased back onto his bed, eyes up at the reporter. "Oh," he called to Dmitri, "have you been following this story? Bunch of people got shot in a hotel right here in town the other day. Crazy scary!"

Dmitri sat back into his own chair and listened to the somewhat-startled anchor spilling the media's suppositions and shortcomings.

> "The death toll has now risen to nineteen victims, as police confirm finding even more bodies at what has been marked as Australia's deadliest act of gun violence since the Port Arthur Massacre in 1996.
>
> "The Holden Hotel and its immediate surroundings were closed to the public and marked as a crime scene on Thursday afternoon and the restrictions have remained in place while investigations are ongoing.
>
> "Detectives have declined to comment so far, but it is believed the police are investigating the possibility that as little as only one man is responsible.
>
> "The police are investigating all leads in the manhunt and are encouraging any members of the public that may have any information to call Crime Stoppers on eighteen hundred, triple three, triple-"

The report was interrupted by the swishing of the curtain.

"Everything alright in here, Mr Terrace?" A young nurse Terry hadn't seen before leaned over the bed and turned off the nurse call light.

"Yeah, all going well. Must've pressed it by accident, sorry. Hey, actually! Is there any chance I could get like a day pass or something – is that a thing? I know the doctor wants me in here for a while longer, but I'd love to go out just for a walk. I mentioned it to her yesterday, but I haven't heard anything back yet."

Terry continued when the nurse squirmed, and he flicked a glance over at Dmitri. "Just, my friend's here and I'd love to go and grab a coffee. Right mate?"

It was Dmitri's turn to squirm, apparently lost in his thoughts, then lost in the news, then finally put on the spot. "Ah, yeah. I mean, if the doctor says it's okay."

The nurse was outnumbered and uncomfortable.

"No problem, I'll see if we can page Dr. Tetherman for you."

❖

The explosion of light slowly started to fade into blurred shapes. Multiple muffled voices were droning over the top of each other, waves folding and crashing together, gasping for the surface. And indeed they each sounded like they were under water.

Occasionally one would break into clarity, only for a word or two, before diving back under the torrent. The foggy images in front of his eyes repeated the same pattern.

There was dirt. Blood. *What are you doing?*

Then a clean clinical floor.

A woman crying. *No, I can fix this.*

Then the green wash of a plastic curtain. *Are you okay?*

The two scenes juxtaposed over each other. *I can fix this!*

The dirt again. Blood on his hands, his shoes.

Dmitri? Are you- the speckled vinyl floor. Bare feet in front of him. A man in a hospital garment.

Don't touch me! Blood on her skirt, her neck. *I can do anything! Anything! Just shut up long enough- I can fix this!*

A hand on his knee. *Sir? Are you okay?*

His name's Dmitri. No, I don't know, sorry.

Dmitri? Can you hear me?

"Hey, Dmitri? Can you hear us? Are you okay?"

The room came back into focus.

Terry. Benjamin.

Benjamin Terrace.

And the nurse.

Dmitri swivelled around expecting to see the bushland again, but he was still sitting in the hospital, his knuckles bleached white with his grip on the plastic chair. White, not red. No blood.

He released his grip and stared into his clean palms. Looking up into their concerned faces, he tried to wash away his own panicked expression.

"Yeah," he coughed. "Yeah, I'm fine. Why?"

"You just flipped out there for a bit," Terry said. "Like you were having a fit, or sleep talking or something."

"Really? Why? What did I say?"

"Nothing - just muttering, mostly. And writhing."

The nurse chimed in now, "do you have a medical condition, sir? Dmitri, is it?"

"Ah, no. I mean, yes. Yes it's Dmitri. No, I don't have a condition. I'm not sure what happened. I- I think I need some fresh air, that's all. I'll meet you downstairs, kid."

The nurse took a step after him but he had already strode into the corridor. When she turned around, Benjamin was sitting on his bed, struggling to slide his shoes on with his good arm.

"Do you think you could still organise that day pass, please?"

Chapter 21

Higher Powers

Detective Peter Oswald woke at his desk.

From time to time there came those long days on the force – not the type bred from boredom where minutes felt like hours.

There was a special kind of exhaustion reserved for those days where time itself no longer became a concept. Whole days vanished gathering details, taking interviews, informing families, blocking reporters. But as the sun cycled in its loops around the firmament it dragged with it the very meaning of minutes, and it stripped the seconds back so that nothing ticked. Time didn't pass, fly or drag.

It simply was and was not.

And eventually when enough energy had been spilled into the vacuum, the clock would tick again, and Oswald could realise how far behind he was, yet again.

The phone had been ringing for a while, and Oswald let it continue tolling as he worked his tired fingers into his eyes. His mind was heavily burdened by the crime scene at the Holden Hotel. As the detective, he was not the first on the scene, but he was there soon enough after for it not to make much of a difference in what he saw.

The hotel of horrors contained enough violence to fill out years of most cops' careers. Hell, in one inning this made the worst massacre in the nation in the last fourteen years. And indeed with chilling similarities in efficiency.

Nineteen victims splashed out in one place, all dead, most of them shot, one strangled and dumped. All within a few minutes of each other. All targeted. No stray bullets. No mistakes, and no trace.

So far.

"Detective?" Zoe Sullivan was at the door. "Sergeant's on the line for you. Says he's having trouble reaching you."

"Thanks, Zoe. I'll pick it up from here."

And evidently this would be as far as Detective Oswald would get to take the case. Naturally the Australian Federal Police had swarmed in, more specifically, the SRS – the Specialist Response and Security Team.

Frankly, Oswald had been surprised they hadn't been called in already so far, with the increased gun violence in the city. But if, as Oswald was starting to suspect, these cases were linked somehow, each scene had left practically nothing to pin on the killer and no clue as to the next target. Assuming, of course that there was some one-man band out there choosing and executing these targets.

And that was why the phone hadn't stopped ringing. Officially, the higher powers wanted a proper handover from Oswald, though in practice, he knew he had nothing solid to offer. He didn't really even have his own theories. They'd take his notes, and they'd do as they saw fit from there. He picked up his handset.

"Oswald speaking."

"He lives," from the mouth of anyone else, it would have sounded like a joke. Somehow the Sergeant made it sound more like an accusation.

"Hello, Sergeant Griffin. How can I help?"

"Picking up your phone was a great start. God knows mine's barely been off the hook the last two days. Some of the lads from the SRS will visit your precinct later in the afternoon. They're to be briefed on the details of all the recent gun-related cases you've been chasing – closed or otherwise.

"I've been considering what you told me outside the Holden Hotel, and I'd like to explore the possibility of a link in the efficiency in some of the recent shootings. The men you meet will look like a tactical team, but their roles are multi-faceted. The SRS operate with more autonomy within their cells so it's important they have as much intel as is available to make the right call on the ground. Understood?"

"Certainly. Still, I wish I had more to give them. Has anything come of the reception CCTV?"

"I understand they're having some difficulty, but that won't concern you now, detective. Everything's being handed to the AFP to take care of effective immediately."

"Sir, with respect, I think it would be more beneficial if we were able to work alongside the AFP, especially while we still don't know exactly what we're up against here."

The deadpan voice on the other line answered with a tone that implied he'd not only anticipated such a request, but that he'd been tapping his foot until the spiel was over.

"It's out of my hands, Oswald. Hand over the intel and get yourself some sleep."

The phone clicked and the line went dead.
Get myself some sleep. Sure. Like it's that simple.

❖

Unit Leader Leon Chapman let out a low whistle as he kicked an armoured tyre of the new beast. His own kevlar-shrouded boots bounced back heavily. He was dressed in full tactical gear, from his helmet to his boots, a patch around his eyebrows and cheeks the only part of his white flesh showing through the breathable balaclava, like he was wearing a reverse domino mask with everything *except* his eyes disguised. His arms cradled his R93 Blaser Sniper Rifle - the sights protected by covers, the 10-round magazine empty, but ready to be swapped for a loaded one on his belt should they be called to action.

"I'd heard rumours. I thought Boss-man said we were years off getting anything like this."

"Yup - amazing how an emergency can cut through the red tape and bullshit, eh?"

"What are they calling this beauty? Looks like it's gotten a few upgrades since the '90s model I saw with the yanks."

"Still the Bearcat. Just a little newer and a lot more improved."

"Christ Gav, it looks like the bloody Batmobile."

"Pretty much! This bastard's basically bulletproof, blast proof and equipped with enough comms equipment to be classified as a mobile radio station." Gavrilo was wearing his combat boots and tactical trousers, but from the waist up his white t-shirt shone in contrast to his mellow olive skin. As he leapt up and held onto the roof railing of the new tactical vehicle, he looked the part of a world war two commando, as if tanned by the African sun rather than his mixed European and Middle Eastern ancestry.

He flipped open what looked like a turret hatch in the roof. "It's even got a man hole here that Prince will want, no doubt. You can fix a machine gun to the top, though I doubt they'll be giving us one of those. But he should have enough fun just manoeuvring his assault rifle from up here. Meanwhile, Guiteau can literally ride shotgun, given all the firing holes in the side."

"Ha, nicely played, Godse," Leon parried, "I notice you've kept the driver's seat for yourself then."

"You're just jealous cos you won't be on board when the action starts. Unless you want to swap places with Prince and try your luck sniping from the hatch?"

Leon had to admit he was a little disappointed at the prospect of not being along for the ride, but his specialty in the long range rifles usually set him apart from the thickest of the action. *Not far enough, sometimes.*

"Hey, how are you going, anyway?" Gavrilo probed, "being back, I mean."

Leon Chapman had taken some personal leave after a cock-up in communications had left him rattled about two months earlier. He was sure it would've gone differently if it had been Gavrilo Godse doing the negotiating on the ground that day. Instead he'd been lumped with the imbecile who'd panicked and spoken out of turn into the team mic. Ruining everything.

SRS had been called out to a siege - a drugged up young guy who'd got his hands on a firearm. Police had set up a four-cornered scene guard, but the bloke had slipped out somehow and taken a hostage – a young woman. The SRS team had been able to rearrange themselves around the new position and Leon was even fortunate enough to have a clear shot lined up on the man through a window.

Through his sights he was even confident of a clean enough shot to clear the danger of hitting the hostage, his crosshairs fixed firmly on the man's ear.

But the greatest tool in such situations is the negotiator, and that day that tool was blunt.

The fugitive was not backing down and Leon, ready for action, had called in, "clear shot – advise."

Before his unit leader had even had the chance to approve it, the idiot negotiator, face to face with the mad man, had called aloud, "No, wait! More time, more time! Hold fire!" And through the magnified window of his scope, Leon had watched the cogs turn in the druggy's head. The man who hadn't known he was in a sniper's crosshairs – hadn't realised exactly how screwed he was – put the pieces together.

And with nothing to lose, he had pulled the trigger. The woman's skull had opened up only a second before Leon's instincts took over and he'd fired the shot that moments earlier could have spared her.

Leon had seen the psychs after the debriefing. He'd broken the events down and worked through the logic of it all. The decisions hadn't been Leon's to start with.

He hadn't been the coordinator on that siege.

He reacted the way he'd been trained.

He'd followed orders.

So on and so forth, with no comfort.

Despite the sessions, it just didn't sit well with him, and he was glad that this time around, whatever exactly this team was being brought together for, he'd got to pick who he was working with, and he got to call the shots.

"Yeah," he said at last to Godse. "I'm good. Glad to be working with you, Gav. Let's pick up Prince and Guiteau and get over to the precinct."

❖

James Guiteau's demeanour could be summed up in one word – imposing. He was a broad-shouldered, barrel chested boulder of a man, who would have been intimidating even without the bandolier of shotgun shells over his chest, the revolver at his hip or the black combat fatigues he was dressed in.

Beside him stood David Prince. A more traditional looking special forces operative, if there was such a thing. Instead of raw power, his presence was intimidating in the way he held himself, an air of confidence that out shone the fact that his Remington R4 Combine was comfortably supported in one hand. Without his helmet and balaclava on, his sandy hair was longer in the front so that it waved just enough to suggest that should the AFP ever compete with the Fireys for a calendar, he should be picked for a prominent month.

Beside Prince stood Gav, suited up properly now, his MP5 sub machine gun slung over his back, his hands free to work a notebook and pen as Leon made ready to officially start the handover.

Detective Oswald considered the men respectfully as he slid several manila folders onto the table.

"Sorry to tell you this boys, but there's not a great deal in the way of leads," spoken like a scout leader having to disappoint his cubs. *This area's just no good for camping.* "I've compiled the information on several recent gun-related crimes in the area, along with interviews, suspects and so on, few though they may be."

The uniformed AFP officer who had introduced himself only as 'Ray' stepped forward now.

"Detective, I understand Sergeant Griffin has explained that this would be an exclusively federal case, moving forward. However, I think it may be helpful to keep the channels open for the groundwork you have already done so far. Say, for instance should someone remember something helpful, they may be more likely to speak to the investigating officer."

The man's voice dripped with honey. It didn't fit his uniform, Oswald reflected. He sounded more like a salesman, or an attorney at best. The words themselves didn't match the tone, and Oswald found it hard to place whether this was said in acknowledgment of his work or in spite of it.

Nevertheless, he had to admit he was not ready to take his hands away from this case, awful as it was, and this may be the only opportunity that would present itself.

"I think that sounds very wise," he replied. "Some of our tests from the crime scenes are still being processed, for example."

"Yes, I understand forensics have been exploring some possible DNA samples from multiple victims at the Holden Hotel. One of the advantages of it becoming a federal investigation is that we are able to speed some of those processes along."

Again, he sounded helpful, but Oswald was aware of some hidden poison in the words.

"Furthermore," Ray continued, "we will cross-match the findings with some of the people already taken into custody, namely a Darren Booth, was it?"

"Ah, yes," Oswald started at the name of the man he'd arrested in the countryside. "I know you will need to do your own investigations, but I believe that one stands out separately from the rest. A bit more cut and dry."

"Yes, and I understand you visited the incarcerated Paul Keeghy recently, did you find anything of use there?"

"No. That is, I didn't actually end up talking to him. I was called away to the hotel shooting. But he is facing charges from over two years back, looking at it again now, I don't see how it could be connected."

"Lastly," Ray pressed on, "I think I'd like to speak with one Benjamin Terrace. I see he was a key witness at one of the scenes, and has been recently hospitalised under violent circumstances, is that right?"

Oswald could feel his composure slipping now. So, they would be going back through all of his work. The kid was innocent, Oswald was sure enough of that, but he had a way of being in the wrong place *all* the time.

At last, one of the SRS men spoke.
"In the meantime, Detective," Leon said. "We will be conducting our own investigation into possible target locations or persons of interest, monitoring communication and so on. You can call me directly should something warrant it."
Oswald thought he picked up on a slight intonation on the word 'directly', and took it to mean 'excluding present company should the need arise'. He wasn't sure what to do with the implication, but it went a long way in making him feel more comfortable.
"Before we finish up," Leon continued, "I'd like to ask you some details about some of the murders in particular, so that my team and I know what sort of person or persons we're up against."

❖

When the interview finished, Oswald dialled the hospital on his mobile, but by the time the call was answered and he'd keyed in the options of where to be directed, he was already at his car.

When he arrived, the bed was empty, but Terry's name was still written above his bed. Oswald figured he must be out for some tests, so he took a seat with the curtain open. At least half an hour passed before he heard a shuffling pair of feet in the corridor do a double take and come inside the room.
"Officer, good afternoon. I'm Benjamin's doctor, Kate Tetherman. Is everything alright?"
Oswald stood to greet her. "Yes, thank you, Miss Tetherman. I just wanted to clarify some things with Terry if he's around."
"I authorised a day pass for him earlier today, I'm sorry. I was told he had a visitor and wanted to get some fresh air."

Oswald sucked his teeth absentmindedly.

"Sorry, was that wrong?"

"No, no, not as such. He's not under arrest or anything."

"I know I shouldn't ask," the doctor said taking a step forward, "but what sort of trouble is Benjamin in? This bashing he's been a victim of – was that a random attack or something more sinister?"

Oswald smiled and took out his notepad. He scribbled some numbers and tore off the page. "Of course, I can't say much, you understand. But he is under police protection... of sorts. In the future, if you wouldn't mind, could you please give me a call with any updates? I'd be interested in knowing who today's visitor was, or if he has any other days out for instance."

The doctor took the slip of paper from him, but she was clearly at a loss.

"Yes. Yes, of course, Detective."

Chapter 22

Trade Secrets

"Tell me about your family, Terry."

The question had come out of nowhere.

It had only taken about half an hour or so for the day pass to be approved, and Terry, his right arm in a sling, had come downstairs to meet Dmitri. They'd met on the footpath outside and walked in near silence at the impressive pace Dmitri was setting. Not far down the road they'd found a small coffee shop and sat inside.

Dmitri seemed off, somehow, Terry thought. Clearly, he had no intention of explaining his little episode in the hospital. And he kept looking furtively around the room. At one point he seemed to be staring down a pedestrian going past the window. His lefthand fingers drummed the table every so often, his right hand in his trouser pockets, fidgeting with what sounded like keys.

"My family?" Terry responded, confused.

"Yeah, I mean, they've been to see you at the hospital haven't they?" Dmitri tucked his chair forward as the coffees arrived. He brought both of his hands into view as he poured half a sugar packet into his cappuccino.

"Well, I've just got the one brother. Jono. And Mum and Dad, of course."

Dmitri raised his eyebrows to urge him on. "So are you like, Benjamin Junior? You know, shared names."

Terry frowned, confused at where he'd gotten the idea from, and unaware of the probing tactic.

"No, Dad's name is Lee. Mum's name's Miranda."

Dmitri only tapped the side of his coffee a few times in response. In the silence, Terry pushed the conversation forward. "How about you, then?"

"What do they do?" Dmitri quizzed further, ignoring the question. "I mean, you mentioned a while back that you're a web designer, is that a family gig?"

Terry chuckled, "Hardly! Dad's an accountant. It was his first job after he was qualified and he's been at the same firm since the stone age. Mum's got a creative streak I guess, but it's more with crafts and gardening. She just works part time now in customer service. Shopping centre concierge, you know.

"She used to be a secretary or something. I think that's how they met, actually. She did some temp work at Dad's firm in their younger years. That's it. The exciting story of the Terrace family. And Jono's three years younger than me."

"Close, though?"

"No. World's apart. He's super into his sport, makes Dad proud. Or at least he did, before I *'filled his head with nonsense.'* Apparently it's my fault he discovered his phone and Xbox. Now he's some lazy lout and I'm to blame. Here, this is us."

Terry reached into his pocket clumsily with his left hand, and clumsier still fumbled to find the camera folder in his phone. He passed the mobile over to his curious comrade.

Dmitri studied the picture briefly, then looked back up at Terry.

"This really them? They look nothing like you."

Terry was stung by the comment. Admittedly, he'd just described how alien they were to him, but it still felt wrong coming from an outsider.

Dmitri continued, still holding the phone. "Three years younger you said... so he's what, twenty?"

"Twenty-one. He just looks younger." Again, Terry hadn't picked up on the subtlety of whatever maths Dmitri was calculating in his head.

"So that'd make you twenty-four."

"And a half," Terry replied defensively, as though the qualifier excused him from some shame of youthfulness.

"Hey, it's no race, kid. Hell, I must be pushing nearly forty soon enough. No, wait, I'd already be just past it."

"Old enough to forget, huh? Done much with the years?" Terry chuckled, happy for the chance to sting back. What had this guy said he was about a week back at the Barrel and Bray? A travelling salesman or something?

Dmitri relaxed back into his chair and his attention was lost out the window.

"I have done... much... with lots of years, yes. Though that's something for debate isn't it? Sounds like your old man would say I'd wasted them, right?"

"You know, I heard somewhere once, wait, let me remember the right wording..." Terry scratched at his temple, "Ah yep, got it –that the measure of the right decisions lay in the answer to just one question: if you had your time over, would you make the same choices?"

"*That* one I can answer easily," Dmitri was beaming. "Yes. Time and time again. Yes."

"Well there you have it," Terry said after a swig of his latte. "According to uh, well whoever said that, you've made the right choices all through life."

"Ha!" Dmitri sculled his cappuccino and drummed both hands on the table now. "Hey, finish your coffee. I want to show you something."

Dmitri led them outside and toward a park.

"Think about what you said before, Benjamin, about doing things over again."

Terry was thrown off by the use of his first name. He was pretty sure Dmitri hadn't used it before.

"Imagine," the man continued, "if that was possible. What would *you* use it for? Of course, people's first response would be to change things, right? To make things better. But what if you actually used it for yourself? Imagine living a life free from time and a particular space where you could do what you wanted and then just – vanish."

Dmitri was really getting on board with this theoretical discussion, so Terry tried to keep up. His arm was starting to ache in the sling from all the walking.

"Well first thing that comes to mind, I wouldn't mind going back to avoid getting my arm busted."

"A good start," Dmitri chimed in with a chuckle. "Show that crazy fucker a thing or two instead, eh?"

Terry started to feel uneasy about where this conversation was leading, never mind where Dmitri was leading them as they walked. He hesitated before he replied.

"I... guess. Sure. But I just meant I'd avoid being surprised by him."

"Right," Dmitri drawled, "but what if, say, you went back now, to the bar. So your arm's not broken yet. Say it's just after you started heading out the door. *This* time, you know where the guy is. You don't have to walk the same path, you can sneak up behind him this time around and *wham!*" Dmitri smacked a fist into an open palm. "You keep walking, arm intact, it's just another night, but this time *he* has the headache instead of you."

Terry grinned, joining the fantasy. "Yeah, that does sound pretty nice right now. I mean, I don't have to bust his arm to make it even, I'm just making sure I get to walk home safely."

"Exactly," Dmitri nodded, sage-like.

After a few more steps, Terry continued. "Though that's the problem with these discussions, isn't it? The whole 'meant to happen' thing. I mean, how would we ever have this conversation, walking here together, if you hadn't had to call the ambulance for me? There's a lot of things that would change."

Dmitri's bubbling mood turned reflective again. "Yeah, you're right. That would've changed *a lot actually.*"

"Anyway," Terry broke the conversation, uncomfortable in the cryptic frown that focus had painted over Dmitri's face. "Waste of time thinking about. Impossible stuff – like people planning out what they'd do if they won the lottery."

Dmitri stopped walking. He looked at Terry like he was appraising him. Considering.

"I don't know if that's the impossible part," he said at length.

Terry stared blankly – at a complete loss as to why Dmitri wanted to push this topic further, but hooked nonetheless.

He couldn't remember the last time he'd had a conversation with someone about a metaphysical, hypothetical situation – at least outside of internet forums. He'd always pictured the people online to match the stereotypical people in his profession. Someone who didn't move much from his swivel chair and survived mainly on potato chips and pizza.

Terry was self-aware enough to know he himself didn't fit the mould, but he was starting to think he still needed to shift his own mental depictions of his peers. Dmitri certainly didn't look like the type to consider these things on any sort of level.

"I'd say the impossible part is explaining it to someone. Convincing them you could do it."

"True enough," Terry replied. "You mean, I couldn't go back to the bar and convince you I'd just got the drop on Rudley cos I knew where he'd be this time around."

"Exactly! How would you convince me that your arm had been broken by him the first time? Wouldn't I just say you attacked him for no reason?"

"Hell, how would I convince you that you'd called the ambulance the first time? You'd have just been in the bar minding your own business, right?"

A shadow flashed over Dmitri's eyes for a second.

"Right. I'd just be there. And I'd have no idea what you were talking about."

The pair started to walk again.

"Let's say it was really important that I believed you, in that scenario," Dmitri pressed. "And you really had to convince me that you'd come back and taken out – who was it? Rudley? You'd have to *show* me somehow, if explaining it didn't work."

Dmitri steered them off the path now, along the grass of the parkland and toward another path further ahead.

"You'd need proof," Dmitri said, and he took a few strides ahead, toward a man who had just sat down on a park bench, his back turned to the pair of amateur philosophers.

The man had taken his wallet from his back pocket and sat it on the seat beside him before opening up a book he'd been cradling. Instantly lost in the pages, he didn't have a chance of spotting Dmitri lean down from behind him and snatch the wallet. Without so much as a glance, Dmitri flicked open the wallet, withdrew a driver's licence and held it at arm's length behind him, toward Terry, all the while keeping his gaze fixed on the back of the man's balding head. When he spoke, he had assumed a mock refined English accent:

"William Jensen, I presume? Of 12 Larson street, Canberra. Licence number 80 636 221?"

Terry was able to read the details in Dmitri's outstretched hand as Dmitri was saying them aloud.

"Carry on, sir, and do be more careful with your possessions." He finished the drama with a bow, submitting the wallet and the licence back to the man who had now stood and pivoted round to face him – his face flushed in a mixture of anger and confusion.

Dmitri marched onto the path now, with Terry following close behind, and the man by the bench muttering and shaking his head as he checked nothing was missing. Terry was sure he'd heard the man swear at them when they were far enough away, but he was at too much of a loss for words himself to listen properly to the angry pedestrian.

The path led along a thin creek and over a small arch bridge. Evidently still caught up in the flourish of showmanship, Dmitri stamped his feet at the top of the bridge and spun on a heel to face Terry.

"So? What do you think?"

"Think about what? Did you know that guy?"

"Never seen him until now," Dmitri mimicked offence. "Why? Did he seem to know me?"

"No– what? How did you know his driver's licence details without reading them?"

Dmitri descended the bridge.

"Well that's not entirely true. I *did* read them. A few minutes ago. Except *those* minutes didn't happen this time around. *This time* was just for show. *I* can still remember the first time, but you can't. Why not?"

Terry took a step backward and surveyed Dmitri's face. If it was some sort of joke, this apparent madman was well and truly sold to it.

"What are you trying to say? You went back in time just to read his driver's licence?"

When Dmitri replied, his voice showed he was stung by Terry's criticism. His shoulders slumped ever so slightly and some of the enthusiasm had died off.

"No," he said. "I'm trying to tell you I read it, memorised it, and then went back to –how can I put it?– reset the stage!"

"To tell me what... that you think you can... travel through time?" Terry spelled the words out slowly waiting for a smile to break the joke.

Dmitri made no response.

Terry continued, giving Dmitri another chance to deliver whatever great punchline was waiting up ahead, "So, what now? Since your proof doesn't seem to have worked, are you now going to go back and... 'reset the stage' again?"

"Mm, there's a complication there."

"Convenient."

"I didn't say impossible, just, in the 'theatre' of the moment, I gave him back his wallet. And that was my doorway back in. My last checkpoint is too old now. Days ago. We'd have to have this whole conversation again."

There was silence as the two continued to regard each other.

"Checkpoint," Terry said at last.

"Best word I can think of for it, at least."

"Like a savegame?"

Dmitri frowned at that, puzzled.

"Okay," Terry continued, starting to smile. "So how do you create these checkpoints?"

"No, no. That's too much detail for now. Especially since you don't seem even remotely convinced."

Terry stared hard at Dmitri.

"You're really serious, aren't you? You believe this?"

"Whatever, kid. Let's start getting you back to the hospital before they send out a search party."

Dmitri brushed past Terry, heading back the way they'd come across the grass. The balding man had left, taking his book and his wallet with him.

The minutes dragged by, the silence so great it was almost audible itself, drumming in Terry's ears as he walked, broken only by the stabbing sensation coming from his busted elbow.

He was disappointed his friend had turned out to be more than a little crazy. He thought about what would happen when he went back inside the building. Would this be the last time they spoke? He'd clearly offended the man, but what else was there to do?

Pretend he's not crazy just so I can pretend I have a friend?

That's *crazy*.

❖

They'd reached the front of the hospital.

It was the late afternoon now, and there was a slow stream of doctors, nurses and patients going either in or out of the building. It was possible to spot the difference just by the posture, mostly. The exhausted staff heading out to the carpark after a long shift. The fresh staff coming in, bracing for whatever may lay ahead for them in the next however many hours. And of course, the wide variety of afflictions besetting their customers, most of which being the smokers getting in their last few puffs before it got too cold to come back outside.

Terry couldn't help himself. He had to break the silence, even if it meant risking more insult.

"So, how far back are we talking, anyway? Our *hypothetical* idea of me going back and stopping Rudley breaking my arm, is that the sort of thing you mean? Or is that too far back?"

Dmitri chuckled. "Not too far back at all. Only two problems – firstly, what you already said about how it would mean us not meeting in the first place – it'd be a little redundant. Secondly is the checkpoint issue. Again, the one before that night was a while back. Only a few hours, but still. Oh, and one more possible hitch, I've never tried taking anyone with me."

They were talking by the main entrance now, and Terry found himself still with questions to ask, if only for the sake of hoping to let the man see how crazy it all sounded.

"So, how do you remember all the checkpoints?"

Dmitri went solemn again for a moment.

"They stand out. They have to, to work properly."

"So how did this guy with the wallet stand out? I mean, I didn't even notice him there until you spoke to him."

Dmitri reached into his pocket and took out a something small.

"Tell ya what," he said with a flicker of a grin starting up again. "How about you try to get another day pass for tomorrow, and I can show you something that I think might change your mind about the whole thing. Hold onto this until then. Call it a trust exercise if you like."

In his outstretched hand was a single brass-coloured key.

Somehow it didn't seem that Dmitri trusting Terry was the right way around for this trust exercise to go. Nevertheless, the boy was still a slave to the curiosity that had led him inadvertently to this building's emergency wing in the first place. He took the key, and his friend walked off into the growing darkness.

"See you tomorrow, then, kid."

❖

Riding the elevators back up to his ward, thoughts were racing around Terry's mind. Most of them made no sense at all. He made his way over to the reception desk, his mind switching now to exactly how much his arm had been hurting. He was looking forward to his next round of painkillers.

As he explained his day pass to the nurse at the desk, she cheerfully presented him with a clipboard and a pen to sign himself back in.

"I can fill in the details for you, if you like, love. Might be a bit of a time saver, hey?" she winked at his slinged right arm. "You'll just need to make a signature, if you can, beside it."

"Sounds great, thanks," Terry replied, just before something caught his eye. "Hey, what's that on the other page? Do visitors have to sign in for this ward?"

The nurse considered briefly before replying. Her tone was still friendly but hushed, as if sharing a secret. "Not everyone on this ward, but for special guests like yourself we need to. Matter of security for well, victims of violence."

Once she finished writing in the date and time of Terry's return, she lifted the folder to the counter. Terry wasted no time scanning through the small list of names as he pretended his attention was where he needed to sign on the page opposite.

He saw his family's names at the top, but it was the bottom two that caught his attention the most.

The last entry read "Dt. Peter Oswald."
So he'd been here while I was out. Hope that's okay.

The line before that made the hairs on his neck pick up slightly, though.

"Dmitri Thyme."
Son of a bitch really believes his own bullshit.

A voice behind him made him jump on the spot. Feminine, but unexpected in his reverie, and with more than a hint of panic in her voice.

"Benjamin," his doctor called, "we need to talk."

Chapter 23

Doctor-Patient Confidentiality

Constable Zoe Sullivan was out of her uniform. Dressed in a dark skivvy and jeans, coupled with her light leather jacket, she would have appeared to anyone passing by as just another patron of the nearby Barrel and Bray Irish Bar.

She'd parked her car on the side of the street. She'd been careful choosing her park, though, driving very slowly alongside the footpath. Away from the pub, toward a fence line and a vacant block. She'd closed her car door behind her, but left it unlocked and had her keys ready in her hand in case she needed to make a quick exit. After all, the very reason she was here in the first place was an allegedly random attack. She didn't fancy the idea of being another victim.

But it was that word 'allegedly' that called her to do some extra fact-checking. Even if it was currently off the books.

She took her phone in her left hand and risked the glow of the screen as she reviewed the images she'd snuck in the office earlier that day. She hadn't checked for sure, but she could take an estimated guess that snapping photos of case files on her personal phone was illegal. Especially a case your superior is working on.

If it's a dead end, then fine – I'll walk away. But if there's something to be found here, well hey, I'm the only one looking.

According to the file, Benjamin Terrace had ducked through a missing section in the fence to avoid the man in front seeing him on the path. Zoe looked down the street ahead of her car's headlights. Certainly, the street light would have given away someone walking on the path. And if you did want to stay out of sight, then sure, the vacant block would work.

Still begs the question of why *he needed to stay out of sight though.*

Zoe stepped through one of many gaps in the fence and tried to retrace the steps. It'd been just shy of two weeks since the incident - most likely too late for her to find anything useful, thus why she hadn't bothered putting this request up the chain of command in the first place.

She'd done some amateur digging online, her own studies not offering much the way of forensics. Following footsteps would be pretty much useless this far along. Even though it hadn't rained - and she'd checked that too – she'd have to be very lucky to find a footstep still preserved. And considering how long the grass was in this little field, any natural sign of someone passing would have vanished within twenty-four hours.

The off-duty officer stumbled through the rough terrain regardless, keeping her eye out for anything that may give evidence to the speed this unlucky pedestrian was putting into his unusual stroll in the shadows. Walking through the grass with only the dim glow of her phone, shadowing an imaginary attacker on the footpath beyond, Zoe could only see herself as a hunter in this scenario, not the hunted.

At the end of the fence line, there were again more missing fence palings. Checking the notes again for accuracy, she stepped through back onto the path, at the edge of the streetlight's refuge. She knew from the report that the site of the attack was not for another hundred metres or so ahead – well out of the street lamp's light. The two had been completely covered by darkness.

But if Rudley's ahead, walking along the footpath all this time, I'd have to be almost sprinting to catch up to him that far ahead.

Zoe couldn't place why it bugged her so much – sure, this Benjamin Terrace was unarguably the victim of a senseless beating, but how he got himself in that position was still beyond her. People didn't generally run *toward* the scary guy in the shadows who's walking away from them.

She stopped when she found what she was looking for. A crimson stain on the footpath. Not a puddle, but a few dried splashes that served as a signpost that this was where whatever game Terrace had been playing had come to an end.

Zoe stooped down, switching her phone and keys for a glass vial and a pocket knife.

She wasn't sure if it would work, but it was worth a shot. Detective Oswald was sure the kid was innocent, and he was in charge of this case. But Zoe couldn't help thinking of the famous old Russian proverb.

Trust, but verify.

Canberra Hospital
6pm, 11 July, 2010

Doctor Tetherman's eyes were red and sore. She had clearly been crying. When they had walked into his room, Terry waited as she took several silent gulping breaths. When no words came, he spoke.
"What's happened?"
Worse than the silence now, the words cascaded out in wash of senseless babble.
"We're not safe. How did you even meet him? What were you doing? The police were here again, and I had no idea you were with him. I need to call them. No. Wait–"
"What are you talking about?"

She took a breath.
Her composure restored, she tried again.
"How do you know the man you were talking to outside? How did you meet?"

Terry frowned. "I think we're jumping ahead a few steps here. How do *you* know him? In fact, go back one more – what business is it of yours who I talk to, doctor?"
"Look, I can't explain it all right now, but you just need to trust me. Don't talk to him again. Stay away from that man. Just trust me, okay?"
He looked her over, as if trying to find where the cracks in her persona were coming from. What had split and let her sanity leak out? It was then he noticed that as they'd spoken, she'd only wiped her eyes with the one hand, only gestured her phantom urgency with that one hand. The other was tucked conspicuously behind her back.
"Doctor Tetherman," he pacified, "could you please show me what you are holding behind your back."
She took another deep breath, and slowly started to move her hidden hand into the light.
"I thought he might be following you."

The sentence was delivered simply, as if those words should make perfect sense, and she loosened her fingers and revealed the syringe.

If Terry had felt like he was calming a wild animal with his last words, now he got the sense he was dealing with something closer to a madman. He spoke very slowly.

"You thought someone was following me. And so, you are holding a syringe."

"I can explain."

"I thought you said it was something you couldn't explain. You know what, I think I should just go."

"You can't!" In response to what must've been a look of alarm painted over Terry's face, the doctor elaborated. "Not out there, not to him, it's not safe. I can explain it all later, just please trust me, Benjamin."

In a matter of seconds Terry thought over the last few days of his recovery. His transfer as an in-patient for what could have been fixed at home, his over-zealous doctor checking in on him as if there were no other patients, their long discussions on her seemingly endless shifts. And the picture he was piecing together in his head seemed all at once very dangerous.

Easing his weight back a step, Terry started to move away. He didn't know what exactly he was dealing with here, but he knew it wasn't normal.

Maybe he should have gone straight out the door then and there. Maybe he shouldn't have stopped to look over at his possessions by the bed. Maybe he should have called for help, but that's always the way with hindsight.

It always comes too late.

It was clear he wasn't going to stay, the good doctor could see that. It was clear he didn't believe whatever it was she was trying to convince him of.

It must've been in the short time he'd broken eye contact that she'd done it. Really, he should've expected it when her composure changed.

When her voice broke from panic to regret.

Either way, it didn't hurt.

"I'm so sorry, Benjamin. Please believe me."

Just a pinch.

And the sensation of falling.

Chapter 24
The Candy Man Can of Worms
Storage Locker 217
Canberra
8am, 12 July, 2010

The righthand side of the honeycomb shelf was still quite bare, Dmitri concluded to himself. He'd placed the stainless steel dove on its side in one of the hexagons after the massacre at the Holden Hotel. He doubted he'd be going back there, at least for a while.
Wait and watch how the man hunt turns out first.

Yet another advantage of the time travelling killing spree – if the need arose, one could go back and remove whatever bread crumbs had been accidentally left behind. Dmitri had spent many evenings wondering what happened in the world in the meantime. If it took a few months for the police to discover something incriminating, well, a lot of life happened in between.
Of course, he had the chance to jump straight back there, and seamlessly flick back to the present. He kept his eye out for small differences – small shreds of evidence that the universe had changed at his whim. But he often wondered how the minutest details of people's lives altered because of his decision to go back. To remove evidence, hell, to remove more people! And on the rare occasion, give a victim a free pass to live out their life unaware of their brush with death.

It didn't leave much room for thinking of an afterlife, he'd reflected. If life and death were dealt out by his hand, a flick of a knife or the squeeze of a trigger, surely he couldn't pluck them from some Paradise just because he went back and chose *not* to kill them this time.

And, he could comfort himself, if no unseen force controlled his victims' passage in or out of this world, then he had nothing to fear of some supernatural recompense for his own actions. He had the luck of living life, and the sport of removing it from others. And that was about as deep as the universe needed to be.
Thinking of it all again now, Dmitri found himself cradling the glock he'd retrieved in one such 'repair job'. The gun itself was not his focus object, the tether to that time, but an unexpected

trophy on a successive kill he'd had to go back for to cover his tracks.

In his other hand was the counter top bell from Quirky Kirk's Quality Sweets. Dmitri rolled it over in his hand, deciding whether it was worth going back there today or not.

Playing over these incidents again and again made an impact on Dmitri, too, ever learning. It taught him to look out for his victim's secrets before striking – such as the case of Yavuz Firat's under the table dealings that were keeping his carpet store in business (or the other way around, as the case may have been).

Call it a charity on Dmitri's behalf maybe, removing a drug dealer from the streets. But charitable or not, it was always easier to get away with killing someone with a lot of secrets. There were so many ways the investigation could go, and so many rich angles for the media to salivate over.

Quirky Kirk just happened to have a worse secret than most. And that first time, Dmitri had stumbled onto it completely unawares.

The First Time Around...
Quirky Kirk's Quality Sweets
4:30pm, 7 December, 2005

The man was stooped over, bending to pick up a crate of those imported soft drinks that tasted like children's medicine. Dmitri had stepped in silently, the door creaking only slightly as it swung closed behind him. Quirky Kirk, if he was indeed the company's namesake, hadn't noticed his entry, and was hefting the carton towards the back room, disappearing behind opaque plastic strip curtains.

Dmitri let his finger hover over the little domed bell on the counter, deciding whether or not he'd obey the little handwritten sign that read: please ring bell.

He'd already known his purpose here before he'd entered, but his incentives were not as noble as the media would later suppose.

Kirk stayed out the back for some time. Dmitri looked back out through the shop window and onto the street, where a black minivan was parked, the letters S.P.B. marked out in thick gold type along its side.

Dmitri checked his pockets again deciding how to play out the drama. He'd tried to imagine the chaos of a loved local shopkeeper being killed in his shop. He'd thought about how to act it out so that it looked as if a local disgruntled teen had decided to clockwork up his choc-orange.

Yes, he'd imagined the headlines already.

So it was going to have to be violent.

He let the bell ring out under his finger, before pocketing it as his checkpoint artefact. Somewhere in the time he'd been gone, Kirk had made a phone call. He stepped back through the strip curtains with a mobile phone to his head. Dmitri only caught the tail end of the one-way conversation.

"...because it's still parked right outside my goddam shop, that's why. Look, I have to get going. Just move it, alright."

As the shopkeeper reached the counter, he pocketed his mobile phone, stretching his leathery face into a smile.

"How can I help you?"

It was one of those rehearsed smiles – his grey half-lidded eyes not following the signals sent up by his wrinkled cheeks.

Whatever his story really was, it was clear that at it had been quite a while since this grumpy and decidedly creepy old candy man had taken a sunrise and sprinkled it with dew.

Dmitri mumbled incoherently. The man instantly frowned and leaned forward slightly, resting a hand on the counter.

"Eh? Say again?"

Dmitri moved a little closer and mumbled a little louder.

Just a little closer, buddy.

"Can't hear ya, mate."

Kirk had twisted his head to one side, frustration clearly painted over his face in his effort to hear. He was now facing the window as he leaned in, so he didn't see Dmitri's hand shoot up behind his head, but he felt it as another hand swiped away the arm propping him up. And he felt the crack as his head bit into the glass counter top with a fierce jerk.

He collapsed onto the floor, barely conscious, as Dmitri rounded the countertop to stand in front of him.

As he slipped his hands into thin woollen gloves from his trouser pockets , Dmitri looked to the shelves around him for inspiration. Glass jars filled with various colourful goodies lined the shelf. Still entertaining himself in the drama, he searched the labels for something ironic to use. Sherbets, marshmallows, jelly beans, fudge... nothing stood out. He paused for a moment to consider the large 'gobstoppers', but his concern wasn't that the man would be telling anyone anything. There were simpler ways to silence your witnesses. He reached for the closest glass jar.

If it was to pass for a violent robbery, it was going to have to be a little messy.

Shattering two, three, four jars over the man's head took a lot of energy. It didn't leave a lot left for prising open the till, so Dmitri, ever the practical man, combined the two tasks. There was a definitive cracking sound as the till hit the man's head, and the bloodied fingers that had been stationary throughout his unconscious beating gave a quiver of a twitch.

In the silence that followed, Dmitri looked toward the back room, his curiosity piqued by the snippet of the phone call. But though curiosity led most of his interests, survival won out and he decided with the noise he'd made, now would be a good time to leave the scene.

He'd walked out with his hands in his pockets, past the van and back down the street. All there was left to do was sit back and wait for the newspapers.

Except the headlines didn't read the way he'd planned.

There was no mention of violent teens, no discussion of a senseless crime. Instead, it seemed like some black market operation had been exposed and was removing loose ends. The puns in the headlines were about the candy man who left a bad taste in everyone's mouths.

One particular paper disclosed a little more than it should have under the headline:

SWEETS TURNED SOUR – KIRK'S SECRET QUIRK.

> In an exclusive interview, Police Officer Mark Corday has shed some light on the mysterious murder at Quirky Kirk's Quality Sweets last Wednesday afternoon.
>
> Officer Corday had been part of an investigation into Quirky Kirk's suspected clandestine operations, following leads of an underground trafficking network for whom

police believe the shopkeeper had been a 'front man'.

It is unknown exactly how much involvement the man was responsible for, but Canberra Police had investigated a number of recent abductions suspected to be linked with the network. The victims of the trafficking ranged in age, but allegedly included minors, while reports of abuse and misconduct of children had indirectly pointed to the candy man's supposedly innocent sweet shop.

Officer Corday was first on the scene, having in fact been operating on surveillance on the candy store that same afternoon in an unofficial bid to track some of the collaborators.

"The store owner had been badly beaten," Officer Corday revealed. "I had been able to respond to the disturbance before an emergency call had been made, as I happened to be nearby at the time conducting surveillance.

Unfortunately, I was unable to change the outcome of the situation for the victim, even with the timely arrival of paramedics, but the cordon we set up did give us the chance to investigate not only the victim's brutal death, but also his premises in relation to the allegations levelled against him.

In a dark tinted minivan parked outside his store, we were able to ascertain evidence of misconduct, and the incident has led into a full-blown investigation into the foul network that the store owner is alleged to have been working within. Incriminating details were found within the van that will give us the chance to storm this network and shut it down permanently."

Officer Corday offered this urgent message to the public in relation to identifying the perpetrator of the candy shop killer:

"A Caucasian male in his late 30s had entered the premises only minutes before the violent attack. We suspect the perpetrator to have been a disgruntled member of the same underground network, and we would like to stress to the public in what some have expressed as an act of vigilantism that this man is not a friend to justice. He is to be considered very dangerous."

The dark-haired man was last seen exiting the store calmly on foot, wearing blue jeans, a black t-shirt and a lightweight jacket. Officer Corday also expressed his regret in not following the man originally, but he explained that while he had responded to a commotion, there was at that stage no evidence to suggest a crime had been committed.

"Our first priority at this stage," Officer Corday said, "is to speak to this man. His cooperation will go a long way in unravelling this network of trafficking and debauchery."

Debauchery, Dmitri had mused. *Who used that word anymore?*

Well, as far as entertainment had gone, he could certainly say this one had ticked the boxes. As to the man's involvement in this trafficking affair, Dmitri considered whether it changed the flavour of the kill for him.
This Officer Mark Corday was right. He wasn't a vigilante. He wasn't about to fill his head with notions of making the world a better place.

Though he had to admit, it did make it a little more satisfying to know the guy was a good candidate to meet a violent end.
The deciding factor, however, was the presence of a description of himself, however vague in nature, printed in a paper and backed up by a determined police officer... that was the sort of thing that could start the steady descent to demise.

And that would ruin all the fun.

The Second Time Around
Quirky Kirk's Quality Sweets
4:30pm, 7 December, 2005

Take two.

Dmitri had already rung the bell, the artefact already sitting in his pocket. In the moments he knew it would take for Kirk to come out mid-phone call, he thought it best to slip the gloves on a little earlier this time. They would be pulling this place apart very thoroughly in the weeks to follow.

And right on cue...

"...because it's still parked right outside my goddam shop, that's why. Look, I have to get going. Just move it, alright."

As the shopkeeper reached the counter, he pocketed his mobile phone, stretching his leathery face into a smile.

"How can I help you?"

Dmitri mumbled incoherently. The man instantly frowned and leaned forward slightly, resting a hand on the counter.

"Eh? Say again?"

Dmitri moved a little closer and mumbled – "I said you deserve this, you fucker."

"Can't hear ya, mate."

The rest followed the script to Dmitri's satisfaction. Only as he stood again over the twitching fingers did he add a little flourish.

"Valiant Officer Corday," he said into the air, taking a jar of chocolate-orange marbles from the shelf and adding its contents to the fragments of glass, caramels, blood and gummies. "Maybe you could say he tripped and fell."

He knew he only had a few moments to get into position. For the chaos to be completed properly, Dmitri would have to be very fast. In his best chances, the officer wouldn't have his gun drawn yet. He said himself there had been no evidence yet that a crime had been committed. He was just responding to a commotion.

Dmitri looked around the store for a good place to get the drop on him. There was a tall stack of soft drink cartons near the front window he could crouch behind, but if the cop was alert, he'd likely see Dmitri hiding there before he even found the body.

He chose instead to slip through the plastic strip curtains, holding the strips up as if held up on a hook. If he was going to spring out to take him by surprise, he didn't want the noisy plastic announcing his presence. In the meantime, he'd be out of sight behind the wall, even if it did mean his hands were full.

It must have only been a minute or two he had to wait, but it felt much longer, heart pounding out a parade in the silence of the store. Finally, he heard the creak of the door swing closed.

The officer didn't call out, he just walked slowly through the store.

"The hell?"

Dmitri guessed he'd spotted the broken counter top.

Walk around… walk around…

The police officer's boots crunched on broken glass. Closer and closer, he came around the far edge of the counter, closest now to where Dmitri was waiting.

"Ah, shit."

The next few events seemed to happen all at once. Dmitri swivelled out the doorway. The officer was facing away, still looking at the crumpled form of Quirky Kirk, but his hand was reaching for his pistol. The holster strap popped free at the same time the plastic strip curtains beat their way into each other in the pendulum swing.

Dmitri already had his right hand over Corday's, holding the pistol in place, while his left reached up and under the officer's chin just as he'd started to turn to his left. Exploiting the momentum, Dmitri twisted hard to his left, and swung Corday crashing behind him and into the doorway beneath the curtains still flapping and clacking over the entrance. Dmitri had meant to grapple out the pistol at the same time, but he had to settle for second best as it crashed to the floor beside the officer's leg.

More like an animal than a man, Dmitri pounced onto his prey, digging his knees into the man's inner thighs, and slamming his shoulders down with his hands. There was a short scuffle as the officer tried to free himself. Dmitri was able to work his arm around to reach the gun, all the while trying not to make any direct strikes at the officer's face in order to preserve the story.

Afterwards, Dmitri would reflect on how admirable it was that the officer hadn't made a sound – hadn't tried calling out to people he knew weren't there to listen. He'd flailed his arms desperately, his corked legs useless in the fight, but in the end the pistol came to rest under his chin.

150

Then fired.

The plastic curtains were painted a dark crimson behind the prey as the lion roared its victory.

Satisfied he'd covered his tracks, Dmitri left. Since no one in the empty street had heard the shot ring out, it would be well over an hour before the first responders would arrive at the scene, investigating the last known position of an officer who hadn't called in to finish his shift.

Reading his paper now he found none of the puns the reporters could get away with in the wake of a paedophile's death. Instead the front page news was of the violent murder of a police officer and the mysterious death of a local lolly shop owner.

It was suspected, the papers read, that the store owner was being monitored for his suspected involvement in some illegal activity.

The grim-faced image of a Sergeant Griffin was featured beside a short exposition.

> "We understand Officer Mark Corday had been conducting unofficial surveillance at the premises following unconfirmed reports of the store owner's sexual misconduct involving a minor.
>
> We are at this time unsure exactly how the events played out that led to the brutal death of the store owner, and especially how Officer Corday's handgun was stripped from him and subsequently used to end his life. Though so far we have seen no evidence to suggest misconduct on the behalf of the officer, we are investigating all angles at this stage. It is likely a third person of interest is yet to cooperate with the police investigation.
>
> Members of the public who may have seen a van in the area are urged to come forward with any information they may have."

The article concluded with a final statement:

> Among his notes, deceased Officer Mark Corday had mentioned the presence of a black Mazda MPV minivan parked outside the store, but by the time the

police cordon was set up at the scene, the vehicle had gone.

Alright then, Dmitri mused to himself. Admittedly, the flavour of semi-vigilantism didn't stick so well now that no one had proof of Kirk's particular Quirk. And evidently the takedown of this trafficking industry would be taking a setback for now as well.

Whoever Kirk had been on the phone to had obviously come and gone without venturing inside the store. The police suspected a third person involved in the crime, but had nothing to go off but a missing gun.

Dmitri had indeed contemplated making it look like a murder-suicide, but the inconvenient trademark of those particular crimes was that they tended to leave their weapon of choice behind in plain view. Dead men are pretty lousy at covering their tracks.

Not to mention, a police issue glock could be a handy piece of equipment in the hands of the talented time traveller.

Years later, and time and time again, this gun would find itself at the chin of the university Dean, needing less shots to be fired on the way up the more often Dmitri visited the learned professor's office.

Each successive visit he'd learned more of the grounds' layout, and the most efficient method.

Dmitri would never know the long term result his return trip to the lolly shop would bring about for Darren Booth and his daughter. Or how many others would be caught up in the otherwise unhampered trafficking scheme.

After all, how far back can blame really be carried? Perhaps the seed of semi-vigilantism sown was simply harvested years later by another man on a chalky country road.

Delivered with two shotgun shells and propelled by revenge.

Dmitri decided today wasn't a day for revisiting after all. Remembering was enough.

Today was a day for discovery.

He placed the small shop counter bell back in its place in the honeycomb shelf and stood up. The glock was a lot lighter to carry than the desert eagle. There were a lot of ways today could go, so Dmitri decided to keep with the more adaptable option.

Where to for this discovery though? How far?

And at that point his eyes fell on the handle from the back of a wagon from years far further back than his own. The wagon that belonged to Theodore and his talkative daughter.

It wasn't that Dmitri was inspired to visit that particular place for his test, but rather that he remembered how he came to own that item in the first place. It was one of the few items that took him back further than his own experiences could. To a time when others had left their imprint on the otherwise mundane object.

He pulled a prepaid mobile from his pocket and called for a taxi as he let himself out through the roller door and clicked his padlock into place.

He'd see how Benjamin was feeling this morning, and he'd see how he felt about some antique shopping.

It'd be the perfect chance to test his little theory.

Chapter 25
Out on a Limb
Canberra Hospital
9am, 12 July, 2010

Terry groaned.

His eyes opened groggily, and he took in the now all-too familiar view of the hospital room. Quickly he closed his eyes again as he remembered the needle prick pinching his arm. Someone was in the room with him – he could hear the clinking of small objects being shuffled. The footsteps were light though, like those of someone trying not to wake someone, but he could hear their clothes swish in the way clothes only do when you're trying to be quiet.

So, the mad doctor is keeping an eye on me now, is she?

Terry thought through what he'd say as he lay perfectly still miming his unsolicited sleep. He'd be leaving, that was certain, and after her little attack there was no way she'd be calling the police on him or Dmitri, whatever she had against the guy.

The steps moved closer to the bed, and something was wheeled softly. Terry could feel a bead of sweat forming on his temple with the strain it was taking to lay still – terrified of whatever was being plotted for him while his eyes were closed.

Terry thought about lashing out and making a break for the door, but without having had the chance to look around properly, there were just too many unknown factors. For all he knew he could have been moved to a different ward altogether.

A voice called in from the corridor.

"Heading down to Oncology, Tom. See you there?"

The figure beside the bed forgot all about the sleeping patient and called back, "yep, I just have two more beds then I'm done."

The voice was male, old at a guess, and best of all 'Tom' was decidedly not Doctor Tetherman. Terry sat up.

"Sorry to wake ya, mate," the food services officer said, "breakfast is served though."

Terry only nodded in response, his mind on what he'd need to take with him to get out of here. He stretched his legs and was relieved to find them working. The syringe must have only been a sedative after all, not a full-blown muscle relaxant.

The only surprise was that he found himself back in a hospital gown, when he'd come in fully dressed from his venture outdoors the day before.

By the time Tom was wheeling away his food cart, Terry was out of bed and scrounging at the drawers hoping to find his clothes with his good arm. He bundled them together, along with his wallet and his long-dead mobile phone, and he peered out into the hallway.

An all-out sprint would only serve to raise suspicion, and the staff may even try to stop him. Instead Terry had to steel himself once more as he tucked his busted arm back into the sling, and tried to walk as casually as possible past the desk.

Terry even managed to nod a greeting to the nurse at the desk. It was the same nurse who'd been there the night before, and he hoped against hope that she wouldn't recall his sign-on sheet or ask any questions.

The walk to the elevator felt like an eternity – on the outside he looked to be going for a groggy stroll to stretch his legs, while inside was all the tranquillity of a school of salmon senselessly thrashing their way upstream all the while dreading the hungry bears.

At last the elevator doors dinged shut, and Terry was on his way down. He slipped into the first bathroom he came across at the ground floor and began riffling through his clothing bundle.
You're kidding me.

It occurred to him for the first time that his family had never dropped off fresh clothing for him. He'd been out the day before with Dmitri in these bloodstained clothes and he hadn't even realised. Now that he was trying to blend in, the splatters down the front of the shirt seemed more like a beacon to say something wasn't right.

He decided he'd risk going past the gift shop on the way out and see if they had any shirts for sale. For now though, his biggest callout was something that would be harder to part with.

Wincing, he eased his arm back out of the sling, and slipped it over his head. Bundling it with the hospital gown, he dropped both into the bin, and then gingerly let his right arm drop to his side. Every slight twist sent stabbing pains shooting up his arm, but if he concentrated hard enough, he could push through it.

Terry caught a glimpse of himself in the mirror and realised how bruised the whole elbow area was.

Better make that a long sleeve shirt.

In the end, he'd bought a cheap pair of sunglasses and a blue cap to complete his disguise. He'd managed to find a thin promotional jumper with a print of The Tale of the American Eagle emblazoned on the front – the tattered Stars and Stripes in the silhouette of the bird of prey, ironic when Terry felt more like a field mouse trying to camouflage desperately into the long grass.

Once outside, he appreciated the need for the little shopping spree at the gift shop – the chill of the wind a welcome distraction as he eased his tender arm through the sweater.

Now it was time to start thinking about where to go next.

"So you're all better?"

Terry turned sharply, certain he'd been caught already.

"Dmitri, it's you! Thank God! How did you get here?"

"Well I was thinking–"

"No," Terry cut him off. "I mean, do you have a car here?"

"Uh, no I came by–"

"Let's get a cab then," Terry cut him off again.

"Yep. That's what I was going to say."

Terry waved hurriedly with his left arm to get the attention of one of the waiting taxis. Dmitri watched as Terry twitched his head backward constantly in furtive glances toward the hospital.

"So they've released you then?"

"In a way, yeah."

"Only I can't help but notice you seem to be in a hurry."

The cab pulled up beside them and Terry got into the front seat.

"Let's just say I no longer require their services." In reply to Dmitri's silence, Terry continued, "Look, it's not a prison. I'm allowed to leave whenever I like."

The driver looked over at Terry expectantly. When a shrug still failed to further prompt the passengers, he asked finally, "so where are you off to?"

Terry spoke over his shoulder to Dmitri in the back seat.

"Over to you my friend."

The detective answered his mobile phone.

"Oswald speaking.
Yes, I remember. Miss Tetherman.
What exactly do you mean by *gone*, doctor?
Alright, I'll swing by his family's house on the way and check if anyone's heard anything.
Call me back if you hear anything at your end.
Oh? Sure. What was the name again?
Okay, I'll check it out.
I won't be far away."

Detective Oswald clicked off the phone call.

"My apologies, gentlemen," he addressed the SRS crew before scribbling down a note.
"Anything we need to know?" The question came from the attorney-like AFP officer. Oswald addressed his reply instead to the SRS team leader, Leon.
"Not at this stage but I'll keep you posted. However, that was Benjamin Terrace's doctor. Apparently he's no longer at the hospital. He wasn't formally released. I think I'll go do some following up. Keep whatever channels you have open in case anything comes through though."
As Oswald reached the door, the AFP officer spoke tersely.
"May I remind you, Detective, that the case now belongs to the Australian Federal Police and the Specialist Response and Security Team? Delegating who follows up leads and who is waiting on standby is no longer your jurisdiction."

"No reminder is necessary, sir," Oswald volleyed. "I am simply looking for a missing in-patient. One I've just been advised about on a private call. You said yourself it would be wise to keep communications open between the original investigating officer and potential witnesses. I shall let you know if there are any further developments, don't worry."

The door closed behind him. As he passed Constable Sullivan, Oswald passed her the note he'd written.

"Zoe, do me a favour and look up someone for me? Just between us at this stage – could be nothing."

"Only for you, boss," Zoe smiled back but he was already out the front door.

"Alrighty, mister," she addressed the note. "Let's see what you've got to hide then…

Aaron Tetherman."

❖

The taxi rolled to a stop.

Through the glare of the window, Terry read the name on the front of the run-down country store and smiled: *Collector's Eclectic Collector*.
"Antiques, Dim?"

In the hour of driving no one in the car had said a word, though the driver had slowed down curiously by the Dreamer's Gate Sculpture and craned his head to look at it as they drove. Despite himself, Terry felt a chill down his back looking at the mythical and decidedly eerie woven Homage to the Dead Bushranger. They were further down the road, but the edges of the structure were still in view.
"Dim?" The back passenger handed over two fifty-dollar notes to the driver and the pair left the vehicle without waiting for change.

"Yeah, you know, short for Dmitri. What, you've never had 'Dim' as a nickname?"
"Guess not."
"Must have as active a social life as me," Terry laughed.

Dmitri's face was serious as he surveyed the shopfront.
"Now, I know you weren't fully on board with what I was talking about yesterday," Dmitri started, "but I'm hoping this place will convince you otherwise. It's something I discovered by accident. Another way of accessing 'checkpoints', or *savegames* as you called them."

In the panic of leaving the hospital, and the relief of having a way out of the grounds, Terry had forgotten that their last encounter had ended abruptly with his opinion of Dmitri somewhat downgraded to 'delusional'.

"Hey, you know I should probably be laying low," he said. "I'm technically in police protection or a witness or something. They'll probably come looking for me before long."
"Relax," Dmitri said. "If I'm right, this place will be perfect."
"What? We'll be hiding in here?"

"Trust me, it'll be like you don't even exist."

❖

Oswald's notepad was unfortunately empty.
"So you haven't heard from him at all then?"
"Not since the other day when we were down at the hospital. I mean, we expected he'd be home any day now, but we figured he'd call us beforehand if he needed a lift," Mrs Terrace spoke matter-of-factly, though her face was pained with emotion.
"So what's he done?" the father called out, impatient, "gone and vanished without even telling his doctors?"
He was still shaking his head as he rose and came to where his wife was standing with Oswald.

"What's the matter with him, then?" the father ranted.
"Oh, Lee, not now please," the mother pacified with a glance over at the younger son sitting on the couch. Jono's face was half covered by his hair, his attention absorbed in his phone.
Oswald interjected, "Benjamin does seem to have a knack for making things complicated, though doesn't he?"

The prompt had worked and, goaded on, the father continued, "you wouldn't believe the half of it. He puts his head where it doesn't belong and then wonders why the guillotine's dropping on him. He's always done it, you know, ever since he first–"
"Lee!" the mother hissed, glaring now. She jerked her head towards the oblivious boy on the lounge chair.

The father took a moment to recover his thoughts. "Ever since, well, always. He must get it from his, er, mother's side." Lee made a pitiful chuckle to try to validate his joke, but his head was down, defeated, his eyes apprehensively on his apparently wiser wife.

"Bit stuffy in here, Detective," she offered with a curt smile, "perhaps a word outside?"

"Absolutely," Oswald beamed, backing down the front steps. "Let's have it all out in the light, eh?"

Chapter 26
Testing the Boundaries

Stepping into the antique store was indeed like stepping into the past, and a troubled one at that. What must once have been a well-intentioned and quaint little store was now a glorified garden shed with rusted and obsolete paraphernalia littered anywhere it could fit.

Amazingly, one or two other customers could be seen pilfering about in the heaps, hoping to strike lucky with the one-man's-trash principle.

Still, it seemed Dmitri had brought them both there for just such an exercise, too.

Seemingly at random, he would dig into a pile, handling the objects far more than was appropriate for standard browsing protocol. From old oil lamps to typewriters, strips of hardened leather to the rotted mesh of old meat safes, Dmitri would take the items in his hand, turning them over as if feeling for some code in braille that would identify what he was looking for.

His next words brought no relief to Terry who once again looked on as if he'd befriended a madman.

"It's rare to find them, you see," he said as casually as if he were just looking for an out of print book. "And they're hard to identify."

"What exactly *are* we looking for?" Terry ventured.

"The object itself could be anything. A door knob, a shoe, a piece of jewellery. It's the *imprint* I'm looking for. You just sort of *feel it* when you find it."

"And you say this will allow you to..." Terry lowered his voice, remembering the madness of the words, "to travel... through time? To that time?"

Dmitri nodded as he continued to probe at the piles of old junk.

"Supposing I did believe you," Terry continued. "What good would going back to an earlier time prove right now? We'd still be in this shop. If you went back to last week, it would look just the same. Probably hasn't changed in decades," he thumbed an ancient looking chess board with most of its pieces missing.

Putting the rook back down onto the board, he moved his attention absentmindedly to a once-ornate feather quill. The detailed nib was intact, but it would be unfair to birds everywhere to call the rest of it a feather.

"No, that's the beauty of the objects. When they are imprinted, it binds them geographically."

"What, now you're telling me you travel time *and* the world? Look, Dim, it's been great, but–"

Dmitri was muttering as he continued poring over the worthless items and didn't seem to be paying much attention if at all to Terry. He continued over the top of him, "on occasion… England, mostly for me, a lot of the really old items here have come from there one way or another. 'Course Australia only goes so far back, as we know it at least. Pretty sure I was in Germany at one point, but I didn't stick around. Language barrier isn't something you want to face if you're– what's that?"

Dmitri snatched the feather quill from Terry's hands and eyed him suspiciously for a moment.

"And you say you don't believe it, ha!" A switch seemed to have been flipped within Dmitri, and suddenly he was standing upright. He was beaming with an energetic bravado and showmanship that Terry had glimpsed the day before when he'd bowed to the stranger on the bench.

"As far as I'm aware," he bellowed in a voice far too loud for the little antique store, "belief has nothing to do with it! Now, take my hand."

"S-sorry?"

"Oh come on, man, let's have a little trust here. I'm not going to do anything strange. I've only ever travelled solo, but I'd imagine if you're coming along too, we'll have to be connected somehow. Now, take my hand, and don't speak for a moment. I'll need to concentrate."

A madman, Terry's warning voice boomed inside his skull. *You've gone and found yourself a madman for a friend. Exactly how far into this madness are you going to take us?*

Terry's head was shaking to himself as he closed his eyes and grasped Dmitri's hand in a firm left handed handshake.

Well, I'm already talking to myself.

And of course, just as expected, a great nothingness happened.

After a few seconds, Terry opened his eyes. None of the other customers were looking at them, at least. He looked at Dmitri, whose face was contorted into the most serious frown.

In a flat, fun's-over voice, Terry spoke, "Dim?"

Dmitri only frowned more, somehow closed his eyes even harder, and raised a finger to silence the non-believer. Terry saw his other knuckles were white with how hard he was gripping the quill.

And then it happened.

There was no pop, no bright light, no tumbling sensation. The walls didn't melt away, fade or transition in any way.

They were simply at the antique store, and then they were not.

Before, they *weren't* standing in an old-fashioned study, and then all of a sudden, they *were*.

Bewildered, Terry locked eyes with Dmitri, whose face was now a manic, wide eyed grin. He released Terry's hand from his grip and began looking around the room. Naturally, Terry looked down at himself to make sure everything was where it was meant to be. A sharp pain from his right arm shot up to meet him.

Not a dream then, I guess.

There was a dark wood desk in the centre of the small room, surrounded by tall bookshelves with ancient looking covers. On the desk, large sheets of parchment were sprawled over the surface, littered with trappings from an age long past. The room was lit by a small arched window at the far end.

Moving toward it, Terry looked out onto what must have been a roof, and beyond that, a dusty dirt track that led away into the distance. A horse whinnied out of view.

"Any clue *where* we are?" Terry whispered, seeing but still not believing.

"Not so far. Temperature's a bit warmer. Probably still in the land of Oz."

Terry shook his head at the deliberate reference.

"It's always hard to tell exactly *when* it is when you use the objects to travel. At least when I travel with my own checkpoints I can remember them, but it's always a bit of a headache trying to work out the times and places in the big shifts. There's a trap door here, most likely leads down into the house."

Where does one start when faced with this sort of situation? Is the priority to find out how to get back? Is it important to know exactly when and where you are? Is it a matter of securing shelter or supplies? Or is this the time to find out exactly *how* you got here?

Terry went with the latter option.

"The object... how does it work?"

Dmitri, satisfied there was no one coming upstairs any time soon, rounded the desk and lowered himself into the chair. He left Terry to pace. Pacing helps.

"It's all about the imprint," he said at last. "Look where it brought us – a feather quill led us to this writing desk. I'll bet if we looked through these parchments, we'd find countless letters to family members, maybe business dealings, something that someone has spent a lot of energy focusing on. Emotion too, which is why I say family letters. Say one day he's writing to settle an argument, or inform someone of some bad news. Do you believe in ghosts, by the way?"

Terry was at least a full sentence behind, still processing what Dmitri was trying to say. "What? Ghosts? No. Why?"

"Well actually that's not so important. A popular theory with ghosts, especially repetitive haunting style ghosts, is not that that they're trapped, sentient beings, but rather imprints left on the world. So maybe once a year at a certain place the same *geographical location* lines up, I'm talking on a planetary scale, you know, with orbits and what-not. Lines up with some terrible thing that happened, or something mundane that was repeated over and over again until it left an imprint in that space. Still with me?

"So, maybe, and I say maybe because who do I have to ask all these questions to? No one. I didn't even mean to discover this ability, it just sort of, happened. Anyway, I'm going off best guess here from what I've seen.

"Some objects have strong imprints on them, like this feather quill. Maybe days from now this guy carks it, and no one uses his feather quill again. The last meaningful imprint was in this room, at this time. And it finds its way over who knows how many years into the Eclectic Collector at Collector, or whatever the damn place is called."

"And you said you found this by accident? And then all the rest by trial and error? What happens if it goes wrong? I mean, how do we get back?"

"Well that's actually much easier. Your mind knows when 'now' is meant to be, and so it takes a lot less concentration to go back to it. Think of it like waking back up. It's actually why I prefer to work closer to what I call 'true present'. It provides more of a challenge. Let's say the old guy is waiting for us downstairs with say a shotgun, or whatever weapon they have in whatever time this is, a musket or a crossbow or something. I think we're clear of spears by this point at least. Anyway, with enough warning we should be able to blink back to true present before he can fire a shot."

"*Should?*"

"Hey, nothing's perfect."

"Speaking of which, my arm is still broken."

"Funny that – what of it?"

"Yesterday… or whatever *yesterday* means now, you asked me what I'd do if I could go back to before my arm was broken and get the drop on Rudley instead."

"Ah yes, sorry, think of that more like theatrical exaggeration rather than exposition. We go back however we are in true present. As I age, I go back at my actual age. When I was seventeen, I travelled back as a seventeen year old, when I hit thirty, I was a thirty year old time traveller, at forty, well you get the idea. As far as I'm aware we're aging still normally right now. I don't actually know, I haven't spent long enough in the past to find out if I aged incorrectly. At any rate, whatever condition you're in at true present, you're in it when you go back, with whatever you're holding or wearing. I mean, pretty sure neither of us was alive in this particular time, so we're not winding back the entire universe's clock."

"Seventeen, you said? You've been doing this since you were seventeen?!"

"Yeah, thereabouts," Dmitri now rose from the chair, visibly uncomfortable with the new direction the conversation was taking.

"So when you went back to your childhood, you'd be a fully grown man? If you went back right now, you'd be the same age as you are now? How did *that* go?"

"I can't–" Dmitri stumbled for a moment, correcting himself. "Uh, I *don't* travel back to those times. I wouldn't know."

"Really? You can travel through time and you don't revisit your own childhood memories? Relive them like everyone would love to do?"

"Look that's not how it works, alright," Dmitri was agitated now, and he was moving toward the trap door. Terry took a chance.

"You told me about Rudley to introduce me to this gig, but you knew that part wasn't actually possible."

He let the silence sit for a moment.

"What else aren't you telling me, Dim?"

There was a scuffle downstairs. Muffled voices started to call out to each other.

"Someone up there?" the voice was worn, aged. Male. Someone thumped the lid of the trap door from below. "Come down now and there will be no need for trouble."

Dmitri brought a finger to his lips to silence the conversation. After a moment of looking around the room, he hefted a heavy box and gently placed it over the trap door. As he straightened, wood splintered from the trap door as a shot rang out from below. The sound ricocheted in the tiny study, and Dmitri stumbled back and fell.

"Fuck, definitely packing more than a crossbow! Come on!" He waved Terry over toward the window behind the desk. "Get it open – let's not stick around to find out what the hell he's got loaded down there."

To his relief, Terry found that the window was hinged, but it evidently didn't get opened often. Metallic clicking and sliding came from below as the gunman reloaded.

"Show yourself, brigand, and I shall let the peelers deal with you instead. Keep hiding and you shall find yourself six feet under somewhere out in the bush!"

"It won't budge," Terry said.

"Use something, use something then!" hissed Dmitri.

Terry turned around and looked for an object hard enough to beat against the swollen wooden window frame. On the desk was one of the thick volumes of some most likely priceless text. As he raised it up with his one good arm, he flicked another glance at what Dmitri was doing. To his horror, he found him crouched at the desk, arms out in front of him pointing a pistol steadily at the trap door.

What the hell?!

Another shot from below brought the box down with a crash, along with the fragments of the trap door. Some muttered cursing came through the gap in the floor, followed by the solid thud of a ladder being propped against the splintered floor boards. Spurred on with the urgency of the approaching attacker, Terry forgot about Dmitri's pistol and crashed the book with all his weight into the window. It swung out free and the book clattered down onto the tin roof.

Screaming with the effort it took to bring his arm through the small window, Terry poked his way through and was scrambling to get his legs out. He heard glass smash from further inside the house and more cursing from the home owner of this bygone era.

Dmitri gave him a shove and Terry rolled through and onto the roof, followed closely by his time travelling comrade. Terry screamed again as he landed in a spasm on his busted arm.

By contrast, Dmitri looked perfectly in control. He slid down the slope of the roof, dangled at the makeshift gutter and dropped gracefully to the ground. Terry moved to lay on his back to take the pressure off his arm, not yet able to think of a way off the roof.

Below, and inside the house, he heard heavy footsteps as Dmitri stormed the front door, a woman's scream cut short by the blast of his pistol, and barely a second later another two shots rang out. Something heavy fell to the floor.

Now there was only silence.

Terry's mind raced to keep up with everything that had just happened.

A minute or two later, his stunned reverie was broken by the top of the ladder appearing beside him on the roof.

"Climb down," Dmitri called. "I'll hold it steady."

❖

Inside the house, the silence was overpowering. Terry stepped through cautiously. On his left, in the little nook with a wooden bench was what must have been a kitchen. No taps or plumbing, just a basin of water. Slumped against the supporting beam, the lady of the house, well dressed at least by modern standards, sat lifeless, a single bullet hole streaming a crimson line down her face and dripping onto her frilly dress. Crumpled on the floor below the shattered trap door, the old man lay in a pool of blood. One hand over a wound in his leg, the other twisted under his body where the second shot had dealt the mortal blow.

"Not very smooth," Dmitri said, surveying the same scene. "I'm sorry about all that. I was hoping we'd have a cleaner run for your first time. Three bullets, though, that's acceptable."

"You killed them," Terry heard the words as if someone else had spoken them.

"And he was about to kill us. Look at this monstrosity of a gun! What is this, an old blunderbuss? *That* would've been messy!"

"Dmitri, you killed them. How– who even were these people? I mean, how many people have you actually just killed? Did they have children? Were those children meant to grow up and have children and grandchildren and great grandchildren? What if you just stopped someone really important from being born? You know, someone who discovered some cure for a disease, or invented television or something?!"

"Oh wow," Dmitri snorted, "the unbeliever gets a taste of time travel and now he's an expert on chaos theory. Well here's something to think about, what if their great, great grandkid was going to be the next Hitler and I just saved the world? Even better, think about this one – what if it was always going to happen this way? His imprint on the quill led us to this day. Why not tomorrow? Or the next day? Maybe because this was always the last time his imprint was on it. Dead before we got here. Literally history."

Dmitri took a waterskin from a hook on the wall and gave it a sniff. Taking a few big gulps, he continued in a softer tone.

"Realistically, Benjamin? Look at them. How old are they? Any grandkids – sinners or saints – are already out there. They just have a sadder back story now. Point is, for one, don't make the mistake of thinking I don't consider these things, and secondly, let me promise you, thinking of all these things is crippling.

"It's crippling in a normal life to think about all the possibilities, different realities, alternate choices. *What if.* Well it turns out if you find the answer to your what-if questions, it just creates more. Life is complex. It just is, no matter what you do."

Minutes ticked by.

"Could you change it?" Terry asked finally.

Dmitri mulled over his answer.

"That depends what you're asking. We could probably go back, yeah. But we'd be going back to the same spot. A minute later, he'd be banging on the trapdoor again. More importantly, if you're asking about yourself, about whether you could forget being here, then no. Not without going back to before our taxi ride to Collector. Even then, who knows, I've never travelled with someone before – maybe you'd still have the memory – some extreme déjà vu or something, who's to say. But here's what I think:

"Let's say I could go back. I go back to last week or something. You don't know anything about what I can do, you don't know this ability even exists. I never tell you, never show you. *I think* you wouldn't take that option if I offered it. You're far too curious. I think we're a little similar that way."

Terry didn't speak. He had to admit to some truth Dmitri's words.

Dmitri continued, "It's always traumatic, by the way. Killing. Not on this level, not the difference between being shaken or being able to stand in the same room as two corpses. I mean emotionally. Killing someone always leaves its mark on you."

Terry looked up now, confused, but he didn't interrupt.

"Imprints, you know. That's the point. To show you this much meant I had to show you the rest with it. You asked me what else I'm not telling you. Well, I didn't know for sure that this little jaunt into wherever we are would go messy, but I also didn't expect it to go smoothly either, being honest. But I knew eventually we'd have to talk about this part. The imprinted objects offer a way to travel without having to make your own imprints, and it means you can go further back or abroad than your own experiences."

Still, Terry sat silent.

"But, the 'normal' way I travel, I make my own imprints. An object helps, but it's only a focus. It isn't everything. The object itself isn't where the *ability* lies. Like I said, it's just ghosts of past events. I just tap into that."

Finally, Terry spoke, his eyes still fixed somewhere between the two bodies. "Your usual *checkpoints*... They're kills, aren't they? Kills you've imprinted on a mundane object from the scene."

It was Dmitri's turn to stay silent. He was unaccustomed to opening up in general, but opening up about murder, well, that was something else again. It felt a bit too much like confessing. Like not getting away with it.

"How many– no, actually. Don't answer that." Terry took a deep breath. "How did it start?"
Dmitri stood.

He walked to the open doorway before turning around.

"Not here."

Chapter 27

The Honeycomb

Detective Oswald was already back at the car. He dropped heavily into the driver's seat, pinching the bridge of his nose in frustration.

After leaving Terry's family home, he had driven to the hospital to continue his conversation with the doctor. His head had already been swimming with what he'd been told, but somehow it seemed the extra puzzle pieces were just making the overall image fuzzier. Especially when he went up to Terry's ward to find he wasn't the only one missing.

With no note or message to say where she was going, and barely even a goodbye to the other staff, it seemed Doctor Kate Tetherman had simply abandoned her post.

The nurse at the reception desk had apologised to the detective.

"She made a phone call about an hour or two ago, then she just left. I thought maybe she was just taking a bathroom break, but she bundled her ID card and stethoscope and dropped them at the door on her way out."

"A family emergency, perhaps?" Oswald had offered.

"Maybe. Strange she wouldn't say anything though."

It is strange, Oswald decided, gripping the steering wheel. Gently, he lowered the sun visor to look at the photograph again. Frozen in her relative youth, his wife looked out at him.

"I am officially too old for this," Oswald said aloud.

Why would someone phone me personally to tip me off with a name, and then run?

Ultimately it came down to two options – *guilt* or *fear*. A guilty accomplice dobs on the main offender and then hides before it comes back to them. Possible, but it didn't seem likely. Fear of the offender on the other hand made a little more sense. Running from the police didn't add up, though. Maybe it was a careful blend of the two. Not for the first time, Oswald reminded himself that the world was rarely black and white.

At any rate, chasing down the doctor seemed the least worthwhile lead. She'd already given a name, even if she'd bailed before explaining its significance. All Peter Oswald had to go off at the moment was that whoever this ghost was who shared Kate's surname –her husband perhaps?– he was apparently linked with Terry's disappearance.

Oswald took out his phone.

"Sullivan, any luck on that name?"

"Ah yes, sorry sir, I got distracted. There's been some back and forth with the lab results from the Holden Hotel. Nothing solid yet, as far as I can tell. They're dealing mainly with the powers that be, now, so I'm having a hard time getting in the loop.

"Anyway, the name. Aaron Tetherman. He's somewhat of a ghost. There's a file on his father from over twenty years ago. He was killed in a farm accident in Broome, you know, Western Australia? Then this guy just vanishes. Officer at the scene described the death as suspicious but pending evidence – no trace of a suspect. A witness at the scene was able to detail events convincingly, but there's no mention of where Aaron went to, innocent or otherwise. Must've been pretty gruesome – reporting officer took some stress leave not long after.

"That's not on here, of course. I did some extra digging. Not that there's a great deal to find, it's all old paper files that have been digitalised. We're talking 1985 here – hell I wasn't even born yet."

"Okay, thanks for the reminder, Zoe. I know we're all dinosaurs. How about the officer? Is he still serving? Any way we can contact him?"

"Actually, you're in luck there. Stress leave got extended, and he ended up quitting altogether. He moved, too. Guess where?"

"Please just tell me."

"Penrith, Sydney. Seems he changed his line of work completely. He helped establish a child adoption agency centre there, specifically crisis and respite foster care."

Oswald started the engine.

"How far away is that? A couple of hours?"

"More like three, I'm afraid. I'll keep eyes and ears out here in case Mr Terrace pops his head up."

"Amazing work, Zoe."

"Don't mention it, sir. Unless I ask you for a reference in a few years for your position," she chuckled before ending the call. "Good luck."

Oswald pulled the car out of the hospital car park with a renewed energy. The picture was starting to clear up again with these new puzzle pieces. And a few of the last ones started to make a little more sense, too.

Dmitri released his grip on Terry's hand. They were back in the antique store.
Nothing around them had changed.

Everything else had.

Dmitri thought back to his last personal checkpoint and weighed up the pros and cons of just going back and living out the same days again until he caught up to the present. Forget Terry and forget about their little confessional excursion.
Except he already knew he wouldn't do it. He'd talked big about not letting the what-if questions run your life, but he knew it was exactly what drew him to this life in the first place. It continued to force each decision, still. Having a partner in crime, so to speak, would at least make it interesting.
Still, there's nothing wrong with having a safety measure in place.

"Can I help you two find anything in particular?" the severely bent over shop keeper had shuffled her way to their side.
"No thanks," Dmitri chirruped, "just browsing. Hey, any chance we could use your phone? We'll need a cab back into the city."
If the old woman was bothered by them not making a purchase, she didn't show it.
Probably just glad to have something to do.

Back outside the door, the taxi met them almost immediately.
"You two again? That was quick."
This time Terry went straight to the back seat without speaking. Dmitri sat in front and tried to dodge the driver's questions.

173

"I thought I'd give it half an hour or so before I drove back. Went to check out that sculpture – figured there might be tourists around who want a lift somewhere. Couldn't believe it when the screen lit up again already. What's it been? Five minutes? Ten? Well, anyway, where to? Back to the hospital?"

"No," Terry chimed in from the back.

"No thanks," Dmitri said, "this side of the lake. Maybe drop us off near the CSIRO Centre?"

"You got it."

He's in a cheerier mood than before. Probably hoping for another cash fare.

As the antique store rolled into the scenery behind them, Dmitri turned reflective once more. The antique store had gone almost identically to the first time he'd discovered how to jump back on someone else's imprints.

Terry would come around.

He just needed to spend some time thinking it all over.

Hopefully he'll focus on the fact that I helped him get out alive. I've never had anyone watching my back.

Chances were he'd focus on the objects. That for the objects to work, they needed the fresh imprint. Dmitri decided that for now, at least, it would play out better to keep the first few years of discovery to himself. It wasn't necessary to share that taking the objects had started *after* he'd gotten away with murder, multiple times over. That in fact, they'd begun as trophies after a kill, not checkpoints before them.

Concentration alone, recalling the details of the scene, really holding it in his mind's eye – that was enough for the travel. But details wash together over time, and the memory has a way of blurring things – especially once you've gone back and made small changes. As his focus started to slip on more than one occasion, he took to holding small trophies from the kills – a ring, a book, a piece of clothing. Suddenly in half the time he was back there. The imprinted object making up for what his mind was letting slip.

In all but one detail.

He'd collected the trophy *after* the kill. To go back lost its sport. Where before he would focus on rebuilding the scene before he'd attacked them, now he was transported instantly to the anticlimactic moments after their death.

It was in just such an instance that he'd picked up the silver cup. It was a different antique store of course, and it was many years ago.

He'd already left the body out the back of the store and was marching back through to the front door when he'd scooped up the ornate goblet. Another customer had brushed past him to go inside as he'd left. Hours later, worried that the customer may have seen him, and in order to trim any loose ends, he'd focused on the silver cup –his literal trophy– to go back to when he'd collected it.

Except it wasn't the antique store he'd been transported to. Instead, he found himself at the top of an elaborate wooden staircase, spiralling down to an unreasonably large foyer area.
Candle sconces lit the hallway along the split-level corridor, and at intervals between the heavy wooden doors stood arrays of silverware and pottery of intricate detail. In sharp contrast to the decadence he was surrounded by, however, was the acrid odour of what could best be described as pig manure.

He let the silver cup fall from his hand as he walked, floor creaking, alongside the banister. One of the wooden doors hinged open and a cleaning woman stepped out in what would have to be the most authentic of maid costumes – certainly hemmed with a considerable amount more modesty than your typical cosplay outfit.
She stood aghast and looked him up and down, apparently appraising his apparel and clearly deeming his t-shirt and jeans most unacceptable.

"What is this place?" he ventured.
In reply, the woman gave him a horrified stare.
"This is going to sound strange," he continued, "but could you tell me what year it is?"
She choked out a reply as she backed into the wall, dropping her wooden bucket and splashing grey water over the floor boards.
The words themselves were a garble of noise, and Dmitri furrowed his brow in his attempt to catch a single one.
"Say again, sorry?"

And she was off.

Her screaming filled the large hall, interrupted only by the barking of some consonant-heavy language Dmitri couldn't comprehend.

Without thinking, Dmitri sprinted after her. It was only when they rounded a corner that Dmitri was brought to a sudden halt by the open window. The street below was something from a history book. Cobbled stone lined the road, pale except for the filth streaming along the edges of what Dmitri would call a gutter. Straw-thatched roofs lined the space between the roads, propped up on thick black beams.

The scene before him was clearly not from his own lifetime, and certainly nothing he had imagined on his own. The thump-thump-thumping of the woman's feet down the stairs was enough to wake him from his wonder though. He thought about pulling the plug, reverting straight back to where he'd been before his repair job at the antique store, when inspiration struck.

He ran back over to one of the many trinkets displayed, and he took them one at a time in his hands. At a gilded cross, laced and woven in a delicate design, he paused.

And closed his eyes.

Now *that!* That was what Dmitri wanted to show his friend. Trade staring out the window of the cab to wandering untapped landscapes writhing with opportunities, leaping centuries at a time, finding new artefacts at each stop to jump back even further still.

Reliving all the glory days of civilisations long gone with the insurance policy of the modern world strapped to your belt with a few fresh clips ready to be loaded if things got out of hand.

Didn't that put everything into perspective? Didn't that trump the precious sensitivities and the rules this society imposed? It was the ultimate what-if!

He turned his head to look at his travelling companion.
What would happen?

"Here we are," the driver announced. He read the sign aloud, "C-S-I-R-O Discovery Centre. Very nice. Go broaden your minds, my friends."

"Oh, you have *no* idea," Dmitri jeered, passing on more cash and broadening the driver's smile even further.

When the cab left, he spoke to Terry.

"We're actually walking from here. It's not far."

They rounded a corner and walked into a small field of storage sheds.

"Still got my key?" Dmitri called out over his shoulder.

"Shit," Terry stopped and patted down his pockets. "I hope so!" As his fingers closed around it, he was relieved he hadn't bought new trousers along with the jumper. Luckily it had escaped the attention of his all too handsy doctor, too.

"So, what? If I focus on this key, we'll jump to some other time where you store all your artefacts?"

Dmitri smiled and held out his hand for the key.

"Something like that, yeah."

Terry hesitated for a moment. Then dropped it into his hand.

Dmitri turned and put into the padlock of Locker 217. It clicked free and he rolled up the door halfway.

"That's it?" Terry asked. "No magic? You just had me hold your key for you?"

"Yep. I told you; it was a trust exercise. And this isn't magic by the way."

Dmitri rolled the door back down, once they'd ducked under it, and flicked the light switch.

"I don't know *what* it is, exactly, but it's not magic."

Terry looked over the spartan furniture. The desk, the roller chair and the array of hexagonal shelves along the left hand wall. Dmitri spread his arms as he walked up to the honeycomb. Choosing a place toward the far end of the hexagonal shelving, Dmitri took the feather quill from his pocket and placed it neatly in its own place. A new item added to the gallery.

"New Age science, maybe. You know, out of curiosity, I think I'll revisit this one later, on my own, and see if you're still there too. It'd be most intriguing."

He was back in his lyrical tone, performing in the spotlight to no one in particular. He finished with a *humph* to himself, then collapsed onto his roller chair.

Terry looked over the immense display of items. What gruesome stories lay behind each one? He had to look away. Above the desk he noticed a power point with a variety of phone chargers attached. A thin blanket was draped over the back of the chair Dmitri was sitting on.

"Dim, do you *live* here?"

"Live here? No. I stay all around the place. Motels, you know. That sort of thing."

"Right," Terry said, inching closer to the power point and sliding his good arm into his pocket to get at his phone. He was weighing up his chances of plugging the phone in without being spotted when Dmitri unintentionally gave him the perfect cover. Turning to the white desk, he lifted the top of it, putting a wall between the two men. Terry wasted no time plugging in the mobile and letting it rest between the criss-crossed steel beams.

His heart skipped a beat when he saw Dmitri stand a moment later and whip the pistol from behind his back. To his relief, the man slid out the clip and stored the item inside the desk, without so much as glancing at Terry.

"Isn't that a bit risky, storing that here? I mean, do they do inspections?"

"On occasion. But I figure the Swedish open plan minimalism gives the place a hidden-in-plain-sight quality."

Terry raised his eyebrows when Dmitri paused.

"That," he continued, "and the false bottom. Take a look."

Terry rounded the desk and looked down at an arsenal of easily concealed weapons. To be fair, he'd expected more of them, but it stood to reason Dmitri could do a lot with a little when he knew what was coming next.

"Here," Dmitri said, holding out the handle of a black pistol.

"Why are you showing me all of this, Dmitri?"

Dmitri considered before answering. "Call it another trust exercise. Hell, Terry, cards on the table: I want you in on this. There's so much for you to see! I can't even begin to describe it all, it wouldn't do it justice. I know you're interested – I can see it. I'm not gonna make you do anything you don't want to do, alright? If things go bad, I'll take care of them. But *I'd* feel better knowing the guy next to me is packing more than just a broken arm in case *I* meet any surprises. Make sense? Here, take the gun."

In a second, Terry found himself reflecting over his last few weeks again. Talk about the unexpected paths life can lead you down. *Screw it*, he thought at last and took the pistol in his left hand.

"It's lighter than I expected."

"That's a 9mm beretta. U.S. Military love this one. Perfect for you, especially at the moment – I read somewhere it's meant to be just as easy to take off the safety whether you're right or left handed, though I wouldn't try it while we're in the shed."

Dmitri shuffled some items around the drawer before closing it. He pocketed some extra clips and then joined Terry over at the honeycomb shelves.

"It's a lot to take in," Terry said at last, letting the pistol drop to his side, his fingers well away from the trigger. He flexed his right elbow, wincing through the pain.

"You know what'll help, old boy?" Dmitri leaned on his shoulder. "A full stomach. It's not too long of a walk from here up to Telecom Tower. Or, Telstra Tower, whatever they call it now. I don't care. The Great Syringe. There's a restaurant up there I've heard good things about."

That threw Terry completely. "I thought we were talking here."

"And we have been," Dmitri replied. "Let's just finish our conversation from somewhere with a view. What better place to oversee our new kingdom– no! Empire!"

"I *am* pretty hungry," Terry admitted, turning now and taking a step closer to where his phone sat on charge. The foggy outline of an idea started to form in his mind.

Was it worth being spotted?
Even a bad plan is a plan, at least.

"Here," Dmitri offered, "let me show you how to keep the pistol out of view. Yep, safety's on, so now you just want to–"

"Wait– we're taking these now? Out in public?"

"It's just a precaution, Benjamin, don't worry. It's not like they have metal detectors or anything up there. Keep it in your pants and there's no drama, eh? Words to live by," Dmitri chuckled.

Terry stayed by the desk as Dmitri rolled the door back up halfway.

"Coming then?"

Sucking in a breath, Terry snatched at his phone and pulled it free the second the lights went out. He had to hope the few minutes it had had on power would be enough.

Chapter 28
Where It All Began

The two men were close in age.
Maybe I have a few years on him, Oswald conceded.

The man sitting opposite him was the type of person you could instantly find likeable. He didn't have to charm you with a joke or regale you with tales about his humanitarian ventures. You didn't even have to see him with the foster children to know they'd find him approachable. And genuine. His eyes held no secrets nor his wrinkles suspicion. He was just one of those few people who honestly did what he did because the world needed fixing so here he was, doing his part.

But when the detective introduced himself and explained why he was there, the man's composure dropped visibly. He slumped into his chair like a man who'd spent a lifetime waiting for the hammer to fall. Oswald gave him a moment before pressing.
"Gerard?"
Still the man sat with his head drooped, cradled in his cupped hands and turning slowly from side to side, refusing to bring up the memory.
"Gerard, people have been dying," Oswald urged. "We're running *very* low on leads, and we have no idea who we're up against right now. I've seen your file. I understand there was some... confusion, about events at the scene back in '85."

Oswald stood. The almost-three-hour drive had made him irritable. He needed answers and he needed to get right back on the road to do something with whatever he found.
"This isn't some sort of internal investigation. I promise, I'm not here to dredge up the past and expose some error in your report, alright? There's just a missing piece I need in order to figure out what is happening, and I believe you're holding it. I didn't come here to talk to the Gerard Hagan who finds homes for children born into bad circumstances, who's spent the last twenty-five years doing some *penance* for some error in judgment, alright? I need to talk to the Constable Gerard Hagan who was there that day on a farm, out in the sticks, who saw something so terrible and took part in some secret so great it convinced him he could

no longer be an officer of the law. Come on, Hagan, I know you're in there. Talk to me."

Trembling, the man uncurled his hands from his face, staring into his shaking fingers as though they were dripping with blood.

Where earlier his eyes had shone with his gentle nature, now they were wide with the horror he was reliving. For a few seconds all he could do was gasp wordlessly as the images flashed across his vision.

"It was… horrible…" he breathed at last. "There was so much blood – everywhere! She begged me not to tell anyone what he'd done. Begged me! *Why?!* It was an absolute mess! Mess everywhere… It wasn't human."

"Your report said there had been an accident. On the farm. Was it machinery? You listed it as suspicious."

"Accident. That's what she'd asked me to do. Write it down as… an accident. She cleaned herself up, pretended she was fine. She was just a kid! And he… I knew him, you know that? Not well, but I'd seen him come into town with his father. He was a good kid, a normal kid, I thought. And then that day… he just turned on them."

Oswald scrambled for his notepad, retaking his seat. "Who, Hagan? Was this Aaron Tetherman?"

"With an axe. A *wood axe*. He turned his own father into that pile of… mess. She'd screamed at him, and he turned on her. She had blood all over her when I got there. Hers, her father's… He'd become an animal. She wouldn't talk about it, of course. She didn't need to tell me, it was written all over her face… what he'd done to her.

"All she said was that he wasn't the same. That he wasn't himself. She just kept saying it. He was older. He was older. He was older. A man, not a boy. A man all of a sudden. I… didn't know what I was meant to do. I hadn't been a cop all that long, certainly never dealt with anything like that. And she didn't want us involved. She hadn't even called the police– she'd called an ambulance. *They'd* called me out after they received the call. We were thin on the ground, in those days. You know, country cops. It was my word on how it went. And she kept begging me. Said he didn't know what he was doing. Said he could fix it."

Oswald looked up from his furiously swishing pen. "Fix it?"

The haunted Hagan locked eyes with Oswald, the ghosts practically visible in his pupils. "That's what she kept saying. He could fix it. He'd said it to her. He could fix it. So she kept saying it over and over. He could fix it."

The room went silent. Hagan's eyes were freely dripping tears.

"She was scared. And confused," he said, "and she still loved her brother. She still thought he could do anything."

Oswald let the new silence sit heavy in the air.

After another minute, he stood.

"Thank you, Hagan," he said, the words came out in a whisper. "I apologise for what I've had to put you through, coming here today. Talking about all this. You have been a great help, honestly."

Hagan seemed to have aged during their conversation alone. The old man cleared his throat.

"I took time off afterwards. Stress leave wasn't such a common thing back then, but I couldn't work. I just kept seeing it all over and over again. Smelling it.

"Somehow, Kate, she, stayed at the farm on her own for a little while. Refused help. God she was strong, even then. It's strange, but *she* pulled *me* through it. I went around to try to help on the farm – figured if she could handle being there, what excuse did I have? Huh. Then of course, well everything changed again when she started to show."

"Show?" Oswald frowned.

"That was when she finally let me help properly. I said she needed to get away from there. Needed to be around support. She had no family left, of course. I knew some folks down this way. Figured getting to the other side of the country might be a good start if nothing else. Built a little support network around ourselves. But there were other things to consider. She was only fourteen, after all. Welfare got involved, and eventually it was decided that it would be in her best interest for us to find her a suitable family."

"For those four years, you mean? Until she was an adult? Did you become her legal guardian?" Oswald had missed something crucial in the story.

"Not for her," Hagan replied. He locked eyes with the detective.

"For her child."

❖

Feeling trapped at her desk, Constable Zoe Sullivan paced in
small circles behind her desk. Oswald's case was being reviewed
in minute detail in the briefing room – the AFP and SRS combing
through to find any plausible link between the figures that had
popped up recently and the massacre that was now all over the
media. No doubt they'd be cursing Oswald's ruinous towers of
disordered paper.

Monuments to procrastination – shrines to chaos, Zoe smiled to
herself, remembering an earlier conversation with the elusive
detective.

She checked her watch. Looked at the phone sitting silent on
her desk. Her monitor open to her emails, waiting for the results
to be sent to her.

"Come on," she barked, "how bloody long does it take to look
at a high priority sample?"

She snatched at the receiver and punched in the number from
memory now.

"Miss Sullivan, yes, how could I have guessed it was you?" the
voice on the other line was friendly, relaxed, and in no hurry.
"As a matter of fact, I'm in the middle of writing my report to
you. The bloodwork's all done. Not that there was much to go
off from your sample. Still, that's why they keep the best of us
down here. We find ways."

"Seamus, you're killing me with suspense here…"

"Right. So I've compared it to the hair samples we were given
from the hotel, and cross referenced with the sweat swab
another particularly bright officer pulled from a victim's skin.
Very clever, that. Honestly."

"Seamus, for God's sake!"

"Alright, alright. Point is, your man didn't do it. Or at least he
doesn't match the samples we've got. Having said that, he might
not be off the hook. Got a familial match."

"What does that mean? Familial? He's related to the killer?"

"In a word, yes. You know, Mr. Burns sort of thing."

"Mr. Burns?"

"Yeah, you know, Maggie Simpson did it, but the whole family's a suspect. Forget about it. Point is, your instincts were on point. Maybe this guy knows more than he's telling. Maybe your lone shooter has a helper on the grassy knoll. Anyway, I'll leave it to you to figure out what to do with the info. I've got a *stack* of other tests to run. You know, from the *normal* ways people send me things."

Zoe was already punching in Oswald's phone number. "Come on, come *on*..."

It rang out.

Her already pacing feet spurred on with a new energy, Zoe found herself outside the briefing room door. She'd been given no order to get a sample of Benjamin Terrace's blood. And she'd overridden standard protocol to get her sample tested as high priority.

Hell, she wasn't even in forensics, she just knew the lab guys from her not-so-distant college days.

Zoe would have to hope the brass were more focused on the results she'd gotten. She sucked in a breath and pushed open the doors.

❖

Oswald looked at the name flashing on his phone screen, then pocketed it to let it continue to buzz against his leg. As he ambled his way back down the stairs, he needed a moment to digest everything.

Hagan had continued the story. How he'd helped Kate Tetherman, only fifteen years old by the time she'd had the baby, find a family to raise her child.

He explained how she'd resisted the idea of adoption at every turn, but that in the end, the legal system had collated the deciding factors of her age and her lack of emotional and financial support and delivered the verdict.

Of course, they weren't to know of the traumatic circumstances surrounding the conception – details she'd convinced Hagan to keep quiet lest it affect the court's decision further. As far as they knew, she was just an underage girl who'd made poor choices in a time of grief.

Hagan himself had inadvertently become involved in the family support system, and as Constable Sullivan had found, within a few years had helped grow an organisation in the Penrith area rehoming children in need. He'd been a support to Kate at the same time, finding housing and schooling, and eventually establishing her in her further study. The contacts in his new career provided her with a myriad of sponsorships and scholarships to ensure she got as far as she wanted to go.

No surprise she'd gone into medical science, Oswald thought to himself.

She'd later moved to Canberra with her position at the hospital, and everything seemed to have worked out in the end – an amazing tale of strength and resilience born in the heart of so much suffering.

Except for the nagging fact of her sudden disappearance. And nagging alongside it was the discussion with Terry's parents that morning. Oswald wanted to believe the two stories were not related. That it was purely coincidence.

But the sickening churning in his stomach told him that maybe Terry's penchant for finding drama started long before his choices had anything to do with it.

The detective hadn't been paying much attention to the speed limit as he'd started his long drive back to Canberra. The road signs were certainly flicking by at an urgent pace, even if in his mind details were swimming around in a slow motion ferris wheel. Chasing each other round and round so that the pieces that fit together never quite caught up.

His phone buzzed briefly in his pocket. A text message.

"Crap! Zoe," Oswald had forgotten to return her call. An exit opened up for a service centre not far ahead, and he pulled off – realising then exactly how much he'd had to squeeze the brakes to bring the Omega back down to the ramp speed limit.

Pulling into the mostly vacant car park, Oswald reached for his mobile. He'd expected the text to be a prompt from Sullivan, but the number displayed was not one he knew.

Any illusions that he'd be following the speed limit for the rest of the trip home vanished as he read the words:

Found Trouble. Telstra Tower. Bring friends.
-T

Chapter 29
Flashbacks

They had been walking for well over an hour. Terry risked a glance down at his phone to make sure the message had sent. He'd been writing it slowly over the time of their walk, whenever Dmitri's attention was on something else long enough, he'd type a few more letters inconspicuously.

It was slow work, especially left handed, but finally it was done. He'd held off pressing 'send' until he could actually see the foot of the tower in front of him. After all, if there was to be a cavalry charge, he wanted to make sure he was on the right hill.

He held down the power button and let the phone die. The last thing he'd want was a notification to go off and alert his companion to his call for help.

Dmitri's shoe scuffed the wavy paver tiles ahead as he came to a stop outside the welcome sign.

"There it is," he said, pointing at the illustration. "Revolving restaurant. Everything and everyone going round and round, seems appropriate doesn't it?"

Terry had no reply, but he squinted up to the giant needle of a building puncturing the atmosphere. Dmitri must have started walking again, because Terry found himself automatically following him.

Once inside, Dmitri walked straight past the intricate scale model of the building with little more than a cursory glance. In another moment, he was at the front desk speaking with the woman behind the counter.

Slowly, Terry turned his head to look out to the carpark behind him. He didn't know exactly what he'd just set in motion, but his churning stomach was telling him the ride was about to get interesting.

Worse yet, the bulge of the pistol nestled into the small of his back dragged with it the burden of the whole bizarre situation he'd found himself in.

What are you doing? You're absolutely insane walking around with a concealed pistol in broad daylight. And, not to mention, in the capital city of one of the countries boasting the toughest gun laws in the world!

Madness aside, the elevator arrived. Dmitri walked straight in and turned to face Terry.

"For such a dated building," Dmitri said as the lift began to rise, "they put in some nice touches to keep it looking futuristic."

The pair watched as a red light rose through the markings on the wall listing out the metres above sea level.

830...

840...

850...

Terry wondered if his silence would start looking suspicious. He wanted to hear more, of course, *needed* to know more about Dmitri, to try to understand how this seemingly normal man with his paranormal gift could hide such a beast within. He'd need to keep Dmitri's trust. Mostly, he'd need to stay alive.

"See all of the phones on the way in?" Terry ventured.

"Oh?"

"Just thinking, they'd have been there a while. Maybe, you know, they'd have imprints."

"Hmm," Dmitri offered. "They could. I'm thinking a little bigger, though. Or rather, older."

The elevator doors split open and the two found themselves more than a little under dressed for the restaurant. In a slow motion rotation, the floor itself revolved to pan across the scenery displayed in each of the tower's windows.

It surprised Terry to see a sheepish expression painted over Dmitri's composure. Only for a second, but it was there. A crack in this killer's veneer.

Then he was back, donning his mask of the man with it all figured out. Almost immediately after they ordered their meals, Dmitri folded his arms and leaned over the table.

"So... questions."

Terry was thrown just as, he was sure, Dmitri had intended. He opened his mouth to speak but Dmitri filled the silence himself.

"Where to? When to? Way I see it, we could jump back to somewhere like that place this morning. Dig through that shack for another imprint, hop back to–"

"Dim!" Terry hadn't meant to raise his voice. A few conversations died off at nearby tables – the deafening sound of people politely ignoring a commotion. Terry continued at a harsh whisper.

"Dim, I want some answers. I'm not going anywhere while I'm still left here in the dark."

"In the dark?" Dmitri slumped his back against his booth seat. "I've been showing you… well, everything."

Terry paused to consider his response.

"Yes," he said. "You've *shown* me. I've *seen*. But you've *told* me almost nothing. You– you're talking about trust exercises and running off into some grim wonderland of– of what? Murder and mayhem, and you think I'm just going to come skipping along for the trip?"

"I told you," Dmitri hissed. "There is a necessary component to the checkpoints. There needs to be a cataclysmic event to imprint the moment. On your mind. On an object. I didn't make the rules."

"No, but you're choosing which ones to follow aren't you. How did it start? How could you *possibly* discover this?"

The two locked eyes for a few drawn out moments. Terry pushed the advantage.

"Who did you kill first, Dmitri?"

A fire burned behind the time traveller's eyes – snuffed out by a professional voice beside the table.

"The quail with orange sauce?"

"Ah, yes. Here, thanks." Dmitri was now all smiles as he faced the waiter.

"And the steak diane?"

"Yep. Thanks." Terry kept his focus on Dmitri instead.

Again, the silence returned as their interest turned to their meals. Or rather, Dmitri seemed entirely focused on his food and Terry temporarily gave up his pursuit of the truth. It was replaced with regret at his choice of a dish which required both a knife and fork and therefore, a lot of concentration to avoid twisting his arm enough for it to send up the shooting pains. The slightest twist in his wrist made it twinge, though admittedly he was getting used to it steadily, and the pain faded more into the background.

With his focus on his plate, Terry didn't see the silent decision being made by his eating partner. Dmitri frowned, then raised his eyebrows. He twisted his mouth up, mulling something over, then grimaced with a faint nod and the slightest of shrugs. An attentive observer might have easily interpreted the string of gestures to have culminated in a wordless surrender: *fuck it.*

"My father," Dmitri finally spoke, through a mouthful of food. "On a farm."

Terry looked up, but Dmitri's eyes were following the steps of someone walking by. Still, he continued.

"You... your own father?"

"Yes," Dmitri pursed his lips having finished the forkful. "It's not easy to think about. You know be–"

"I bet, I mean–"

Dmitri cut him off in return and continued: "because it's the most difficult time to avoid going back to."

Terry swallowed.

"Did you say *avoid*? Isn't that the whole point? Going back? Why would you av–"

"I broke it." He was now avoiding eye contact all together, instead tracing anyone who walked past.

"Broke it?"

"I went back... and I broke it. Changed it. It doesn't work anymore."

"Then why do you have to avoid it?"

"BECAUSE I GET THERE TOO LATE!" Dmitri roared.

All pretense by the other customers to not have heard him were abruptly dropped.

Dmitri's eyes were closed, his brow furrowed, but pain rather than concentration seemed to be twitching out in the jerky movements he was making trying to shake something from his mind.

❖

In Dmitri's head, the voices were screaming. He said aloud to Terry, "things weren't where they were meant to be. And I had to improvise. I thought I could fix it."

Like an over-speed train gunning through tunnel after tunnel, the flashbacks streaked across his eyes.

"What've you done? What have you done?!" She shrieked.

"I can fix it. Alright? I can fix anything! I've done it a hundred times already. Well, not exactly like this. Usually it's the gun. Something's wrong this time. Don't you understand? Just shut up long enough and I can fix this. Shut up!"

A phantom pain stung his palm as he relived the memory – the words back then had been punctuated with a strike. The memory then flashed further forward, to a much worse insult. His most monstrous trespass over that line of hellishness.

"Don't you dare, don't you dare!" She shrieked as the clothing tore. "Don't touch me!"

The sickening feeling in his gut. Deep within his being. Her whimpering sobs in the ensuing silence.

"I'm sorry. I'm sorry. Oh god, Kate, I'm so sorry! I'll fix this."

Dmitri was now holding his hands over his ears at the table. Still the sounds and images came back, carriage after carriage of the cruel locomotive.

"It's never gone like this. Never. Let me think – please! Shut up! Shut your mouth and let me think! I can fix this!"

But nothing was the same.

He'd gone back and relived the moments before those so many times and it'd never gone that way until that day.

The gun was always there.

Always in his hands normally.

He'd fire it, his father would fall, and then Dmitri would run.

He'd try different routes to leave by, different towns he'd pass through and spend a few weeks or even months adjusting to a new life. And then eventually he'd make enough mistakes to warrant undoing, and he'd jump back.

He'd fire the gun again, and he'd go. And his gift of travelling seemed so exact. Always the same way.

Then that one day... it just wasn't. Something had gone wrong. Maybe his focus was off, maybe he thought of the wrong day, or just the wrong time. He couldn't be sure. But when it went wrong it didn't ever come right again.

Dmitri lifted his hands away from his ears and looked at Terry with terror in his eyes. He took a breath. Tried again. He spoke:
"Something went wrong. Something was different. I was in a different spot completely. I was meant to be by the log, but instead I was right behind him at the wood shed. I panicked and found the closest thing I could.

"Benjamin, understand. I needed to complete the checkpoint. It was my first, and I'd done it so many times over. For all I knew back then it was the only checkpoint I had. The only time I could go back to. I had to go through with it every time, or I thought I'd lose my... ability. I thought so, anyway. It's where it all started, so it made sense."

Terry stared, wide eyed, clearly finding no way to process the fragments he was hearing. A farm, a gun that was meant to be there but wasn't. He shot his father? And then didn't shoot him another time? Whatever was going on inside Dmitri's mind obviously made a lot more sense to him than he was saying.

Back in his memory, Dmitri heard it again.

Hack.

Hack.

Hack.

The splashes.

The splitting.

Still it continued.
Hack.
Hack.
Hack.
Hack-hack-hackhackhackhakhakhak.

And then she had emerged from the house.

She saw what he couldn't undo. And in the madness of the moment he had turned on her and he fell further still past the point of no return. Giving in to some primal depravity, and so intense the tearing of his soul that there was no way back to the time before.

He looked again at his open palms on the table.
"Every time I went back," he whimpered to his spellbound confidante. "I was always too late. It had happened. And nothing could be undone. Nothing about it could be changed. And the worst way it could have ever gone was how it would always be.

Forever."

Terry was rapidly trying to fill in the blanks when Dmitri suddenly slumped back once more with a heavy exhale.
"*Phwah*... Fuck. I did it." He glanced at his hands and twisted his head, madly drinking in the details of the restaurant they were sitting in. "I did it!"

Terry frowned, puzzled that these three words of confession were so at odds with the distinctly triumphant expression on Dmitri's face.

"I did it," he said again. "I fought it. I didn't go back. I was so close – I could see it all – but I stayed here, didn't I?"
To Terry's horror, his friend breathed a genuine sigh of relief. Worse, he chuckled. A sinister smile, a gurgling grin. Within seconds of showing his most gut-wrenching remorse here he was, actually pleased with some achievement he'd made.

Terry tried to give him the benefit of the doubt. It stood to reason that if getting something off your chest brings relief, then shedding something truly terrible comes only with terrific relief. Even if he didn't really know what it was Dmitri was getting off his chest.
Still. There was something purely evil about the glint that had returned to the man's eyes, which, he now observed, were slowly tracking another passerby's footsteps.
What the hell is wrong with this guy?

Terry's stomach hung somewhere between pity and horror, unable to comprehend the complexity of this creature he was sitting with. He lay his cutlery down on his plate, the food barely touched. On the other side of the table, Dmitri began ravenously digging into his own meal like he had an appointment to keep.

"Dim," Terry spoke softly. "What are we doing here? Really?"
Dmitri looked up, his cheeks stuffed with food. He raised his eyebrows with a sharp glance to the walkway.
"We," he swallowed, "have been waiting."
He paused long enough to clang down his cutlery and shuffle to the edge of his booth seat. "But we're done with that part now. Come on, time to go."

Unwittingly following the instruction, Terry shuffled along and stood. He looked over to the steward as if to pay their bill, but Dmitri was already walking toward a man in business slacks and a smart chequered shirt. The man carried a wrapped sandwich in one hand, and he headed around the corner past the centre lift shaft. Dmitri had clearly anticipated the presence of the service lift ahead, smiling slightly as the man approached the elevator and used his other hand to stretch out an ID card attached to his belt.
By the time he'd stepped into the lift, touched the keypad and turned around, Dmitri was already with him – Terry not far behind.

"Oh," the man protested, "sorry mate, this one's staff only."
Dmitri feigned ignorance and called back to Terry, holding his arm out over the entrance. "Come on ya goose! I'll hold it open," then turning to the staff member: "sorry, what was that?"
"I was saying, this is the service lift."
Terry entered, and Dmitri jammed a finger into the 'close door' button. "Service lift? Oh, that's cool. So like, you bring stuff up in this one?"
The elevator lurched downwards.

"No, look, you can't be back here. This lift is for the telecommunications floor. Staff only," the man explained, exasperated. "I'll take you back up. You'll need to use the other lift, guys."
He reached his ID card out again, but before he could press anything, Dmitri had his hand on his wrist. It was only when the

man looked down that he saw how far the pistol was from his stomach. Dmitri pacified him:

"No, no, no, no, no– don't worry about that."

He nudged the gun barrel forward:

"We're almost on your floor already. Why don't you give us the tour?"

Chapter 30
The Cavalry Charge
Telstra Tower, Canberra
2:30pm, 12 July, 2010

SRS Unit Leader Leon Chapman and his team were already on alert in full combat gear when the call came through from Detective Oswald. Gavrilo Godse left immediately to have the BearCat tactical vehicle ready to roll out and James Guiteau was making a final check of the weapons. David Prince was engaged in conversation with the AFP liaison officer, talking tactics and, in particular, requesting a change be made to the weapon Guiteau would be shouldering.

"This is a civilian building we're talking about, Prince," the officer urged. "I don't want him firing off a 12-gauge round inside that concrete tube and causing collateral damage left right and centre. He's either gotta suck it up and use the rubber pellets or take an MP5 like Godse."

"No problem. Only someone as crazy as Guiteau would choose the nonlethal pellets over an SMG. I'm sure he'll go for it."

"*Less* lethal," the officer corrected. "Right, that just leaves Leon himself I need to brief. Chapman! Over here a minute, I want to know how you'll be coordinating the assault at the front of the building from your vantage point."

"Well, that's the trouble, Ray," Leon replied, closing the gap quickly with his long strides. "Depending what we're up against I may not have too much of a vantage point. The Detective seems to think the kid's got himself mixed up with the hotel shooter. No evidence so far to say he has anything bigger than a pistol, but if he's got as meticulous a plan as he must've had for the Holden then we've got to consider the fact that he'll see us coming up the Black Mountain Range long before we're close enough to do jack shit. And he'll have the highest ground from up in the tower, too, so I'm not sure my sniper rifle is going to be our best asset today."

The AFP officer considered this briefly. "We can get you a chopper. That help at all?"

"No way I'd chance firing a shot from there, but it'll help with coordinating the team on the ground. If nothing else, it'll give us eyes on the situation earlier. How's the tech team gone with the building schematics? I'm assuming this tower has some form of emergency stairwell."

Ray grimaced, "You'd imagine so, yeah. I don't remember seeing one the last time I was up there though, but I guess I wasn't really looking."

"So you know the building at least?"

Ray explained that he had been up to the tower a few years back with his wife. "It wasn't the most exciting of dates, but hey, if there's a revolving restaurant in your city you have to check it out at least once, right?"

"Back to the civilians," Prince interjected. "Is the building in lock down already? Or evacuated?"

"No alarm as yet. Not even a triple-o call out. Sounds like Oswald's man has tipped him off while it's still quiet. Hopefully it stays that way until we get there."

❖

When the elevator doors opened, Terry was the first to step out, followed by the technician. Dmitri had been very clear on how he'd like things to go on the next floor.

"I'll be right behind you the whole way. I'm going to trust you a lot here, mate – what's your name? Alright, Shane. I'm going to put a lot of trust in you here, Shane. I'm going to put the gun away, okay? And you're going to show us around like we're some special guests. Hang on a moment, Benjamin. Now Shane, if I'm wrong about you, if you raise the alarm or try to run, if you let me down... I'm going to put *a lot* of bullets into your back. Do you understand? Good. Yes, Benjamin?"

"Our clothes. We're hardly going to blend in."

"That's Shane's problem now. He'll come up with something good. Maybe you take the lead, though. Just so our friend here is sure he understands the rules."

The corridor ahead of the service lift was circular. It curved away to the right, with doors opening up on the left along the way. As the trio passed the first door, they peered in with a rising scale of curiosity. By the time Dmitri had craned his head in, one of the businessmen rose from his chair to close the door. The next room was empty, the bright lights shining on a broad conference table. As they approached what was clearly the toilets, a woman stepped out and smiled before hurriedly breaking eye contact, her face hidden behind hair that flicked back down over one side of her face.

Jumping nervously into the role imposed upon him, the technician turned to Dmitri and gestured toward the toilets. "Uh, uh, if either of you need the uh, the lavatories, they are on your left." Sweat beaded down his temples as he twitched out an awkward smile, then he continued down the circular hall.

"Very good, Shane, thank you," Dmitri trilled.

When the corridor opened out wider into a lounge area, the technician stopped abruptly and motioned to a door tucked between the reception desk and the wall.

"This is our uh, staff area. If you would..."

Terry paused a moment to read the brief exchange between the receptionist and Shane. It was the same woman who'd just come from the toilets, only she was frowning now. He wasn't sure what Dmitri had planned, but he got the feeling that the less people got involved the better.

"After you, Shane," Dmitri waved, "you're leading the tour." Terry lingered at the doorway, but the other two started to walk in.

"Wait," Terry said. "Out there. How do we get out there?"

As Dmitri turned he gently touched a hand to Shane's elbow. There was nothing outwardly threatening about the gesture, but Dmitri was sure the message would get through to the quivering man.

Wait.

From his place near the reception desk, Terry was looking past the lounge room, through the windows to a part of a large radio dish he could see. A hand rail tracked the edge. Further in the distance, a fleck of grey in the sky that someone waiting for police back-up could hope was a helicopter streaked across the sky.

It was the grey-suited receptionist who spoke next. "Sorry, sir, that area is limited to service crew only. There is a viewing deck upstairs if you would like some fresh air though."

"Is that right, Shane?" Dmitri cajoled. "So, you can't help us anymore."

"Uh, uh, well..."

The receptionist's frown had transformed into full suspicion. Terry tried to diffuse the situation with a wave.

"Shane and him go way back. He said he'd give us a bit of a tour, but I think we're done. Thanks so much for your help." He smiled and turned, leading the trio back down the hallway.

Dmitri hissed a whisper as they passed the toilets again, "Is that right? Are we done here? Nothing more you can offer here? I'm disappointed. I thought you didn't want to disappoint me."

Still looking ahead to the elevator, Terry wondered briefly which of them the implied threat had been made to.

"Actually, wait," the technician said suddenly. "In here. There's meant to be a service door here, from the Ranges Room, though I've never actually used the one on this floor."

They shuffled into the room and Terry closed the door behind them. Passing the conference table, Shane went to the far wall and fumbled with some keys in his pocket.

Huan Li had already closed the boot of his bright green hired SUV. The rest of the family had gone on ahead up the path, but he'd needed to change the batteries in his flash first. Popping the compartment back into place and sliding the unit onto his Nikon's hotshoe, he held the SLR to his eye to check the auto focus was responding. He hadn't meant to aim anywhere in particular, the driveway up Black Mountain Range had just been an automatic choice, but he was well rewarded for it. Snapping the shutter off, he accidentally got an impressive photo of a hi-tech combat vehicle bouncing over a speed bump and lifting briefly into the air. It was painted matte black with a mesh roll cage over angled windows. It looked like what you'd get if a tank and a hummer had compared notes in a late night study session.

The vehicle pulled up to a halt in the carpark, bouncing softly with the precision of its suspension. Huan snuck in one more photo before the doors opened to reveal a barrel-chested man in black fatigues and a thick shotgun held in one hand. The gun itself had orange highlighted areas on the stock and near the barrel but, taken with the rest of the image before him, there was no way Huan would mistake it as a toy.

He was relieved to see the word 'POLICE' printed over the back of another man who stepped out from the other side. Though it was written in English, the translation wasn't difficult in context. Huan didn't understand the words the man spoke into his radio, or the static reply, but he could see which direction the heavily armed officer was facing and followed his gaze to a helicopter steadily coming into view.

Heading straight toward the tower.

The tower where his wife and children had just gone on ahead into.

To his credit, Huan ran to them.

The winter breeze on the service balcony was freezing in contrast to inside the tower. It blasted Terry's face and instantly turned his cheeks pink. The technician had already folded his arms – his business shirt offering nothing against the icy chill. He shuffled over in the hope the large radio dishes would shield some of the breeze. Where they were standing, there was a long stretch without windows, unless you counted the frosted slits of the toilet windows ahead. No prizes for guessing why the rooms were named the way they were – true to its word, the Ranges Room looked out to the forested hills behind Canberra. Terry could just make out glimpses of the winding road up the range, and he guessed the carpark sat somewhere behind one of the large dishes ahead.

"So," said Dmitri. "Here we are. The centre of communications for a nation's capital city. You'd think it would be harder to access."

Terry watched Dmitri take in the scenery with his jacket blowing softly around him. It wasn't until Dmitri started following the wires and cables with his eyes that Terry began to worry again about the man's intentions up here in the tower.

With a sharp sniff, he turned to the technician. Without warning, Dmitri shoved him bodily into the concrete wall, and tore his name tag from his belt.

"Shane *Remington*," he read, grimacing false grandeur to Terry. He turned the ID tag over a few times, studying it.

Terry broke the drama of the moment, "Alright, come on Dim, let's keep moving. What are you looking for out here?"

"Hang on Benjamin, I do love a good pun. You can't just walk away from these opportunities. Oh, I know – a close shave with Remington, eh? Or, or, it's a Shane we had to meet like this."

The technician had slidden to the floor, winded by the sudden attack. He looked up now in confusion and fear. "What do you want? I've done everything you asked."

"I know," Dmitri answered with a tone of disgust, squatting down to lean over the man. "It's pathetic."

"No, I've decided," he continued, turning his gaze back to Terry, "I'm sticking with the Remington one. Remington's close shave. What do you think, Ben? Except...." he stood again.

"Except that implies that it was only a close call. And you got away. God, you know I don't think I've ever had to work so hard to set up a checkpoint."

Alarms rang in Terry's mind. His eyes widened as Dmitri reached again for the pistol. "Dim, wait!"

He lunged toward the technician just as the shots went off.

❖

"How's things looking down there, lads?" Unit Leader Leon Chapman spoke into the headset built into the helmet. Hungrily scanning the ground ahead of the chopper, he kept one hand on the roof railing to steady himself while his other steadied his sniper rifle on the seat beside him. He'd taken the ammo clip out and pocketed it. There was no scenario where a stray 7.62mm round could fire off in a helicopter and everything would just turn out fine. And of course, he'd already decided there was no way he was going to attempt a shot from a moving aircraft. As much as it pained him, he was up here on overwatch and he'd be advising the rest of the troop from the air.

"No action yet," Godse replied, "but not smooth either. A tourist from the carpark got spooked and sprinted toward the building. Prince is on foot after him, Guiteau is a little behind him. I'm just getting the BearCat ready then I'll be at the door with them. Some uniforms have pulled up behind us, so we'll get them to mind any civilians that come out. I've got AFP Liaison Officer Ray here, too."

"Roger that," Chapman called back. He looked out and down to the winding road. "Looks like you've got a few more squad cars on their way up to you. Damn! They've got lights on already, so stay alert. Could be enough to startle the target into action. We're not far from the tower now. Keep the radio open."

Chapman turned to one of the police pilots and switched his comms to the cockpit only. "AFP Liaison Officer Ray... Is that his first name or his surname? Such a mouthful."

The helmeted heads turned to face each other briefly but made no reply.

"Not important," Chapman said, and he returned his gaze to the tower.

❖

Meanwhile a silver Omega ducked effortlessly between and around cars on the Federal Highway. The driver had one hand holding one phone to his ear.

If you're gonna break one rule, you may as well break a few, right?

"No, I don't have a description of him," Detective Oswald said, bringing the phone down to punch in the horn until the car ahead changed lanes. "Terry didn't say any more than what I've told you."

"Unbelievable," the voice on the other line replied. "This is fucking unbelievable!"

The curse sounded foreign in the voice of the liaison officer. Oswald got the impression the stronger language was reserved for special occasions. He could only imagine how red the guy's face must be.

Hair dishevelled. Collar trussed. Poor guy. Mustn't handle stress well.

"You told me," Ray ranted, "you said he was the hotel shooter! I've sent the bloody SRS up to the tower and you don't even know if it's our guy?!"

"I know it's the guy, *you* choose not to believe me. I'd bet my career that the hotel shooter was the same one who killed Donald Harvey. And his gardener. And Yavuz Firat! Terry was poking around after the Harvey shooter. If he's found him, he's found the one you're after."

Oswald let the phone drop into his lap as he brought both hands back to the wheel. He'd entered suburbia, cutting back some of the speed, and he needed both hands to make the right turn safely.

"Oh, you've bet your career alright. You're going off a text message, detective! I'm here on the ground. Our men are at the doors already and... wait one."

"Look, I'll give you a description of the kid." Oswald said, his own volume dropping as the noise of his engine quieted with the lower speed. "He'll be with him, I'm sure of it. He's got some inner–"

AFP Liaison Officer Ray still had the phone in one hand when he relayed the new information into the radio. The words hit Oswald like a punch to the guts. He revved the engine further, pulling off at last onto Black Mountain Drive.

"Shots fired! Repeat, shots fired! All units report!"

❖

The technician's blood erupted over Terry's face. That close to the barrel of the gun when it went off, his ears rang in a high-pitched drone.

Whether it was by shock or the by the viscous red muck itself, Terry wasn't sure, but it seemed to take an age to unstick his eyelids from each other and prise them open. Not an inch from Terry's own face, Telstra technician Shane Remington's face had gone slack. One of the bullets had broken the jaw on its way into the brain, another had torn open a section of the neck. It wasn't clear where the third had landed but the overall effect was that what once was a skull was now more like a broken egg.

"Shane it had to end like this," Dmitri said, not seeming the least bit fussed by the sight before him. He was holding the blood-spattered ID card at arm's length, reading the name again.

A brief sickly twitch was the only rebuttal from the very dead technician.

"Hey, isn't Remington a gun manufacturer as well? Damn, could've tried something from that angle too. Maybe next time."

Crouched over the corpse, dripping in blood and chunks of things he didn't want to think about, Terry was seething.

"What the *fuck* is wrong with you, Dim?!" As he started to stand, something metal he'd forgotten was tucked into the back of his jeans pressed into his lower back. He locked eyes with Dmitri.

"He wasn't doing anything," Terry said. "We weren't in any danger. You killed him in cold blood!"

"But not for nothing," Dmitri implored. "Benjamin, haven't you been listening? We needed *this*!" He shook the ID card. Now I have a checkpoint. This guy just needed to give it to us. And he has, see?"

"Shane. His name was Shane," Terry barked. "And the only thing he did wrong was... get in your way. Just like..." Terry's heart was already racing, but it jumped ahead even faster still as he remembered Oswald's reproach in the hospital. Terry's left hand reached behind him, his eyes wide with realisation. "Just like the gardener. You... Dmitri, it was *you* from the start!"

The pistol *was* lighter than he'd expected. Too heavy though for his broken right arm, of course. The left would have to do.

The look on Dmitri's face as he was presented with the barrel of one of his own pistols was a cocktail of surprise, contempt and distaste. Mostly it was disappointment.

Worse was what it lacked.

Fear.

❖

David Prince had reached the automatic doors at the same time as the running tourist. The man was clutching his camera and shouting out in his own language into the foyer.

Still moving forward, Prince took in the details of the room before him. Parents held children close in the confusion. One man staring intently at the model Telstra Tower in its perspex case backed away and stumbled on to the floor.

Briefly getting close enough, Prince got his hand on the running man's arm, but he shrugged it off and kept yelling. By the time James Guiteau stepped into the room, nonlethal shotgun in hand and bandolier of rubber bullets over his thick chest, Huan Li, the panicked tourist, had found his family at the ticket desk and was urging them out of the building.

"Control, this is Ground. He's come in for his family. Looks like they want out of the building. Clear to send them out?"

"Clear from the air," came Chapman's reply.

"Clear in the carpark," AFP Liaison Officer Ray said.

That was moments before the shots rang out above them.

If the presence of heavily armed police and a screaming tourist wasn't enough to set the atmosphere from 'suddenly less bored' to 'sheer panic', three loud bangs and an officer's radio barking "shots fired" in a tinny voice will do the trick.

Australians are used to hearing words like 'terrorist' and 'mass shooting' as strictly the vocabulary of the World News. Always far from home. Never part of your average Monday afternoon.

At a stretch, 'shots fired' might be something you hear of in the rougher parts of Sydney or Adelaide, but they're not typically random encounters. It's usually to do with someone already involved in the criminal scene.

So when a city suddenly has a mass shooting at a hotel, and the Police haven't found the man responsible, there's a mixture of feelings among the populace. There are those who will stubbornly say that it won't change anything about their behaviour – the odds are so small it's not worth worrying about. And there are those who begin to think that every small incident is one of those big ones.

Whether they sat on one side of the fence or the other on this particular argument, everyone in the immediate foyer began to panic. And in their alarm they ran straight past the uniformed and armed men whose very presence said, "it's one of those big ones."

The patrons (and a few of the closest staff) though only about twenty in number, burst through the doors and scattered like deaf sheep. The regular police had pulled up in extra patrol cars and were standing by their vehicles. The BearCat stood ready to pounce, and a silver Omega screamed to a halt along the pavers.

A few officers made an attempt to call out to the civilians or direct them away safely, but one direction or another, they were moving. And they didn't plan on stopping.

Oswald barrelled out of his car in a hurry, the door still open and the monotone warning wailing that he'd left his keys in the ignition.

"Don't even dream of adding to the chaos, Oswald!"

The order was barked from behind the BearCat. It was Ray. "The SRS are in there and it's their operation. Unit leader's in the chopper. Stay back, detective. You wanna help? Keep the civilians away. Goes for the rest of you officers!" he yelled out now. "Get a perimeter set up here *now* and I want patrols at the foot of the hill. The civilians are witnesses we'll need to speak to, and I'm not risking widespread panic."

Oswald had to hand it to him, he'd read AFP Liaison Officer Ray poorly. He knew what he was doing.

Looking back up at the tower, grinding his teeth in his grounded position, it was Oswald who saw the silhouettes blink into view briefly on the top radio floor.

"Ray," he started, then continued before the man could protest. "Movement. Third floor. Outside. Did you see it?"

Ray sucked a deep breath through his nose, lips pursed. The gesture said loud and clear: *Alright, but this is on you if you're wrong.*

He called into the radio. "Control, take a sweep in the air. Possible movement on third floor. Behind the dishes."

"Roger that."

❖

"I saw them," Terry pressed. "On your honeycomb. You had envelopes. Yellow envelopes. From Donald Harvey."

Dmitri took a moment to think, then smiled. After all, it was how he'd found Terry in the first place. Going back to work out how he'd been seen.

"And you knew it was *me?*" He pushed. "You knew it was me who saw you. You knew I'd already seen your work. You killed them! Was that just another checkpoint? A little game? You killed them for no reason – none! Just so you could what, travel by blood?! *Traverse time on a pile of corpses?* And then stand here and say it's *necessary?* Some great sacrifice the innocent make for your entertainment? You're sick!"

Terry worked his finger awkwardly over the safety catch – the gun still pointed directly at Dmitri's face.

"And it ends now."

It would be a nice sentiment to say that, for a moment, all the ghosts of the innocent stood behind Terry, triumphant in his vengeance on their behalf. And suddenly the world would be a better place and the violence and bloodshed would come to an end with Dmitri gone.

But in reality, there was just another angry man covered in someone else's blood who squeezed the trigger of the gun he was aiming at his friend.

Except nothing happened afterward.
No loud bang, no painful recoil.

No bullet.

Click!

Then Dmitri snapped. Laughter first, then rage. A belly laugh from a madman who had been trying to hold it in through a most eloquent speech.

"Bravo, good man! Bravo!" he even bowed slightly. "I hope someone got that down – that was – whew, you were so angry! Oh, I could feel it! The passion, the conviction, the...." he peeled back in derisive laughter. "The stupidity."

When he looked up again there was no mirth on his face. Only deathly betrayal etched into his pupils.

"Did you think I'd give you a *loaded* gun?! With all your protesting and pleading and your... moral objections."

He was stepping toward Terry now, slowly. Menacingly. He paused to mimic him in a sing song voice, *"ooh, the gun's lighter than I thought it'd be, oooh-ooo!* Yeah no shit, Sherlock! It's empty! Let's call it a... *trust exercise."*

What had been a distant drone in the background was quickly becoming clearer – a helicopter approaching the tower. And sirens from below.

Dmitri continued walking forwards. Terry continued his retreat until he bumped the rail. Now Dmitri circled him slightly so that his back was to the concrete wall, and Terry's to the railing. He brought his pistol up and pointed it at Benjamin Terrace.

The chopper came level to them now, still a safe distance, but they were in clear view now of the police.

"You've still lost, Dim. The police were already on their way. Countless people have seen your face inside this tower today, and when you pull that trigger there'll probably even be video footage. So go on. Game over."

"Again, mate," Dmitri said, ignoring the loudspeaker demands the police were making. "That's what *this* is for." He held up the blood-spattered ID badge. "I'd really hoped you of all people would get it. Nevertheless–"

Terry lunged for the ID badge with both hands, the pain in his elbow all but gone in the adrenaline. Somewhere in the struggle a shot had been fired, over the edge and well clear of the grappling men, but it was enough for the chopper to raise its altitude and for the police radio chatter to go into rapid fire.

Dmitri brought the pistol down on Terry's back in thumps, while Terry brought in a series of left-handed punches into his abdomen, spearing him with the barrel of his empty pistol. Shoving his assailant into the concrete wall, Terry heard the clatter as the pistol fell from Dmitri's hand.

Dmitri raised a knee up into a strike to Terry's stomach. Bringing his foot back, he found the wall and kicked off it. Smacking his lower back hard into the rail, Terry was weakened, but he made a desperate lunge once more.

This time, Dmitri was ready for him and followed a right hook under the chin with two hands launching upwards into his belly. Terry was off balance, and when he crashed back into the rail he was a foot off the ground.

Toppling back, his equilibrium reeled as the ground became sky.

In the silence, Dmitri picked back up the gun he'd dropped.

Shit...

Chapter 31
Critical Choices

Helpless.

Hopeless.

Nevertheless, Oswald ran.

It wasn't because he'd recognised Terry – he was too far away for that. It wasn't because there was any chance he could help the person falling. It was just the knee jerk reaction of a good man.
A good cop.

Behind him was a scene of chaos – officers either running forward to the building or chasing the retreating civilians. Their orders had been to standby, but even AFP Liaison Officer Ray had left the BearCat and was moving forward in a daze of automated action under pressure.
Ahead of Oswald, the figure continued to fall, infinitesimally small fractions of a second ticking by in adrenaline-fuelled slow motion.

But the figure didn't reach the ground. Not that he stopped either. Nor did he vanish. Simply put, where one moment Oswald was running and Terry was falling, suddenly neither of those things were true.

Never happened.

Not for Oswald at least.

Terry looked around.
He was back on the tower. Dmitri had just slammed Shane into the wall. He was sliding to the floor, winded by the sudden attack.
"What do you want?" he pleaded, while Terry stared in disbelief. "I've done everything you asked."
Terry looked down at his own hands. He had the pistol – the empty pistol.

"I know," Dmitri answered with a tone of disgust, squatting down to lean over the man. He was completely oblivious to what was happening behind him. "It's pathetic," he spat. "No, I've decided... I'm sticking with the Remington one. Remington's close shave."

Terry knew he only had seconds. Dmitri was about to stand, about to fire three bullets into the technician. But Terry could see his jacket pocket, and what looked like the tops of the ammo clips he'd pocketed back in the garage. They were poking out teasingly as the man squatted. Terry reached down, his fingers gingerly touching the edge of the cold metal.
"What do you think, Ben?"
He sucked in a breath, sure it was all over. Again.
But Dmitri hadn't turned his head. As he straightened, Terry pulled the clip free without Dmitri noticing. He fumbled with the handgun trying to release the empty clip and reload it.
"Except...." Dmitri continued. "Except that implies that it was only a close call. And you got a–."
"What the fuck?"

Terry was startled by the change of script. The panicked words had come from Shane Remington. Dmitri spun on his heels to face where the horrified technician was looking.
Dmitri's face furrowed with confusion.

Terry wasn't sure what was happening – did they somehow know what he'd managed to do? He didn't even understand it himself. But here was the killer and his victim looking at him expectantly. Accusingly?
"Jesus, Ben, are you alright?" Dmitri asked. "You're covered in blood!"

Terry looked down. A detail he'd missed as he looked at his hands before was that the crimson gore he'd been coated in – Shane's crimson gore – moments before falling off over the railing, was still on him.
Yet Shane was alive. Skin unbroken. He thought back to what Dmitri had said about going back in the same condition, age and clothes as *true present*.

"Dim, that's... that's it! That's how you can do it without killing! It's *his* blood!"

Understandably, Shane decided now would be a great time to run. Without looking away from Terry, Dmitri extended a hand to shove the man back as he tried to stand. "*Sit* down."

"Dim, you don't have to kill him," Terry said. "The checkpoint still works because you *did* kill him. The imprint was made. But look, I've got his blood all over me from before, but he's fine now. You can go back to the moment before – you said so yourself! He doesn't have to die – no one does! Or at least, not twice."
"Are you telling me you looped back? You... you travelled?"

Shane, certain now that he was clearly in the presence of two madmen, one of whom was suddenly dripping in blood and nonsense, the other intent on killing him. There was no need to sit and wait for their argument to end. He shuffled along the wall awkwardly, out of reach, then rolled into a crawl towards the door.
"I... don't know. I guess so," Terry said, shaking his head. "I was falling. I focused, and... I'm here. And so is–"
The shot came from Dmitri's pistol again.
Only one shot this time.
But it didn't hit his head.
This time, it was aimed at the retreating technician's thigh. The man screamed and dropped to the floor, desperately clutching his leg.

"No!" Terry yelled at Dmitri, "listen to me, you've got the checkpoint, he doesn't have to die now. What about the man at the bench, huh? You got his licence, you read it to me, you said you'd travelled. You– you killed him, didn't you? Then went back and this time he kept his wallet *and his life*. If you could do it then, why not for all of them? Go back. The old couple in the country, Donald Harvey, the... the gardener!"
Dmitri walked ahead of Shane and stood above him.
"You don't get it, Benjamin," he said. "Some things can't be undone. Sometimes I get there too late."
"Bullshit! That's got nothing to do with it. You're not here for answers, you're only here for blood. What, there's no adventure for you in *saving* a life?" Terry fumed. "And now what? You'd blame it on *one* thing you can't undo? Out of all the mistakes you can fix, you'll stand here and say you can't go back because of *what*? The farm? You killed your father and now you can't stop, is that your excuse?"

Dmitri glared at him. Below him, Shane was writhing and whimpering, blood steadily oozing out in a sickly puddle. Still staring at Terry, Dmitri squatted down and placed his gun at Shane's temple.

"You don't get to talk about that," he spat the words, as he pulled the trigger.

What had been a background noise crescendoed into cacophony as the chopper emerged from behind the tower.

As Dmitri rose, his eyes on the police helicopter, Terry nodded to himself.

"Yeah," he said. "Well you're right about one thing. This time it would've been too late anyway."

He brought his pistol up.

Pointed it at Dmitri.

Once more, the look on Dmitri's face as he was presented with the barrel of one of his own pistols was a cocktail of surprise, contempt and distaste. Mostly it was disappointment.

What it lacked was fear.

At least temporarily.

"It's loaded this time, Dim," Terry said, barely audible over the helicopter propeller.

Dmitri brought a hand to his pocket, he looked down and found a bloodied streak where Terry had reached in for the clip.

"This ends now," Terry said.

Dmitri's eyes widened with realisation and he lunged forward.

Too late.

The pistol reports echoed over the sound of the chopper. Two shots? Three? Terry wasn't sure. But there was a spray of blood and his friend fell to the floor, crumpled over the top of the Telstra repairman – Dmitri Thyme's very last victim.

It wasn't an instant death, but it was still pretty quick.

Maybe he travelled in those last moments, Terry thought later. *Maybe he went somewhere familiar.*
His locker perhaps.
Or the farm.
Maybe he breathed those last moments somewhere else entirely, taking the bullet holes with him to some distant past.
Somewhere ancient and wonderful, like he'd described.

But it was unlikely.

Terry, aware that his actions were carried out in full view of a police helicopter, backed up no doubt by the men who *he'd* called for help, lay the pistol down carefully. He brought his hands to the back of his head and knelt at the edge of the rail.

He faced out to the hovering metal bird, his knees in the blood. The side door of the chopper was open, and an officer was yelling into a radio. He couldn't hear the words. He couldn't really hear anything.

All the noise seemed to fade under the weight of his thoughts. Or rather, they were washed out by the lack of them.

In this chaos, he was calm.

Chapter 32
Revelations

He was back in the clinic-green police interview room. The icy chill of the air clung to the steel chair Terry sat on and the steel table he rested his arms on. The touch of ice coursed through the steel handcuffs wrapped around his wrists. His right wrist, in particular, protested to the conditions. The entire arm was swollen and bluish, and the skin was starting to break against the shackles.

Pain had been firing ceaselessly from shoulder to hand, no matter how Terry tried to cradle it. Dried blood broke off, and streaked the polished steel, dissolving in the cold sweat from his palms.

He'd been in this room before. He'd answered questions at this table just two weeks before. Except, this time there was a big difference.

This time, he was guilty.

It had already taken a few hours. Talking, then waiting. Then waiting and talking. The AFP had been the most interested and had started the interviews. When the officer had first come in, Terry had assumed it was a solicitor. It made him wonder whether he was meant to stay silent until he had one present, like in the movies. They didn't seem to mention it, and, having no intention of denying anything, Terry decided it probably wouldn't matter. Eventually the man left, though he left a definite impression that he'd be coming back later.

Detective Oswald had been present from time to time, though his demeanour was nothing like the rapport Terry thought he'd built with him before. He said little and stayed only for short times. The caring father figure he'd cut before had all but vanished, even eye contact had become a fleeting privilege.

Terry had wanted to thank the man. Even as he had been cuffed and dragged at gunpoint from the scene, he'd reflected that a single text message from him had been enough for Oswald to send in a small army. It meant a lot, and had been rewarded poorly.

Terry had explained the events the same way each time. He spoke about how he'd come to meet Dmitri in the first place, in the bar the night he'd been tracking Rudley. He made sure to emphasise the fact that he wasn't to know who Dmitri had really been or what he was capable of.

How he'd gone from innocent bystander to accomplice to murderer was still tricky to navigate. The police were not about to believe that he'd travelled in time.

Well, officer it was self-defence; he killed me first!

No, somehow it didn't seem like a line of reasoning they'd be willing to follow. But without this knowledge, it stood to reason so far that he'd killed both Shane Remington and Dmitri Thyme.

Eventually they'd be able to do forensics on the guns, surely, and that'd clear him of one count of murder at least. Maybe if he could just talk to Oswald on his own, he could try to explain the rest.

He'd sound crazy, but at least the truth would be told.

Looking at the opposite side of the table now though, he knew one thing for sure.

Constable Wilkes was not the prick to open up to.

"So... why'd you do it?" Eddy Wilkes prompted.

How did this guy even get in here?

"Oh wait, let me guess," the ass continued. "You got a taste for it at the Harvey household, then you just had to kill again and again! Am I right?"

"What are you talking about?" The empty string of random questions had gone on for a few minutes already, and Terry couldn't sit in silent judgement any longer. "I was already cleared of that charge. I was the *witness* for Donald Harvey's murder. I was *helping* the police."

"How convenient," Wilkes said with a smug smile. Clearly he thought he was doing a great job of putting the pieces together.

"Does Oswald know you're in here?"

Wilkes frowned, then fired new questions.

"So maybe you just wanted to know what it was like? Killing someone. So, you climbed the tower with your friend and shot him dead. Who'd you shoot first, by the way? The technician or your friend?"

"Look, I've already explained this to the *real* police officers. I didn't kill anyone else. I shot Dmitri to stop him killing other people. I'm not proud of what I did but I stand by it, whatever happens from here."

"Oh, so you're a hero now? You decide who the baddies are, and then you get to kill them, eh? A real-life Batman, huh? Well, guess what! You need to read less comics and leave the bad guy hunting to the police, mate."

"What? Batman doesn't... you know what, why am I even talking to you? Where's Detective Oswald?"

"Okay forget about the Telstra Tower for a moment," Wilkes went on. He shifted in his seat with all the confidence of a man who has no idea how much he's failing by. "Tell me about the Holden Hotel. Were you there that day, too?"

"The Holden Hotel? Wait, is that where those people..."

"Were massacred just a couple of days ago? Yep, that's the one," Wilkes interrupted. "People are starting to think maybe you had a hand in that one Tezza."

Terry ignored the nickname, some ill-fated attempt at rapport delivered alongside a serious accusation.

"Wait, wait, wait, hasn't that guy been caught? You guys have him right, the guy from the news? The one who shot up the hotel?"

"Rattled by news of the hotel shooting, eh? They'll be interested to hear this," Wilkes was nodding to himself, a regular Sherlock Holmes solving another mystery. "Some people think we've caught him, yup, I'm thinking I'm looking at him."

Terry's breathing began to race along with his thoughts. He'd been focused on Dmitri's killing of four or five people. True, he'd assumed there would have been more in the past when he saw the trophies and checkpoints in his storage locker, but it hadn't occurred to him he'd been talking to someone capable of a mass shooting. When must that have been? While he was lying in hospital?

God, I'd even talked to him about it when he visited!

"Where's Oswald? I need to talk to him," Terry insisted. "I need to talk to him *now!* If there's any way Dmitri could have been responsible... God, I don't know... I don't know if I have any helpful information, but there might be something."

"Woah, woah, you're really sold on this idea you're on our side, aren't you, kid?"

The door behind Wilkes opened, but it wasn't Oswald's face. Not at first.

"What the hell are you doing in here, Constable?"

There was a confusing exchange in which the AFP officer barked orders and questions at Wilkes and had him leave. The door closed again and Terry was alone, briefly.

Any doubts Terry may have felt about whether pulling the trigger was the right move were fast peeling away from his mind.

Would Dmitri use his gift for something that horrific? Surely the Holden Hotel had nothing to do with checkpoints or exploring ancient times. From what he'd heard in the news someone had indiscriminately fired on men and women, even a minor… and then vanished.

"Damn it!" Terry slammed his hands on the table and sent a new wave of agony up his right arm. He'd been a fool the whole way through. Played by Dmitri at every turn, and somehow even enticed into some grim game. One way or another, he'd gotten his own hands very dirty.

There was a fresh commotion beyond the door. It burst open again and a woman with bouncy chestnut hair barrelled through. She threw herself onto the empty chair opposite Terry and gripped his hands in hers, tears streaming down her face.

"Doctor Tetherman?" Terry asked, astonished. "What's going on? Why are you in here?"

Oswald followed through behind her, calmly. He turned to nod briefly at the AFP officer then paced over to the wall. He didn't say a word as he folded his arms and leaned against the concrete slab.

After a few concentrated breaths, the doctor managed to compose herself.

"I'm so sorry, Benjamin. I'm *so sorry!* You were never meant to go through this!"

When she looked up again, her tone switched as her profession took over. "Why is he handcuffed like this?" She hissed at Oswald. "Look at his arm! It's swollen and blue, it's probably rebroken! And it's freezing in here. You, you haven't even let him wash off the…"

Her composure dropped again and she sobbed. "Whose blood is this? Was he there when Aaron died? Oh my poor boy… did you see it all?"

"Miss Tetherman," Oswald broke his vow of silence.

"Doctor," she corrected automatically, with a sniff of tears.

"Doctor Tetherman," Oswald began again, "Benjamin Terrace is accused of murder. Police witnessed him shooting a man earlier this afternoon. Our primary concern at this stage is identifying the victims and ascertaining the events leading up to their deaths. It is not—"

"Shane Remington," Terry interjected. "I've already explained it to the other officers multiple times. I didn't kill that man, I was trying to save him from the man who killed him. Dmitri Thyme, who up until today I thought was a friend, he killed the technician in cold blood. Twice, actually. I've been hoping to speak with you, Detective, there is a complicated element I'd like to attempt to explain."

"I think there are more than a few complicated elements at play here, lad."

"Why *is* my doctor here?" Terry asked, unsure of how to respond to her hands gripped tightly to his own. He hadn't forgotten what had happened the last time he'd seen her.

"They called me in," she gasped. "Next of kin. For identification."

"Next of kin?" Terry directed the question at Oswald.

"Her brother," he said flatly. "Dmitri Thyme was not his real name, Benjamin. It was Aaron. Aaron Tetherman. And we have a positive DNA match to place him at the scene of the Holden Hotel shooting, which, I understand *Constable* Wilkes has recently been discussing with you."

He glared at the mirror on the far wall, which Terry took as confirmation that it was one-way glass with a team of officers behind it.

The woman's tears were dropping onto the table, her head pressed against their joined hands, bobbing with the waves of emotions coursing through her.

"There's more," Oswald said. "Though I imagine this will not be easy to hear."

He left his place against the wall and leaned over the table. "We've been able to cross reference with your own DNA. It confirms something that's perhaps best explained by the good doctor here, if she's feeling up to it."

He placed a hand on her shoulder comfortingly. When she nodded, he walked to the door and closed it softly behind him.

Chapter 33
Making Amends

Canberra City Police Station
9:30pm, 12 July, 2010

"What would you do?" Constable Zoe Sullivan asked the officers crammed into the space behind the one-way glass. The question hung in the air as they stared, heads shaking, at the handcuffed murderer and the weeping doctor. "Just imagine. You've just been told you're adopted. Your doctor is really your mother, and the man you just killed was actually your father."

"Don't forget the best bit," Wilkes chimed in after a brief pause. "You're an inbred."
AFP Officer Ray snapped his attention to the Wilkes' comment and opened his mouth to reprimand him, then changed his mind. He turned his head back to the window. "And Uncle Daddy was a mass murderer," Ray said. "Yeah, that's pretty fucked."
Eyebrows were raised all around.

"Maybe we can clean him up a bit now?" Oswald suggested. "Give Terry – ah, Benjamin Tetherman – a chance to wash off the blood. Put him in a cell for the night. We're gonna have a bit of work ahead of us tomorrow at the site. I think we're done here for today."

Inside the interview room, the apologies were coming thick and fast.
"Please understand," Kate begged. "I was fourteen. No court would let me keep you. I didn't know what to do. I'd only ever lived in the country. Back then, there were only two men in my life. Suddenly one was dead and the other was a monster.
"They forced me to give you up. It wasn't a choice. There was never a choice. I managed to track you down over the years, to find you. But I had to watch you grow up from a distance."
A few minutes passed as the two of them blinked through tears. Terry was lost somewhere between rage and grief and was doing his best just to keep listening. There were so many

questions, and each answer only seemed to bring a band of its own questions with it.

"When you came into the hospital," Kate continued, "I thought it was perfect. Now we could be together, even though you could never know who I was. It made sense, you know. Because I'd never met my own mother. She died not long after I was born."

Terry looked at her and tried to think of this woman as his mother. Of course, his own connection with the people he'd always thought were his family was incredibly strained, but putting it down to a secret adoption somehow didn't magic away the problems like it seemed it should.

That's when he noticed the sparkle as the light reflected from something on her neck. She'd reached for it unwittingly as she spoke about her mother.

"What is that?" Benjamin asked.

"Oh," Kate smiled for the first time. "This was my mother's. My father – oh, well, your grandfather – gave it to me when I was still only very little. He told me it was very precious, and a reminder that my mother was always here."

"And you've worn it since?" An idea was scratching at the back of his skull.

"Yes, of course. It's the only part of her I have."

"Doctor... um, Kate," it was the closest to 'Mum' he could manage under the circumstances. "Could I see it? Could I hold it by any chance?"

"Oh," she said, she looked down at his hands briefly. A moment of some inner turmoil played out before she continued.

"Yes. Yes of course, here."

She unclasped the pendant and put it in his left hand.

"Tell me about your place. Where you lived back out in the country. Please, every detail."

In response to her confused glance, he lied.

"I want to know where I came from."

❖

"What's that she's giving him?" the AFP officer asked the room.

"An heirloom, maybe? Should we take that from him?"

Oswald lost interest in the discussion. He'd been listening to the description of the country home with mild interest, but his ears pricked up at the next question Benjamin asked Kate. He'd heard the words hours earlier in his conversation with Gerard Hagan.

God could that really have only been earlier today?

He didn't understand the relevance of Benjamin's words now any more than he had understood Aaron's words repeated in Gerard's office, but he knew it couldn't mean anything good.

❖

"What if I could fix this?"

Kate looked up in horror at those words, rebounded from the folds of history all these years later.

"What? What did you say?"

"If there was a way. To fix everything. What if I had a way?"

Fresh tears brimmed but didn't fall. They weren't the sort that preceded a sob – they were the sort of tears that wobbled before eyes as they glazed over in helplessness. Another family member lost to some madness.

"Please, Benjamin, you're scaring me."

"Just trust me, please. I have an idea."

The door opened, and Oswald led the small procession. They weren't outwardly aggressive, but something must have spooked them, Benjamin thought, for them all to come in like this.

"Doctor Tetherman, we're going to have to call it there for tonight, I'm afraid," Oswald said. "Benjamin will want the chance to wash up a bit and, like you said, those cuffs aren't doing his arm any favours. Once he's back in a cell we can take them off."

"Well, what's going to happen with his arm?" her professional side had spoken again.

"We'll have one of our first aid officers look at it for now, and after he's washed up a bit, we can have him in a sling or something."

"Officers," she addressed them all. "I understand you wanting to have your own people look at him, but I'd certainly prefer to treat him myself. I mean, how often do you have someone's *doctor* in here with them?"

Oswald had to admit they'd all been moved by the emotion of the unorthodox reunion, and the lines of protocol tend to blur at such times.

"Well, I suppose I can't deny a patient his doctor," he smiled conspiratorially. "Okay with you, Ray?"

"Is what okay?" the question was thrown over his shoulder as he left the room. "No idea what you're talking about."

Oswald led them through the corridor and toward a cell. Oswald was taken aback when Kate followed Benjamin in.

"Detective, you know I'm safe with him," she smiled.

"Suit yourself," he replied. "If anyone asks I'll just explain how you avoided police questioning earlier today." He smirked as he brought the keys up to the small aperture and unlocked Benjamin Tetherman's handcuffs.

"What will you need to treat the arm?"

Kate prattled off a few items she expected them to have on hand and Oswald left the pair alone to get them. She took the weight off Benjamin's right arm and led him to the sink attached to the small steel toilet. She looked down at the grime by the sink hole.

"Please tell me you're holding the necklace tightly," she said.

When she looked up, Benjamin had a serious expression on his face.

"If I'm right, this might not matter in a few moments," he said. "But it's important I let you know something. He carried the guilt around with him his whole life. Dim, uh, I mean Aaron. He was truly sorry for what he did. I saw it. Even if I didn't understand what he meant when he told me. He relived it over and over. And he did try to fix it. He just didn't know how."

She twisted her lips slightly, unsure how to process this information.

"But he couldn't do what I can do. I can actually fix *everything*," he said. He leaned in and kissed her on the forehead.

"Goodbye."

He closed his eyes and gripped the pendant.

Opening his eyes, he saw a classic country ranch.
A young man knelt down in front of him, cradling a rifle, his eye staring down the scope oblivious to the silent observer who had materialised beside him. Further up the small worn dirt path, behind the pair, a young woman was walking back up to a ramshackle house, searching the ground for something. Benjamin followed the aim of the rifle with his eyes and saw that an older man was in line with the barrel, and the youth was twiddling his fingers impatiently by the trigger. It was a surreal moment.

The target was the man he now knew was his grandfather. The man lying at his feet was his father, and the woman was his mother.
Or at least, they would be in a few dreadful minutes.

As he eyed up the situation, he followed through with what he knew was the only acceptable solution. The only way to stop all the pain from having ever occurred. The countless people he could save with this one decision.
There was no time to waste with indecision. It was time.

He kicked the would-be killer hard in the side and he rolled over from the unexpected blow. Dmitri was younger than Terry had known him. Only a teenager. And his name was not Dmitri Thyme.
Not yet.
This was Aaron.
Aaron Tetherman.

This is where it had started, and this is where it had to end. Benjamin pulled the gun from where it had fallen, and he

225

levelled it with the flesh beneath the man's chin. His eyes were wide with surprise, but Benjamin knew it had to be done.

He'd already killed this murderer once before.

The difference was that this time they were the eyes of an innocent young man looking back at him.

This time he was killing his own father.

And this time, he knew what would happen.

A voice called out from near the house. It was Kate. "Where'd it go? Aaron, did you see where I dropped–?"

The shot rang out cold and clear in the morning air, and the young woman covered her mouth in time to catch her scream. Grandfather Tetherman was already running up hill, having dropped his pile of wood.

The world would put it down to suicide. Tragic, but common.

The two witnesses, however, would never be able to understand or explain how from opposite sides of the yard they had each seen the same fleeting phantom.

The flickering ghost-like figure of a man who had stood reverently over their fallen family member just moments before fading from existence.

THE END

About the Author

Based in Brisbane, Queensland, Adam Duncan is a full-time primary teacher as well as a part-time writer and artist.

So far, 'Art by Adam' has exhibited in Supanova and Epic Diem, as well as a cube at My Cube in Garden City. The prints for sale feature mainly pop culture parodies and cross over designs, but scenery painting and pencil portraiture has remained a steady staple of his commissioned works.

At the start of 2018, Adam Duncan shared his classroom for two days a week, stepping into a part-time role which enabled him to focus more on some of his other projects.

Thus, *Chaos Imprint,* though given a few different working titles along the way, was swiftly projected from its sixteen slowly developed chapters into the finished book you're holding now.

2019 will see the author back in the classroom full time, but with one book under his belt, this is only the beginning of the tales left to come.

Visit www.adamduncan.com.au for more information.

Got an enquiry? I'd love to hear from you!
Email: adamduncan@artbyadam.com.au

Author Interview – Q&A

What genre would you categorise *Chaos Imprint* under?

My first vision of this story was solely a crime novel. It was originally going to focus chiefly on Dmitri as an anarchistic serial killer who was impossible to catch because he was just doing things to watch the reactions – to see how everything panned out. It was fun for a few chapters, but then it stagnated quickly. The only ending in sight was a descent into madness and finally being taken down as he took more and more risks. The story would take you on a thrilling ride, but when it finished, there'd be nothing exceptional that stuck with you. The bulk of the story sat dormant, the unfinished chapters floundering before they'd begun.

Exploring the idea of throwing in a sci-fi element, however – time travel, of course – gave a whole new life to the novel. Coincidentally, I'd already chosen 'Thyme' as the surname for the killer, and a lot of other elements and scenes I'd already written flowed seamlessly into the new concept. It was as if the book was always meant to be a time travel story – I just hadn't realised it yet.

Overall, I still feel it is pitched to the crime novel reader more than the sci-fi reader. 'Crime Thriller', perhaps – not so much a hybrid of crime and sci-fi as crime peppered with a few spices from the world of science fiction.

❖

We often hear authors speak about the way their own experiences sometimes make their way into their writing. Was that still possible when writing in this genre?

Absolutely. I mean, I should clarify here that I'm not referring to the crimes themselves, thankfully, but quite a lot of the small details come from real conversations or situations. Sometimes they're moments you think back to when writing and you can duplicate small details. Others are a matter of something really sticking with you and you find yourself wondering if there's a way you can weave it into your writing. I'll give you a few examples if you like.

The interaction between Benjamin Terrace and the police officer at the desk on his first visit to the police station was reminiscent of a time in my teenage years when I accompanied a friend to give a statement after he was mugged on his way home from school. Naïve little me, sitting in my smug private school uniform became curious about the people coming and going. The response I received from the officer was exactly the words Terry heard in the early chapters. "They're all baaaad people," drawled out with the same condescension I hope I captured in my pages.

A really helpful moment came one day as I was writing the chapter 'Family'. I was with David Kachel in the library on one of our writing days, and it was the first time I was to introduce Terry's unknowingly adopted mother. I kept writing her lines, then backspacing them instantly. It just didn't feel like how she'd be talking. She'd need to be concerned, but still show that little bit of distance. The real challenge as I sat there, was a small child at a nearby table tapping things at random, yelling out to his mother while tearing up and down the otherwise silent aisles. We were not the only people concentrating nearby, and it's hard not to look when a child suddenly shrieks.

Finally, the mother picked up the child, and announced loudly that she "was sorry we'd have to go now, little one, *some* people here can't read so they don't know the *quiet* section is over *there*."

I smiled broadly at David, not just in amusement, but at the revelation the woman had given me. *That's it! She'd be as passive aggressive as that lady!* Suddenly I had a face and a voice for Mrs Terrace and the pages seemed to fill themselves.

There are a lot of other examples like this; I think that's just the joy of being a writer. Whether the food options the characters order for lunch match the experience of the person you're talking to about their date at the Telstra Tower in their early 20s, or a strange dream has you up at 3am scribbling nearly illegible notes on a piece of scrap paper, there's a part of you that's always thinking about the story. You grab onto anything you can to make it feel more exciting or make it feel more real to the reader.

I'll share just one more scene, since it was the most chilling for me. It may of course have been nothing, but you never know. Years ago in Hobart, I went into an antique store – if you're picturing the scene from Collector's Eclectic Collector, you're on the right track. Passing by the door that led to the back room, my then-wife and I saw a dark crimson stain creeping from under the door, accompanied by a *lot* of blowflies. Looking up we found we were being watched closely by the steely eyes of the creepiest looking shop keeper I'd ever seen. Needless to say, we politely made a swift exit.

We justified it in our minds with as many different explanations as we could think of and carried on with our trip. But even then a seed was sown into what would eventually become a small part of *Chaos Imprint*. Earlier on, I'd imagined writing a scene where Dmitri killed the original shop owner and had to pose briefly as the shop keeper until the customers left. In the end, the scene only got a brief mention when we hear of Dmitri's first discovery of how his gift interacts with antiques.

I'll cling to those justifications that it was okay not to raise the alarm, but if there are any real Detective Oswalds out there looking for any more information from back then, I may be able to offer some helpful dates and times.

Some readers have commented on some interesting choices for names in the book. Could you shed any light on that?

Certainly – just because it's an Easter Egg doesn't mean it has to be secret. I've always liked the idea of names that follow a theme. I chose the theme for the name in *Chaos Imprint* only after naming one or two characters already, so I followed it from there.

There's some extra reading you might enjoy in the bibliography, but maybe it's better if I just list some names that should be familiar, and you can pick out the composites from there…

Lee Harvey Oswald
John Wilkes Booth
James Earl Ray
Gavrilo Princip
Nathuram Godse
Leon Czolgosz
Charles J. Guiteau
Mark David Chapman
Charlotte Corday

❖

How long did it take you to write *Chaos Imprint?*

Ha, this question always gets me. Technically I wrote a chapter way back in 2007 as part of an assignment – the scene where Terry first witnesses the killing of the gardener outside Donald Harvey's home. A year or two later I suddenly got an idea about extending the story further. I did a fair bit of short story writing back then, mostly for my own entertainment, but I hadn't attempted anything larger than a few chapters. The envelopes the killer took with him from the scene were in my original writing, so I decided to build on it from there – what could have been in them if they were linked to something bigger?

And that's about where it stayed for a very long time. Eventually, Dmitri's character started to come into view, and one night somewhere closer to sleep than lucidity, the face of this rugged cop who was instantly likeable came into my mind's eye. Better yet, he came with a name – Detective Oswald.

I wrote a few of the early chapters when I could find spare time and motivation, but it mostly sat dormant in that dreaded 'someday' pile, especially because I had no idea where the story was going to end.

In about 2015, I was meeting up with Bek Payne (nee Giles) for semi-regular writing sessions, and ideas for new stories were sprouting. Trying to focus on this one first, the sci-fi element presented itself, and the story blossomed. I wasn't writing chapters so much as pages and pages of notes about how it would all tie in. I had whole sections written out about how the time travel would work, which scenes would affect other scenes, and finally, a view of how it would all wrap up.

The danger of bringing the plan that close to completion, I found, was that suddenly I felt like I'd already written it. *I* knew how the story went and how it finished, so suddenly I felt like it was time to start working on other projects. Aside from my art, I was filling pages of planning again on another book, and even jotting down a few notes for a third novel – not sequels, these were completely different genres. I thought I had it all worked out, you see. I could work on whichever genre I felt most like at the time.

In reality, that didn't pay off as planned. I had a whole lot of nothing. Finally, at the start of 2018, I basically promised myself that I'd have *Chaos Imprint*, then called *Thyme of Chaos*, finished by the end of the year. November, in fact, I'd said. That'd give me enough time to have it on the shelf for the end of the year.

I know, it was very unrealistic. But, I looked at the planning notes I'd made, took an estimate of the remaining chapters to go, and worked out how many weeks in between I could give each one to stay on track. I ended up with about eight more chapters than I expected, which was great. Better yet, I finished it one evening in late November.

Shortly afterwards, I was checking out self-publishing websites and designed a first draft front cover. When I submitted it for a proof copy, I was given a friendly notification that they would be out of the office between certain dates over Christmas, and that I could expect delivery mid-January. That's okay, I conceded, at least it's been sent off by the end of the year, I can live with that.

So you can imagine how thrilled I was to have it unexpectedly arrive on my doorstep and make its way to my shelf on Christmas Eve!

❖

As the killer's darker past is revealed in *Chaos Imprint*, we discover some pretty confronting details about his family life. Is there any further comment you'd like to make on how his backstory came into being?

This was really one of those moments in my writing where I felt like the story was waiting to be written. In order for everything to wrap up the way it did, and this is the big moment when the sci-fi met the crime story, there were certain things the characters were simply going to have to do. I remember listening to advice for young writers from my hands-down favourite author, David L. Robbins – I'm probably misquoting it here, but he basically said that while you should have a plan for what's going to happen in the story, there should be parts where the characters surprise you. You know, two of them meet, and even though you're the one writing the story, you have to kind of sit back and see how they interact with each other. He was speaking about dialogue, I believe, rather than events, but as strange as it sounds, this was a moment where I was surprised by what the characters did. I had steered Dmitri away from the stereotypical prey-on-young-women type serial killer right at the start, keeping in mind my original idea for him was the impulsive, anarchistic killer who was hard to catch because they were more like random acts of violence. Women might be the victims sometimes, but he wasn't going for a 'type'.

What better way now for him to avoid this pitfall than to be genuinely afraid of reliving the moment? And not only for himself, but for the sake of that person who was so close to him that he wronged so badly. And you get to see glimpses of this softer side when he's faced with similar situations – particularly in the Holden Hotel. It's only brief, of course. Typically it didn't end up with him actually sparing the lives of other women he came across on his destructive path, but it was enough to have that limit there. A precipice he'd only crossed because he believed there was a way back with no repercussions.

❖

So you've written your first novel. Can we expect to see any more stories from you?

Yes. Emphatically, yes! The ideas I mentioned earlier that were coming thick and fast between writing sessions on *Chaos Imprint* are all still in notebooks, word documents and even little notes on my phone. I made a deliberate effort not to get into the headspace of my next book – *As the Crows Fly* – this year while I've been finalising *Chaos Imprint*, but now all those fences can go down and I'm really looking forward to jumping head first into the next book.

Completely different genre, this time. This one will be a Young Adult Fiction, still set in Australia, of course, but this time I'm bringing it much further north, to the Mt Mee and D'Aguilar area. It won't be a sci-fi this time, but if I can entice you with some cryptic hints, you can expect to travel to 18th Century England and Germany for some parts of the story, Australia in the late 60s for others, and just to make it interesting, I'll also get to introduce you to another world altogether...

Bibliography

ACT Corrective Services, (2018). "Cottages"
http://www.cs.act.gov.au/page/view/862/title/cottages-including-detention-for-women

Atlas Obscura, (2018). "Dreamer's Gate"
https://www.atlasobscura.com/places/dreamers-gate

Australian Federal Police, (2013). "ACT Policing: Annual Report 2009-2010"
https://police.act.gov.au/sites/default/files/PDF/act-policing-annual-report-2009-10.pdf

Barnados, (n.d.). "History"
https://www.barnardos.org.au/about-us/history/

Beretta, (n.d.). "92FS: The World's Most Trusted Military and Police Pistol"
http://www.beretta.com/en-us/92-fs/

Buchanan, K., (2015). "Police Weapons: Australia"
https://www.loc.gov/law/help/police-weapons/australia.php

Department of Health, (2013). "Guideline: Managing the Clinical Records of Children Available for Adoption"
https://www.health.qld.gov.au/__data/assets/pdf_file/0030/369066/qh-gdl-063-1.pdf

Ewing, M., (2014). "Hands-on Review: Blaser R93 Tactical"
http://www.snipercentral.com/blaser-r93-tactical/

FindLaw, (2018). "Familial DNA Searches"
https://criminal.findlaw.com/criminal-rights/familial-dna-searches.html

Grist, M., (2010). "The Half-Built Ruin of the Dreamer's Gate"
http://www.michaeljohngrist.com/2010/06/the-half-built-ruin-of-the-dreamers-gate/

Have WheelChair, Will Travel, (2018). "Canberra – Wheelchair Accessible Activities Canberra"
https://havewheelchairwilltravel.net/canberra-wheelchair-accessible-activities-canberra/

James, P. (2010). "The 15 Most Infamous Assassinations in History"
https://www.good.is/articles/the-15-most-infamous-assassinations-in-history

National Institute of Justice, (2012). "DNA Evidence: Basics of Identifying, Gathering and Transporting"
https://www.nij.gov/topics/forensics/evidence/dna/basics/pages/identifying-to-transporting.aspx

Pafferty, J., (2018). "9 Infamous Assassins and the World Leaders They Dispatched"
https://www.britannica.com/list/9-infamous-assassins-and-the-world-leaders-they-dispatched

Rushton, S., (2010). "Familial Searching and Predictive DNA Testing for Forensic Purposes: A Review of Laws and Practices" http://www.anzpaa.org.au/ArticleDocuments/220/familial-searching-and-predictive-DNA-testing-for-forensic-purposes-a-review-of-law-and-practice.PDF.aspx

Sibthorpe, C., (2016). "Black Mountain Tower Revolving Restaurant Floor Still Vacant After Three Years" in *Canberra Times*
https://www.canberratimes.com.au/national/act/telstras-revolving-restaurant-still-vacant-after-three-years-20160914-grg54i.html

Tesltra Tower, (2018). "Design: Technical Specifications"
http://www.telstratower.com.au/design.aspx

Wilderness Arena, (2015). "Animal Tracking and Signs Guide – How to Track Any Animal (Even People)"
http://wildernessarena.com/overviews/animal-tracking-signs-guide

Wyllie, D. (2017). "9mm vs .40 Caliber: How do the Cartridges Stack Up?"
https://www.policeone.com/police-products/firearms/articles/286263006-9mm-vs-40-caliber-How-do-the-cartridges-stack-up/

www.ingramcontent.com/pod-product-compliance
Lightning Source LLC
Chambersburg PA
CBHW050515260626
47157CB00004B/1335